Dearest Blood, A Romance of the Revolution

Jessie Haas

Published by Jessie Haas, 2025.

ISBN 979-8-218-57335-5
Library of Congress Control Number: 2025905625
Cover: Oil on canvas painting titled "Fanny Montresor-Buchanan-Allen-Penniman",
in the Fort Ticonderoga Museum Collection. Used by permission.
Gravestone of William French, in the Old Cemetery, Westminster, Vt,
Design by James F. Brisson
Published by West Parish Press
367 Lettieri Road
Westminster West, Vt 05346

For my father and my town

This is a work of fiction closely based on historical people and events in Westminster, Vermont, in 1775 and 1783. The only invented characters are Elizabeth Alexander, and Isaac Weaver and his family.

Pronunciation note: Fanny was often pronounced "Fanna" in old time Vermont; in letters among the Allen Family greetings are sent to "Miss Fanna." This pronunciation quirk affected other names, including Billy, which was sometimes spelled "Billa," sometimes "Bela."

Friday afternoon, March 10, 1775,
Westminster, shire town of Cumberland County, colony of New
York

Part One:

The Green Joseph

Chapter One

"Crooked house for a crooked man," our hired girl once called it. Each time I stepped out the back door I remembered that and defended Fa in my mind. He was *not* crooked, and as for the house, *oblique* would be a better word. It stood back from the village street and at an angle to it, each corner pointing to a cardinal direction like a compass rose. It had been the only frame house in Westminster when we came here in 1771, and that still held true four years later. Naturally Fa bought it. My stepfather meant to be the most important man in Cumberland County, and the house suited him exactly; he was at counter-purposes to this place from the beginning.

Oblique or crooked, the house made a large, friendly buffer from the street, and I found it difficult as always to leave the back step. I looped up the train of my riding skirt so it wouldn't trail, listening to the innocent sounds of snow melting off the eaves, chickadee song, children playing. From the Court House all was silent: no sound of riot, jailbreak, or seditious assemblies. But listen harder; it was only five months since the Whigs gathered there in convention, just shouting distance from this house, had voted to treat us Loyalists as "loathsome animals not fit to be touched or have any connection with."

We'd laughed it off, Mother and I. Westminster had never welcomed us. We were not the only Tories in town; there were others loyal to the Crown, and many with some degree of loyalty to New York. But they were New Englanders. We were Yorkers. Fa was an ambitious politician, and with Massachusetts Bay in open rebellion just 25 miles away, every political feeling here had intensified.

Still, after four chilly years, how could those insolent words from the Liberty Boys and their ilk make any difference? But they had. It's one thing to know yourself despised, another to have the sentiment codified in a quasi-official document. Still unseen except by the birds, I adjusted my fashionable hat to a more defiant angle, smoothed the sleeves of my leaf-green riding joseph, smoothed them again, until a tiny involuntary sigh warned me: *now or never*. Go forth, or back indoors.

I never went back indoors.

With the usual little heart-flutter, I started down the path. Mother watched from the kitchen window, vigorously polishing a pewter tankard. Did she I wonder what I'd been doing there on the back step, why it always took me so long to come into view? Or did she know? She usually knew. The great thing was to *appear* confident, and I was good at that.

As I reached the stable, Isaac and Cloud emerged from the dark doorway: a sturdy boy of fifteen in a red Liberty cap at the shoulder of a dancing golden mare with silver mane and tail who pricked her ears at the sounds of snowbanks crumbling and blew purring breaths through her fluted nostrils. For all her spirit, she put not the slightest tension on the reins looped softly between her and Isaac.

We met in the center of the yard. Isaac tightened the girth, then bent, clasping his hands to form a stirrup. He didn't once meet my eyes, which was proper. Yet he made doing the proper thing into a form of insolence, too subtle to complain of, too obvious to ignore. Gritting my teeth, I set my booted foot into his palms, and he tossed me up into the saddle.

At that moment Cloud whirled under me. I flew over her back—grabbing for mane, reins, anything—as the snowy ground rushed up at my face.

A fierce grip seized my arm. Isaac yanked me toward him. Somehow the saddle was under me again, and I clutched both horns with my knees, gathering rein as Cloud halted, blowing loud snorts at the horse and rider coming rapidly down the King's Highway—Captain Azariah Wright of the Whig militia, on his black nag.

Like many local men, Wright had skirmished up and down the Connecticut River Vally during the French and Indian War. That ended fifteen years ago, the year I was born, and today you would never guess that most of our neighbors had been soldiers. Only Captain Wright retained that air of danger. Fiery, radical, discontent, he had responded to unrest in Massachusetts by organizing a Whig militia which he drilled unrelentingly at his farm down on the Flats. Late afternoon was an odd time to see him here in the village; I received the strong impression that something was afoot.

Did Isaac know? Probably. His face was blank, and when I glanced at him, he looked off in the other direction. But his rather large right ear was pointed toward the hoofbeats.

"I'm ready," I told him. "Let her go."

My heart still pounded as I rode along the lane to the street. What can be more unsettling than to miss the saddle, when you're being thrown up by someone you don't quite trust? The powerlessness: the conviction that one has displayed a complete lack of grace: the *resentment!* Isaac did help me, though. He could have let me go over the side. He could have snickered. All right. I set that down in my mental account book, one faint check mark in the plus column for Isaac Weaver.

I reached the corner in time to see Captain Wright swerve into the yard of the Whig Tavern, far down the street. Well, well! The Whig captain usually drank at the Tory Tavern, next door to his farm. The proprietor, John Norton, was an old friend who sold good rum, which apparently made up for his politics. To ride up here on a Friday afternoon, and at such a pace, Wright must have some errand of unusual secrecy and importance. We'd soon know what it was. Each faction discovered the other's business with surprising speed in Cumberland County. But the news would come indirectly. We'd have to wait and watch for it.

Not wanting to encounter Wright, I turned Cloud the other way, toward the Court House. Two stories tall, it stood square and fortress-like with its back to thin air at the very rim of the plateau, the embodiment of New York power, and of Fa's power as the preeminent Tory in the county. The road divided at the front door, flowing around the building on both sides to disappear down the steep hill behind. Next to the Court House, topping the sentry box by a provocative couple of feet, stood the Liberty Pole the Whigs put up last fall. When Captain Wright wanted to gather his men in a hurry, he sent a boy shinnying up the pole to place a red cap on top. I'd never seen him do it, but I knew that often, that boy was Isaac.

The setting sun shimmered huge behind the bare trees on the western ridge, lighting the Court House windows a fiery, dancing orange. I was late for my ride. Mother and I had been cleaning all day, getting ready to host the judges and officials during the court session that began on Tuesday: four days of cleaning for one evening of wine and cheese cakes! I was itching for my gallop, but Mother had vetoed that—almost vetoed the whole ride, but I'd promised to keep to a sedate amble along the street and to get back before dark.

I paused near the Harlow cabin, perched on the edge of the precipice just across the road from the Court House; Elizabeth often popped out to talk for a minute when I rode by, but this late in the day, she was likely busy making supper. The cabins and barns below looked like children's toys, and the windowpanes of the Tory Tavern glowed sunset-red. Only four buildings in the village had glass windows—the Tory Tavern, the Whig Tavern, the Court House, and our house. Even the Meeting-house, where everyone met to worship and to conduct the business of the town, had only wooden shutters over oiled paper. The rest were all log cabins with no windows at all. Fifteen years ago when those cabins were built, husbands had doubtless promised wives a frame house soon, with glass panes to let in the light.

But almost no one had even started to build. Glass was so rare that when I turned Cloud around, she leaped sideways in violent fright at her own reflection. I sat it out with perfect security, which made me feel like a much better rider.

"Cloud, don't be a 'loathsome animal'!"

From inside the building someone laughed—one of the prisoners, a poor farmer locked up for not paying his debts, watching me with his face mashed against the cell window. He couldn't have heard my witticism. He simply must have thought it funny to see Crean Brush's stepdaughter nearly unseated. I took one hand off the reins to give him an airy wave, and my loathsome animal bolted.

No surprise. Speed was in her blood, and she loved her afternoon run, streaking along the Flats with all the little Wrights, Nortons, and Holtons crowing from their yards: "Here she comes!" and "There she goes!" as we made the sharp turn onto Sand Hill Road and disappeared into the trees. I never galloped up here on the street—too many people, and the

Meeting-house and Court House frowning down on me. But I was helpless now, wasn't I? Being run away with, and *my*, it felt good! The wind whipped away the cares and complexities of being Fanny Montusan. I was air, I was speed, I was Cloud, I was—

about to run into the Meeting-house, looming there in the center of the street within a stone's throw of our front yard. Cloud veered around it, throwing our shadow huge and black on the unpainted plank walls. Drunk on speed, she aimed herself like an arrow for the far end of the street, each stride longer and stronger than the last. Tears stung my eyes, blurring the cabins and log barns—

"*Sperie*!" a woman screamed, as a child streaked out from one of the yards almost under Cloud's nose.

I sat back against the reins. Cloud's hind feet *shhhed* on the snow and it sprayed up around us. She half-reared, came down, and stood quivering. The little girl ran on, so close I could see the tangled back of her pale hair. Sperie Averill: Experience Averill, granddaughter to Atherton Chaffee, who was Fa's only real friend here in Westminster. Her father, Asa, hastened from the tavern yard, his long strides already shortening in relief. Mary, her mother, had come racing from the cabin. She collapsed against Cloud's shoulder, panting, "Thank God. Oh, thank God."

The snowy fields spun around me. I all but fell from the saddle. Mary caught me by the elbows as my knees sagged, and we were face to face, eye to eye—Fanny Montusan, the Tory's stepdaughter; and Mary Averill, whose husband, father, father-in-law, and brother-in-law were members of Azariah Wright's Whig militia.

Speechless, both of us.

Cloud's breath billowed around us like fog. Her eyes were wide and dazed. Over Mary's shoulder, I saw Sperie's father swing the little girl up in his arms. In the tavern yard, his fellow militia-men turned away from the scene. Disaster had been averted: time to receive their instructions. Wright, frowning, flicked a glance our way: a rough, uncouth man, intolerant of all rowdiness not of his own making.

I said, "I'm sorry. I shouldn't have been riding that fast on the street."

"Of course not. I'm sure you never will again." Mary glanced at her approaching husband, then leaned close, looking intently into my eyes. Hers were warm and brown with crinkling lines beside them: eyes like her father's, frank and friendly. "Remember, Fanna," she said, quite seriously. "Whatever happens on Tuesday, no one means you or your mother any harm. Tell her that!"

"What's going to—"

"*Shh.*" She turned as her husband reached us, carrying the little girl on one arm, and embraced them in one awkward armful. "Sperie, what have we told you about running around horses?"

The child's tiny fingers played with the curled rim of her father's tricorn hat. "You said don't run *behind* horses. I ran in front!"

Mary's eyes met Asa's for a shocked, laughing moment. "Child, you'll be the death of me! Asa, give her here. I need to go see that my pudding hasn't scorched. You help Miss Fanna back on her horse."

"Miss Fanna" wasn't sure she *wanted* to get back on her horse, but what choice was there? Asa Averill, staunch and fierce Liberty Boy, handed his little girl over to her mother and tossed me up into the saddle. No mishap this time. I settled myself more or less gracefully, and he looked up with a complicated expression that could have been stern or grateful or friendly or warning. Maybe it was *fatherly.* "Good day, Miss Fanna."

"Good—"

He'd already turned toward his cabin door. I headed back up the street, wondering what was going on, and how on earth I had managed to stop Cloud in time. I hadn't thought about it, just sat back and resisted, not with seat or legs or hands, but with everything at once, a posture that let me keep her at a walk now, though she wanted her stall and supper. My French riding master in New York had expended many words and frustrated, explosive little French noises, trying to get me to understand something I'd never grasped. Was this it? And what, in fact, *was* it? As a great categorizer of books and plants and Latin verbs, I found it unsatisfying not to know. But at least I could repeat it, and that was good.

Almost nobody was left on the street. Women and girls were indoors making supper, men and boys were finishing chores—and there went a bareheaded figure, ducking between the two cabins next to our house. Did Isaac know we used that red cap to keep track of his whereabouts, and did he sometimes stuff it into his pocket when he wished to be incognito? I'd begun to suspect his brain was by no means as bovine as his countenance. It couldn't be! But if that was him, what was he up to?

Cloud fretted at the bit, beginning to jig. I did the mysterious new thing and made her walk. The rhythm of her hoofbeats steadied my mind. *One-two three-four, one-two three-four: one-day Tues-day, Mon-day Tues-day—*

Tuesday. The day the court would open. The judges and other officials would arrive in Westminster sometime Monday afternoon.

What was going to happen on Tuesday?

Chapter 2

I rode into the yard just at the moment Isaac leaped over the back fence, out of breath, arms and legs spraddled, his bright cap askew on his head. He stepped to Cloud's head to steady her as I dismounted, but gave nothing away, just waited, blank faced, for me to be safely on the ground. I would have liked a moment alone with Cloud, to look into her eyes and see if she acknowledged that anything had changed between us, but she had already transferred her attention to Isaac, nuzzling into his palm for a treat.

Cupboard love! I stroked my gloved hand down her neck once, and watch her led off to the stable, a little ache in my heart. What was most precious to me? My mandolin, my drawing implements, my books, but Cloud was dearest.

"You bought her *what*?" Mother said, when Fa brought these horses home last autumn: stout brown Joost, the Dutch horse, and Cloud, a running mare by the imported stallion Wildair, bred at the DeLancey racing stable in New York. I didn't know any of that the first time I saw her. I just knew how fine she was.

"The *last* thing we want is to attract more attention!" Mother said.

"We already command attention," Fa had answered. "Let it be admiring." And he brought out the package containing the fashionable joseph, made to my measurements in New York. All over golden hairs now. I picked a few off, let the breeze snatch them from my fingers, opened the kitchen door.

Mother was bending over the hearth. The glow from the coals threw a ruddy light on her face, which showed no particular expression. That was enough to alert me. She had many secrets and kept them well, her only flaw being that she looked like a woman keeping secrets. But this was different. This was about me, her weak spot, her biggest secret and as I knew full well, her greatest love. Therefore I could read her anxiety as if it had been printed on a page.

I sank onto the settle and pried my boots off, watching her back. Watched her clothing, really: the sweep of petticoats carefully held back away from the coals, the smooth whale-boned waist, the two large, fine woolen handkerchiefs disposed over her shoulders and tucked into her bodice for protection from the winter cold. This kitchen was warm, but no other room was. The settlers, never more than a few feet from their fires, were more comfortable in those dark cabins than we were. Mother wore a white cap on her head with a scarlet ribbon wrapped around it. The ends of the ribbon trembled.

"You saw," I said.

She turned, meeting my eyes, waiting. It was the thing that mattered most to her, that she could trust me. I waited too, until finally she said, "I saw you talking with Mary Averill."

Now I could admit it. "We—nearly ran Sperie down."

Mother whitened, reaching for a chair-back for support. "The child's unhurt?"

I laughed, thinking of Sperie's blissful indifference to her own peril. "You know what she said? 'You told me not to run *behind* horses, so I ran in front!'"

Mother smiled thinly. "I remember a child like that!"

"Well, you still have her, but I'll never gallop on the street again! She was under Cloud's nose before I even saw her. But I stopped Cloud. From a dead gallop!"

I wanted praise, wanted her to be interested, but she was staring at something not in this room. Eventually she shifted her gaze to mine. "Fan, what would have happened if you'd injured the child? Or killed her? What would they have done?"

I saw again the tangled back of Sperie Averill's hair. "Nothing I didn't deserve!"

"Don't speak lightly. It could have been—" she stopped herself. "We need to be very careful. You understand that?"

"I'm *always* careful!" The words burst out of me, full-voiced. "I've been careful for *years*! I haven't told one single person—"

"Of course not. I'm not talking about *that*."

I swallowed the hot words that wanted to rise. We never did talk about *that*. Mother meant that we were two women alone in a place that didn't want us: wealthy among poor people, Yorkers among New Englanders, Tories in a town where the politics were mixed at best, radical at worst. Loathsome animals, too! The surrounding cabins didn't have windows, but they had many eyes, and Fa, our protector and the one who had engendered most of the ill-will against us, was some two hundred miles away in the City of New York, leading the Loyalist faction in the Assembly in undermining everything Azariah Wright and his Whigs believed in.

So she was right to have riot in her mind. Riots had happened in Massachusetts; the windows of houses like this one had been shattered, libraries full of books and documents dumped in the streets. Still, it made me a little sick that she seemed mainly concerned about us, not Sperie.

But I had to ask, before Isaac came in. "What's going to happen on Tuesday?"

She frowned. "You mean the court session?"

"No. Mary told me, 'Whatever happens on Tuesday, nobody means you and your mother any harm.' She wanted me to be sure to tell you—and she didn't want Asa to hear her say it. Captain Wright brought them some news just now, down at the tavern. There were a lot of men waiting for him. She hadn't even heard it yet, but she already knew what it was about."

"Hmm." Mother turned back to her cooking pot so I couldn't see her face. "John will know what's afoot. Tavern-keepers—"

Isaac's boots came clumping up the path. Like the red cap, those boots always told us where he was.

We ate supper together, all three of us at the kitchen table in the New England way. In our former world, we ate in the dining parlor with a servant to wait on us, a girl who cooked the meal and ate by herself in the kitchen. But life was different here; New Englanders made their hired help part of the family, which was a necessity when most of the rooms in the house weren't heated. Isaac said nothing, and we said nothing much. I would have liked to know what Mother was thinking.

The message from Mary had disturbed her. But she couldn't discuss it in front of Isaac, even though he probably knew all about it. What was he thinking behind that blank expression? I could only wonder and listen to the back log hiss comfortably in the hearth, and the mellow clock chiming in the next room tell the half-hour.

After supper Mother swung a kettle of water over the coals and took the good tea pot down off its shelf. I didn't even look a question, not with Isaac sitting there. A few minutes later, he let himself out of the house on some outdoor errand.

"Do you think he tells them we drink tea?" I asked, when he was gone.

Mother shrugged impatiently. "It can't come as a shock to anyone! *We* have no reason to honor the boycott. The Whigs either, if there was any truth in them! All they need to do is pay for what they threw in the harbor."

"The Whigs didn't destroy the tea," I argued. "I mean—*some* did, but it wasn't even all the Whigs in Boston, Elizabeth says, and the ones up here had nothing to do with it!"

Her eyebrows raised. "What are you saying, Fan?"

"I just think the government shouldn't punish everyone for something only a few people did. It isn't fair!"

"Oh, children always want things to be fair! Will you go tidy the front parlor, please? If there's news, John will be up to tell us."

Children? I thought. *Children!* But that was lost in the larger issue. "*How* tidy?"

"Just set things to rights a little; poke up the fire. He'll understand. I'm sure they're in the middle of getting ready for the judges too."

Court sessions were a tremendous cause of housework in this town, with judges, lawyers, clerks, plaintiffs, and jurors to be accommodated and fed four times a year. Not that I had ever realized that until this winter, when our hired girl left. Mother decided it was the perfect opportunity to teach me to keep house. Who can predict where life may take her? I might not always be able to spend my days riding, sketching plants, and playing the mandolin. A woman should know how to carry out every task her household requires, whether she does it all herself or directs her servants to do so . . . Oh, it was an inspiring little speech, back in October!

Now in my guise as accomplished housewife, I carried a candlestick into the front parlor—which a day of cleaning had reduced to chaos—coaxed the banked coals back to brightness, lined up the polished wine glasses on the table, pushed the chairs in around it, removed a discarded washrag, and angled the armchairs toward the fireplace. That made the room look welcoming, and if the candles were placed just so, the light wouldn't reach deep enough to show the disorder beyond. At the interface of candlelight and shadow, where a person sitting quietly might easily be forgotten, I placed a chair for myself.

As I picked up the candlestick to leave, the light slid over the portraits on the wall: the glossy pleats and ruches of Mother's silk gown and my own simpler one, the fabric stiff-looking, barely worn except for that one sitting. I'd expected to wear that gown frequently to balls and parties. But everything had changed.

When Fa commissioned those paintings, they matched his status. He lived among important people and was important to them. He could afford to dress his wife and stepdaughter richly, have their portraits painted, live in a fine house with a beautiful garden. But almost before the paint was dry, we became his downfall.

Fa was a nimble man. He saved a great deal from the wreckage, but what he salvaged was acreage, and it was here. So here we came, and the portraits came with us, to gaze down on all who entered this room, revealing the extent of our former wealth and perhaps a bit too much about who we were. What chance did Mother have of passing herself off as an ordinary housewife, with that face continually on display? It showed her exactly as she was—clever, secretive, and forceful. What were our neighbors to think, seeing her so plainly, and seeing, too, that we had such possessions, when none of them had so much as a charcoal sketch to adorn their log walls?

I was somewhat less revealed in my portrait: only twelve years old, and I looked it—a little dressed-up doll a trifle too short for her large head. My figure had improved since then, becoming graceful, proportional, and too tall for that gown. But those same eyes still looked out at me every morning from my mirror: sad, thoughtful, apprehensive. I blinked in the candlelight and was almost surprised that they didn't blink back at me.

Chapter 3

It was nearly an hour before the knock came at the kitchen door. I let in John Norton—a sturdy, dark-haired man with a sound of Ireland in his voice that always made me think of Fa. I greeted him with an impulsive kiss on the cheek. He smelled of smoke and cider and the fresh outdoor air.

"Miss Fanny!" He put an arm around me. "I hear you almost ran down a child with that wild mare of yours."

"How do you know that already?" I teased.

"A tavern gathers all news. Experience Averill—and it was the child's own fault, I heard. Even her mother seemed to think so—or at least didn't blame you. I heard you two stood talking for a full quarter of an hour."

I laughed in his face. "It's not *taverns* that gather news, it's tavern-*keepers*! We spoke for two minutes at most! Maybe three. Don't believe everything you hear, Mr. Norton, and only half of what somebody tells you!"

He chuckled. I loved that about John. He was quite unshockable and always appreciated my wit. So did Mother, but not always in public. "Let Fanny take your coat," she said, "and come on through." She led the way with the tea tray, and I brought up the rear.

John glanced at the welcoming fire. "You were expecting me, then. What have you heard?"

"Nothing that could be called news. We rely on you for that. Take this chair, please." Mother seated herself opposite him, and I went quietly to my own chair in the shadows. Mother poured two cups of tea. I opened my mouth to ask for one. She'd brought three cups, so clearly, she was expecting me to remain in the room. But no. Be quiet. Listen. An hour ago, I was a child to her; one wrong word and I'd be a child again, sent away so important

19

matters could be discussed. I sat back, hugging myself. The fire's warmth barely reached me here. Already my toes felt cold.

The smoky, tannic tea aroma blossomed on the air—finest souchong, smuggled into New York by the Dutch and brought here buried deep in one of Fa's trunks. John cradled the cup between his big hands, inhaling the fragrance, and took his first sip, closing his eyes. Mother's mouth tightened impatiently, an expression nearly matching the one in her portrait. Around us, the house began to speak, as it did on cold nights—a creak here, a pop there. It wasn't an old house. It had been built for Westminster's first minister, who lived here briefly before running away with a woman not his wife. The house's groans always made me think of his abandoned children. Did they hear their father's footsteps in those sighs and shudders?

A large swallow of tea, a deep sigh: John opened his eyes and sat straighter. "Don't think I don't hear that foot tapping, General Margaret! Here's the news in a nutshell. The Whigs have asked the judges to stay at home on Tuesday."

My heart did a quick double thump. Mother's frown deepened. "*Asked* them?"

"Yes. About forty men from Rockingham went to Chandler's house and requested that he not open court."

Requested? In Massachusetts, the Whigs *forced* the courts to close. Elizabeth had been living in Worcester then. She'd described the thousands of farmers choking the streets, armed with sticks, like Birnam Wood come to Dunsinane. Crown-appointed officials were marched in front of the crowds and made to apologize over and over, until everyone had heard with their own ears. Magistrates fled their homes to take refuge in occupied Boston. Forty men privately *asking* the chief judge to suspend the court—was that supposed to terrify us?

I was on the verge of saying that, despite my best intentions, when I saw how still Mother had gone: barely breathing, eyes fixed on the steam rising from her cup. Bright color flooded her cheeks, always a sign of high emotion. "What did he tell them?" she asked.

"You know Tom! He managed to have it both ways. Said he'd got a case of murder to deal with, but that the Whigs should meet him here, and if it wasn't agreeable to them, the court wouldn't try any cases after that one."

"So he gave in to them."

"Did he? The Whigs seem to think it's a trap—that the sheriff will bring arms against them, and there'll be bloodshed. Tom gave his word and honor that wouldn't happen, but now he's sent word to the other judges asking what they want to do."

"There's only one thing they *can* do!" Mother said. "Hold court! What reason did the Whigs give?"

John sat back, steepling his fingers. "As to what reason they *gave*, I don't know. But why they're doing it is two-fold. For one, there's no cash stirring, and some people—naming no names—are taking advantage: suing farmers for some trifling debt, throwing them in prison, and buying their land at public auction. There's two men in the cells right now on that account."

"Very proper," Mother said, "if they can't pay their debts."

Very stupid, it seemed to me. I muffled the thought, because there were times when I could swear she heard the very words I was thinking, but I never did understand how putting a man in jail made it more likely that he'd pay back what he owed you. A cruel system, in my opinion, and one ripe for rational reform.

"Proper or not," John said, "it's not the half of it. There's also the embargo the colonies enacted at their so-called 'Continental Congress.' No trade with Britain until Parliament backs down on the tea tax, and a lot of other demands. I don't pretend to know them all. New York didn't ratify, thanks to Mr. Brush!"

"Not *just* him!" I said. John started at the sound of my voice. He'd obviously forgotten I was there. "Judge Wells voted against it too, and at least half of the Assembly! Fa couldn't do it alone. He's only got one vote!"

John looked at me a moment with warmth in his eyes. "True enough, Miss Fanny; the credit's not all due to him, nor the blame. Be that as it may, the Whigs here in Cumberland County voted to adhere to the embargo, and the colonial government voted the other way, which puts us in a funny position. The colonies say no trade with Britain, and no trade with any colony that won't uphold the embargo. Now, which side are *we* on? There is some room for doubt. The Whigs think closing the court will show that Cumberland County means to comply with the Congress."

No, I thought. There's some other reason. But I couldn't quite see it yet.

"We most certainly will not comply!" Mother said. "We *are* New York! A county can't simply vote to overturn the laws of the colony."

"We're New York now," John answered. "But when we bought our farms, this was all New Hampshire, and let the maps say what they will, it's still New England! Where do most of them come from? Massachusetts! Everything that's happened down there has happened to their families. Their fathers and brothers helped close down the courts, or grabbed their muskets and marched for Boston when they heard it was being shelled—aye, and their gray-haired mothers ran shot and ball for them in their preserving kettles! This comes as no surprise to me."

"But why *now*?" I asked. "Is it because Fa's away?"

John put his head on one side, pursing his lips. "Possibly. But it's more than that. I don't know if you've read their proclamations, but I've heard they were very radical. They claim they just want their rights as British subjects—but British subjects have to bow to the acts of Parliament, and that they won't do. I don't know where it ends, honestly. But the court session is the right time for them to show their hand, if they're going to."

Mother said, "You seem very intimate with their thinking, John."

"For my sins! I fought with 'Riah, see. Scouted up and down these rivers with him, camped with him, argued with him. He doesn't have any secrets from me, nor I from him. He's as wrong as wrong can be, but he'll never take one step back from what he believes."

"Would you?" A disagreeably pert question. I hadn't meant to ask it; it just popped out.

John stiffened in his chair. "No. I won't go back on my king and my country. But a soft answer turneth away wrath, Miss Fanny, and you'll hear me give one from time to time. Just bear in mind—I could never beat 'Riah wrestling, but then, he couldn't beat me either."

The clock at that moment chose to remind us of the hour. Nine: surprisingly late. Thinking of law and order, and mistakes averted, I ventured to add another name to the conversation. "What about . . . Ethan Allen?"

Mother's breath hissed; she hated the very name of the man. John looked startled. "What about him?"

"Is he part of this?"

"Why should he be? His concerns lie west of the mountains. No, this is all home-grown, I'm sorry to say. Oh well. Maybe the judges will hold firm, and it'll all come to nothing. That's my hope."

"At least there won't be riots," I said. John's eyebrows went up; Mother's eyebrows went up; my cheeks heated with embarrassment. "They said so themselves, in the proclamation! They're going to discourage mobs, they said, so as not to hurt anyone. Just treat us like loathsome animals!"

John looked uncharacteristically sober. "Treating a neighbor like an animal isn't far off from hurting him, is it? They keep saying they mean us no harm, but if that's so, why are they hoarding gunpowder? They stood Gage off in Salem when he came to get it, they stole it outright in Portsmouth—"

"What about *our* gunpowder?" Mother asked. "The Westminster gunpowder?"

"I don't know," John said. "I haven't heard a thing."

I turned my head. Through the window, I could see the corner of the Meeting-house, standing there empty and dark as the tomb. We were the closest house to it as befitted the home of a pastor, and there, only a few hundred feet away underneath the pulpit and behind a little door, rested the town's store of powder. I thought of it often during thunderstorms. It was not entirely restful, living cheek by jowl with a powder house.

"The powder's everybody's," John said after a moment. "It's mine just as much as it is 'Riah's."

"And if it comes to a fight, you'll share it out?" I asked. "Half to each?"

He laughed. "Who knows, Miss Fanny? Maybe we will!" He rose to his feet. "Doubtless it'll all be fine, if nobody makes a mistake. Thank you for the tea, General Margaret, and the chance to sit still a moment, but I must be off. Good evening." He opened the parlor door. "Oh, there you are, young Isaac! Fetch me my horse, and look sharp about it!"

I glanced at Mother to see if she'd noticed that. *There you are, young Isaac!* Close enough to hear everything, I shouldn't wonder! But she only stared into the coals. I took John's chair. The fire had died down, but warmth from his large body still lingered. "They did promise no riots," I said, when the silence had gone on awhile. "And Mary said they mean us no harm."

"This will harm us."

Her voice was sure and quiet. I heard the kitchen door bang shut behind John Norton—our friend, the man, of all others, whom we turned to in emergencies during the long months when Fa was away at the Assembly. The house was empty now save for us, and Isaac. I had to ask.

"Is . . . *he* . . . still in Boston?"

He. Captain John Montresor, military engineer in the British Army, barrack master for North America, drafter of the definitive map of New York City, veteran of Fort Duquesne, the Halifax expedition, the sieges of Louisbourg and Québec, and the relief of Fort Detroit, designer of the fortifications at Niagara and Fort Erie, as well as the gravity railroad there. Gallant in war, faithless in love. My sire.

Chapter 4

"I don't know where he is," Mother said, not looking up.

"Really?"

"The last I knew, he was in Boston. Fortifying the Neck. Don't think of him, Fan. He's not a factor."

"I don't think of him. Only—"

"There is no 'only.'"

"*You* keep track of him. You and Fa always know where he is."

"It's best to know—but don't think of him as coming to our rescue. You know better than that."

Now I looked down. I knew nothing, really, only what I'd been told. That Captain Montresor led that giddy girl Anna Schoolcraft astray when she was just fifteen—abandoned her, pregnant and alone, with nothing to eat and no firewood. After I was born, and she had died, and her older sister Margaret—Mother—had rescued me, this officer and gentleman repudiated all responsibility for my maintenance and support. It was exactly what one would expect from an Englishman of the upper classes; they were moderately faithful only to women whose families could enforce good behavior, or when they had something to lose. My little mother was an artillery officer's daughter, respectable enough if she'd behaved herself, but she had not. She was a convenience who could be tossed aside like a broken toy when his circumstances changed. If things went wrong on Tuesday, there was no chance that John Montresor would come to our rescue.

Mother picked up the tea-tray and paused in the doorway. "I'm going to bed. Will you to bank the fire, please? I'll take up a soapstone for you." In a moment I heard her in the kitchen, speaking a few words to Isaac; then her footsteps sounded, slow and heavy on the stairs.

I hugged myself, shivering, and got up to stand closer to the glowing coals. It would be warmer in the kitchen, but Isaac was there. Oh, for the days when we had a hired girl to carry up the warming pan! But if I waited, the hot soapstone would take the worst chill off the sheets and provide a place to toast my toes.

I turned to warm the backs of my legs and caught my own attention. Fanny on the wall, Fanny on the hearth, gazed at one another. I knew her look. I could feel it on my face now—because was it happening again? Was the world turning upside down? That was what those dark, dilated eyes in the painting saw. A nice little girl just starting to appear at dances and parties, just learning the panache it took to wear silks and powder, discovers that her life is a fiction. She is not the daughter of the woman she calls Mother. There's another mother, no longer living, and the father whom she'd thought dead is the handsome officer across the room in his scarlet dress uniform, with his beautiful, wealthy wife—also named Fanny, because sometimes life has a bitter sense of humor.

The two Fannies couldn't exist in one ballroom. That was too embarrassing for the man in the middle, and since he was a brilliant military engineer, highly valued by those in power, he was able to make one Fanny go away. He didn't care where we went, and Fa, not without influence himself, was able to parlay social exile into a substantial grant of land here at the raw edge of New York.

But those were black days. I'd had much to absorb: the change of place and expectations, a real mother and father, neither of whom were admirable. Mother—I continued to call her that; it was her name—had worked dawn to dusk, settling us into our new life. But it was hardest for Fa. Outwardly he swaggered around Cumberland County, flashing his fashionable attire and his brilliance. He inspected his new lands, laid down rules to his tenants, began to sound out the local politics.

But at night he sat with the decanter at his elbow, frowning at the walls. His hand acquired a tremor it never had before. Land, even six thousand acres of it, was only wealth if it could be sold, and most of Fa's could not. There was nobody to buy it. Cumberland County was a backwater, a place of no influence or power. He was like a fish out of water here, flapping helplessly.

I asked him once—only once: "Is it my fault?"

He raised his head as if it were very heavy and looked straight at me. "No. I knew who you were when I married Margaret. You are entirely innocent, and your mother was too, very nearly."

"But if it wasn't for me—"

He stirred his shoulders as if shrugging off a greatcoat. "That's true, Fanny, but it doesn't matter. Your birth is only a circumstance. Don't let it affect your happiness." He never said how that might be accomplished, and it did affect his, but that moment sealed my loyalty to him forever.

Then came the day when he returned from visiting Judge Chandler with the old sparkle back in his eyes. He was said to be an ugly man, with his rough, pockmarked skin, but when that look came over him, he seemed lit from within. You might hate him, and many did, but you had to admit he was *something!*

"Chester is much too out of the way to be the county seat," he told us. "The jail is a pen made of hackmatack poles! The prisoners push the ceiling up when they want to get out and go visiting. Westminster, now, is much more central. On the river for easy travel. A beautiful village—you smile, Fanny, but one day it will be beautiful, when these cabins are gone and we have families of substance living here, in houses like this one. The wealth and prestige of Cumberland County will be greatly enhanced by having Westminster as its shire town."

Over the next three years, with little else to do and a strong inclination to distract myself, I watched as he went to work step by step, pulling political wires, calling in favors, planting suggestions in just the right ears. His skill, his vision, his progress consumed me like a novel. As our neighbors began to shun him, I only grew more fascinated. They were right to feel as they did; I could see that. He intended to replace them or turn them into tenant farmers. The Crean Brush estate would rival those of the Hudson Valley patroons. His wife and stepdaughter would sparkle in a setting worthy of their brilliance.

But in the meantime, the locals benefited. Soon Westminster was indeed the county seat, with a grand Court House perched on the bluff like a castle. Next Fa raised the idea that Cumberland County should have representation in the New York Assembly. Once he'd accomplished that, he got himself and

Judge Wells elected, and there he was, back in the thick of things, at the top of a pyramid of his own building.

The moment he was in the capitol again, he made himself useful there, and hated here, by drafting a law to put down the Bennington rebellion: Ethan Allen and his cronies outlawed, riotous assemblies banned, punishments for such assemblies enhanced. "The Bloody Acts," our neighbors called them, and now when they talked about the hated Yorkers, Fa was their prime example.

It didn't matter. He was himself again, with his old sparkle, his old satisfaction at making things happen. These people couldn't possibly understand a man like him—but they could damage him, and if they did, could he put himself back together again? He'd done it in his thirties, when he came to New York, and again in his forties, when he came to Westminster. But he was fifty now, and that tremor in his hand had never gone away.

I took up the poker and began pushing ashes over the coals, so they would live till morning. *This will harm us.* Our family, Mother meant. Our prospects in the world. Fa's spirits. They blazed up hot and quick, but they sank back just as quickly, smoking and hissing, and then nothing could cheer him—

Or was that completely true? There was that time after his first Assembly session when he sank again, morose for reasons we couldn't understand. Then came the letter from Ethan Allen, his worst enemy. I remembered him unfolding it, and as he stood next to the window reading it, his eyes lit with amusement and appreciation. It was a turning point. The darkness never returned, and from then on, I had a soft spot for the outlaw, in spite of everything.

Where was that letter? Still in the same drawer?

I took my candle into the cold, dark study, sat at Fa's desk, and rested my hands for a moment on the polished wood. I remembered sitting here to witness a deed for him, putting a botanical drawing in front of him, playing a ballad for him on the lute, translating a passage from Latin to French to English while he listened and made minor corrections. Even in his dark time, he made sure I had books and music.

The letter was where I'd last seen it, in a drawer Fa left unlocked. With the passage of time, it had been snowed under by other documents. I lifted them out carefully, keeping them in order. I spread the letter on the desk, and brought the candle closer, running over the familiar words from almost a year ago.

May 19, 1774.

Sr

I have Sundry ways recd Intelligence of Your hatred and Malice Toward the n. Hampshire Settlers on the west Side of the Range of Green Mountains and particularly Towards me. The repourt You made in behalf of Mr. Clinton is Noticed by the Green M Boys. They have Also Took a retrospective View of a Number of Learned Attorneys and Gentleman (by Birth) Interested in the Lands (by N. York Title) on which they dwell . . .

All those "Learned Attorneys and Gentleman By Birth" were Fa's colleagues and kind friends to me. I'd borrowed books from their libraries, taken cuttings from their gardens, yawned over their long speeches, and been delighted by their little gifts.

. . . Deludeing the Assembly Part of the Members of which Undoubtedly are Honestly Disposed and Beguileing them Into a false Opinion that Those People You Call the Bennington Mob are Notorious Rioters &ce. You Know better and are Sensible that they Onely Contend for their Property and that they have No Design Against the Government any further than to Protect the Same.

I know it was the Land Schemers Influenced the Assembly to Pass the 12 Bloody Acts of March Ult. (Mr Saml Wells was Very officious bringing it About) they then Laid a Trap for the Lives of those persons Proclamated for and Wells and You are but busie Understrappers to a Number of more Overgrown Villains which Can Murther by Law without remorse.

"Murder?" Mother had said, furious. But it was true that the Acts made Allen and his lieutenants liable to be transported to England and hanged.

I Have to Inform that the Green Mountain Boys will Not Tamely resign their necks to the Halter to be Hanged by Your Curst Fraternity of Land Jockeys who Would Better Adorn a halter than we, therefore as You regard Your Own Lives be Carefull Not to Invade ours for what Measure you Meat it Shall be Measured to You Again.

P.S. Mr. Brush, sir/

As a Testimony of Gratitude for the many unmerited Kindnesses and services you have Done us the last Sessions at New York &cc &cc we Intend Shortly visiting your Abode, Where we hope to Have the Honour of Presenting you with the beech seal—which we Beg your kind Acceptance of as a Mark of the high Esteem we have of your Person and as a Token of our Approbation for the Eminent Exertions you Displayed of your Abilitys in Bringing about the Salutary act of the 9th of March last—We have the Honor

Sir

To be yours sincearly

The Green Mountain Boys

Fa laughed aloud when he came to that part. "What exquisite insolence!" he said and explained that "the beech seal" was a flogging with a branch from a beech tree, a severe punishment indeed. He cleaned his pistols and carried one with him always, and for several weeks never omitted to glance out the windows before leaving the house. But he liked the letter. It woke him up and amused him. He and Allen had never yet met, nor even seen each other. I was the only one in the family who'd even had a glimpse of the outlaw—just a lithe back and shoulders clad in hemlock-green, disappearing horseback over the rim of Court House Hill. That had been one of the days he visited his friend John, our friend John. Did he know he passed right by Fa's house? He must! I had a feeling they would like each other—or at least, would enjoy sneering at each other in ornately polite language.

Maybe John is wrong, I thought, replacing the letter in its drawer. Closing the court would cross a line. New York would have no choice but to re-establish government by force, on behalf of itself and of the Crown—and once troops were here, they could be used to put down the Green Mountain Boys. Allen might have an interest in preventing this action.

It seemed far-fetched, though, even to me. Really, everything depended on Judge Chandler. If he stood firm, all might yet be well.

Chapter 5

In the night I dreamed of hoofbeats. Twice? Three times? But in the morning, the street seemed empty, innocent. The only people about when, shivering, I peeked out my chamber window, were boys bringing in wood and water. Smoke poured from cabin chimneys as the fires revived.

Watching the village wake, I layered myself into my clothing—stockings fastened on with a broad ribbon, stays laced comfortably for working, farthingale pad and pocket tied on, a light petticoat and a heavy one, each with their attendant knots, then a short work-gown—more lacing— and two large handkerchiefs tucked in to keep my neck and bosom warm. There! Wouldn't it be nice to have a maid-servant!

Mother was at the hearth, kindling a fire in the bake oven. "Good!" she said, seeing me. "I want to make an early start on the cheese cakes."

So we weren't going to talk about it. Not surprising. Mother was a woman who could keep her own counsel, and there were the cheese cakes. She served these crumbly, savory little morsels with wine on the evenings during the court session when the judges visited. A few of these, a glass or two of Fa's wine, and even important, cautious men tended to expand, reach for another, and say a little more than they'd meant to. The cakes were a lot of work, though. "I miss the bakery," I said to her bent back. There was a pause before she answered, long enough for me to hear what that sounded like and start to apologize.

"We *are* the bakery," she said, running over my words.

"I didn't mean—"

"I know what you meant. I miss it too. Every morning!"

We'd breakfasted on bakery buns in the city, with the finest butter. Here we ate johnnycake or pie or, like this morning, fried mush—which couldn't compare with a soft white bun but did taste good with butter and maple sugar made by Isaac's father. Fa held the mortgage on the Weaver's farm. Isaac's father was paying it off slowly in maple sugar, firewood, hay, and Isaac's labor. Isaac made sure to get as much maple sugar as possible this morning, layering it thick on his fried mush before he bolted it down.

"I'll need more oven wood after breakfast," Mother said, ladling him out a second helping. He nodded shortly, managing, as usual, not to say a word to either of us through the whole meal. But as he lowered his head over his bowl, I noticed a glitter in his eye, a flush to his cheeks. He was excited. More excited than he'd been last night. Had there been some further development?

There was no time to find out. Soon we were all at work. Isaac stacked the oven wood at the hearth. Mother fed her fire, while I marshaled everything we'd need for a baking—we'd make several pies and some bread as well as the cakes—then cut and trimmed a large slab off the big cheese and settled in to grating. My shoulders tensed up in a way that felt all too familiar. "It seems like just we made these yesterday!"

"Three months ago," Mother said.

"It feels like three weeks—*ow!* I've grated myself." I put my thumb in my mouth; the warm iron taste of blood seeped onto my tongue. When I looked, though, it was only a tiny flap of skin nicked partway off at the edge of the knuckle. I smoothed it straight with the other thumb. "I see why the farmers complain. Dropping work every three months to serve on juries—"

"Nonsense! They enjoy it." Mother was up to her elbows in pie crust. "It's a chance to get out and see people and pass judgment on them—a perfect ending to a long winter! Do you need to wrap a rag around that? I don't want blood in my cheese cakes."

"No, it's fine." Just one more insult to hands already roughened by scrubbing and polishing. It had been days since I opened a book or picked up a pencil or touched my mandolin. As I attacked the cheese again, I couldn't help saying, "I miss Anna. We should find help again."

"I can't think who," Mother said. "Nobody wants to send their daughters to a Loyalist household."

"I know. 'Loathsome animals'!"

Mother didn't dignify that with a response. *Slap, slap.* Already she was rolling out a crust, with quick, deft strokes of the pin. In a moment she folded it in half, laid it into a pie plate, and opened it up like a book. It fit the plate dead center, the way her crusts always did, and she began another. "We're two able-bodied females with no men or small children to tend. I'd feel ashamed of myself if I couldn't manage in that situation—or if I failed to teach you to do the same."

I stopped listening. I knew this speech by heart. A woman should be able to do everything: a poor woman because she must, a rich woman so she could instruct her servants. "Whether it's a mansion or a cabin—" I heard her say, and as I carefully grated the last heel of cheese, I vowed *mansion*. I'd rather advise some other poor girl not to shred her knuckles than risk my own. Already we lived in what amounted to a mansion for Westminster, and things would only get better if Fa could make the land pay—

". . . get one to butcher next week."

"*What*?"

"I didn't think you were listening! I was saying, I ought to get a hog or a sheep to butcher in the next week or two, before the weather warms up. You won't learn any younger."

"But animals aren't fat enough to butcher in the spring. I do know that much! I'll learn some other year."

"Maybe, but I don't want to send you into marriage ignorant—"

"Of *hog butchery*?"

"Or anything else."

I was ignorant of *so* much else! Not completely. I wasn't a fool; I understood the fundamentals. But what took one past flirtation into real love? What led my little mother to her mistake, and why was it so easy for him to leave her and foreswear me? How did you find your way inside a person, to see that the handsome, manly, and accomplished Captain Montresor was a hound, and that the pockmarked, red-faced Crean Brush was true of heart? To marry without knowing that would be—

And then I really heard what she'd said. "Wait—why are you talking about marriage?"

"These are tumultuous times, Fan," she said, never pausing in her work. "We think it prudent to have you settled before war breaks out."

It was dawning on me that this was not one of those theoretical conversations about housewifery sometime in the distant future. The air in the kitchen seemed to congeal, thick and unbreathable.

"Have me *settled*?" I managed to say. "Like an *account*? Like a *debt*?"

"Like a young girl who could come to harm without protection." This came out of her mouth in a calm, matter-of-fact tone, as if it were not the most outrageous thing she'd ever said. I wanted to laugh, because this couldn't be real. It must be some kind of game she was playing, some kind of test.

"How would it *protect* me to give me to some person I've never even—" Some motion of her shoulders made me realize the truth. "Wait, I *have* met him?"

"Yes. I doubt you'd remember. You were little more than a child—"

Suddenly my hands were shaking. "I'm *still* a child! You said so yourself last night! If my mother was too young at fifteen to be walking out with a man, I'm surely too young to be marrying one!" She flinched, but didn't answer. "Who is he? And what would he get out of marrying a girl he doesn't even know?"

"It would be a gamble, like any marriage. If your fa prospers here, your husband may become a wealthy man."

"Based on my inheritance!"

"Or you may become wealthy based on his. He's not well-off yet, but the family is, and he's positioned to prosper in the business, whether in war or peace." All in her every-day voice, as if she weren't saying something fantastic.

I forced myself to speak calmly. "Can I say no?" This was a game. It had to be, and the right question would reveal that.

"You can say anything," she said, "and if I see my way clear, I'll heed your wishes. But if it comes to war, Fan, none of us knows what will happen or where we'll be, together or apart. As a married woman, the wife of an officer—"

I sat down hard on the settle, sick to my stomach. "He's an officer."

"Yes."

My lips felt numb. "My mother was an officer's . . . sweetheart." I had to swallow; my chest felt like it had a bubble of air stuck in it, just to the right of my heart. "Look what happened to her."

"He's a man of family, Fan. A family that has a position to maintain, and that has agreed to take us in if needed. Both of us."

Both of us. Her and me. "What about Fa?" But I knew the answer to that question. If war came, Fa would be pursuing fresh opportunities. We'd be on our own.

"When did you decide this? It wasn't in Fa's letters! I read them all!"

"It was, just not so you could see it." Another pie took shape under her flying fingers, which never hesitated. Only the color in her cheeks showed that she was agitated. "Last autumn when things got bad in Massachusetts, he started to think that the Whigs would go too far. We decided he should look around while he was in New York this winter, and he has, and—he's come to a tentative agreement."

"But—" My mouth was dry. This couldn't be happening. "I don't . . . I can't—"

"I'm sorry," she said. "I should have found a better way to tell you."

Tell me. Not ask me. I was at their disposal. Had I always known that? Just at this moment it felt as if I had—but then why was I so surprised?

Knockknockknock came at the kitchen door.

Chapter 6

We stared at each other. How strange. There was still a world outside this house.

The knock repeated. Mother glanced down at herself. "I'm all flour. Would you answer?"

Could I? Let an outsider into the house? This wasn't the time for that. But Mother kept crimping as if the world ran on pie crust rims. I went toward the door, blinking against the dazzling brightness inside my head. *Married?* How did this lightning bolt strike me here in the kitchen in the midst of grating cheese, foreclosing all my hopes and imaginings? Dances, flirtation, acrostics done in Latin: music figured into it, sleigh rides, and an agreeable sense of danger. I would test and probe, I'd always believed, until I was sure I had met my match: someone who delighted in my wit, whom I couldn't easily best, who would have to get up early in the morning to best me. He would be unorthodox, an original mind. A rider, a thinker, a man of letters.

He'd already been chosen for me. He might be anything—a rake, a drunk, a brute, a dullard—

I opened the door.

For a moment, I literally didn't recognize her. The blue homespun gown nearly matched her eyes: so pretty on this fine-boned, self-contained young woman smiling at me, and now not smiling, looking puzzled—

Elizabeth, of course: Elizabeth Alexander from down in the Bay, who came to Westminster last winter to help her cousin Rhoda Harlow with the children and the spinning and liked me instantly, though she was four years older and a Whig.

"I'm sorry," she said. "I thought—but I see you're busy."

"Hello, Elizabeth," Mother said behind me. "Did you come to take Fanny off for one of your walks? I can spare her a little while. My fire's slow this morning."

I didn't want to go. I felt weak and dazed, almost unwell, like someone who shouldn't be exposed to the outdoor air. But Mother was already draping a cloak over my shoulders. She turned me around and tied the strings as if I were a small child. Our faces were two inches apart, but all I could see of her was the top of her cap. "There!" She almost pushed me out of the house.

"Well, that was easier than I expected!" Elizabeth said, starting along the lane. "Which way? Willard Hill or up to the springs?"

"Oh. The springs." I followed her the way one sheep follows another, mindless, crowding close.

"But that's cruel, when Billy's been saving himself for you!" She'd been teasing me about Billy Willard since she introduced herself at Meeting, her first Sunday here.

Then as now, she'd been dressed in homespun, proud to show herself a Whig. Back then, in the early days of being shunned, I'd taken pleasure in needling them. "Don't you know Mother and I aren't fit to be touched? We're enemies of American liberty. You're supposed to treat us as loathsome animals!"

"Are you quoting from something?" she asked, eyes sparkling.

"Oh yes, the resolution of October twenty."

"I don't know anything about that," she said. "And I don't obey kings *or* committees. I do as my own conscience dictates." Which would have been a stuffy, pompous New England thing to say, except for the saucy smile that went along with it. It was that which made us friends, immediately, and from her that I got my education in the Whig point of view. She knew all about the protests in Massachusetts, and the reasons people there were so roused and indignant. I was driven to admit that I might have felt the same, and had to fall back to the last-ditch defense, loyalty. Mine was to Fa, New York, King George. Hers was to America, and our rights as British subjects—of which, she said, Parliament was depriving us. For good reason, I said, and she said we Americans were being reduced to a state of slavery, which was illegal and treasonous, and *I* said I had met slaves and the comparison was absurd—it went on and on, and we both enjoyed the battle, and the chance, as intelligent, educated females, to talk about something other than spinning, sewing, and the other domestic arts.

This morning, though, I walked beside her half-blind, my mind beating against the cage of the word *marriage*. We turned onto the side road, striding along briskly, and I didn't notice that she'd gone quiet too until she suddenly said, "Fanna, can you tell me—is Judge Chandler to be depended on?"

The words seemed to come from a great distance. I couldn't make sense of them. "Why?"

She hesitated. "I guess it's all right to tell you—everyone seems to know. He promised to meet us—the Whigs—at court and listen to our grievances. But now they say the court party means to get here first and bar the doors. You probably think that's good news!" she added with a laugh. "But what do you think Judge Chandler's likely to do?"

I struggled to collect my thoughts. *Was* it good news? The Court House was like a fortress. Whoever got inside first would be able to hold it indefinitely. Did that mean nothing was going to happen? "Judge Chandler . . . sees both sides of things. He tells you what you want to hear, and he means it. Then when he's with somebody else, he means something else. He's not dishonest, exactly. Just soft."

Elizabeth snorted. "Soft as a wet cow-pat, it sounds like! He gave his word and honor no arms would be brought against us. *His word and honor*!"

"Fa doesn't rely on him. Not unless he's right there to brace him up."

"I see." She gave me a complicated look and half-smile, and I knew what she was thinking. Nobody here trusted Fa either, not ever. Even if he was doing the very thing he'd promised, people assumed he'd turn it to his own advantage later on. And he might. He thought three steps ahead of everyone else and could see advantage and openings where others saw nothing. It made him useful to New York government, but not loved.

I looked away, because talking about Fa wasn't comfortable even with Elizabeth, and spotted a genuine oddity: Reverend Bullen out in front of his house, talking with Azariah Wright.

I felt Elizabeth's elbow in my ribs. She'd seen them too. We didn't slacken our pace. Reverend Bullen gave us a tiny nod in greeting, briefly taking his eyes from Captain Wright's face, and the captain himself paid us no attention whatsoever. In a moment we were past them. Elizabeth murmured, "Do you think he's going to hit him?"

"Listen!"

But there was no sound of a blow behind us. Captain Wright had been a great friend of Reverend Goodell, the faithless former minister. Reverend Bullen he despised, for reasons unknown, and he would slap the minister whenever they came face to face. Bullen took it. That had astonished me at first, but Azariah Wright was considered a dangerous man, and people let him go his length.

And yet, now they stood talking together quite calmly. There could only be one reason. Bullen was Whiggish in his politics, and politics must have gained the upper hand over personal animosity. They must be talking about whatever was planned for Monday, and I didn't like it. Azariah Wright in control of his emotions was an even more dangerous element. I glanced at Elizabeth, wondering how she saw it, and found her watching me seriously. "Fanna," she said. "What's troubling you?"

I drew a deep breath, or tried too. Something stopped it, a tight band around my chest. "Elizabeth, I . . . might have to get married."

She stopped in her tracks. "Whatever for?" Her gaze dropped to my belly. "You aren't—"

"Of course not! But Mother thinks—Mother says—I'd be safer married. If war comes."

"Married to *who*?"

"I—don't know who he is. She told me just before you came. An officer."

"A *British* officer?"

"We're all British!"

"You know what I mean. Is he from England?"

"I don't know. I don't know anything about him!"

"Marriage should be for love," she said sternly, beginning to walk on.

"And it should be for older people than I am!"

"Yes, it should! Girls do marry at your age, occasionally, but . . . you'll let them do that? Marry you to someone you don't even know? I know New York ways are different than ours, but—"

"*New York ways*? We aren't *that* different!"

"You aren't? What about those Hudson River families. What do they call themselves? 'The Patroons'? Your mother grew up there, didn't she?"

"Yes, but—we aren't like them." Though we wanted to be. The Patroons, with their vast estates, their hundreds of tenants all paying rent, their mansions and servants and aristocratic lives—who wouldn't want to live like them? Love existed among that class, but marriages were alliances, meant to consolidate power and wealth. Patroon of the Connecticut is what Fa wanted to be, and Mother shared the ambition.

But I couldn't bear the appalled look on Elizabeth's face. "It's not like that, Elizabeth, really! This isn't about money, it's to keep me safe. His family has promised to take us in if a war starts."

"Us," Elizabeth said flatly.

"Yes, Mother and me—don't look like that! You don't understand. I didn't just *happen* to Mother and Fa. I'm not their child!"

She shook her head in bewilderment. "You're *her* child, aren't you? She was a widow when she married your stepfather—the widow Montusan."

"No. We say that, but it isn't true. My father's name is John Montresor. A British officer. My—*real*—mother was his mistress. Mother's sister, Anna. She was my age." My voice wobbled. "He abandoned her, and she died when I was born. Mother found me or I would have died too, and when she married Fa, he adopted me. They didn't have to."

"*Somebody* had to!"

"No, they didn't. Babies like me die all the time. Mother *saved* me. I owe her."

"That much? Think about it, Fanna! It's your whole life, probably. Very few husbands are so obliging as to die young!"

I pressed one hand to my throat, shuddering. "I don't even know if he's young. He probably isn't. A young man would want to choose his own wife!"

"A nice young man would! What are you going to do?"

"*Do?*"

"Yes, do. Defy them? Run away? You do own a very fast horse!"

"But who would I go to? There's no one—except my grandfather, and Mother would just go there and fetch me."

"Then you must simply refuse. But honestly, why is this necessary? Wars happen all the time without people rushing to get married. What about your father? Would he take your part?"

"No, he arranged it."

"Your natural father, I mean."

A laugh choked out of me. "*Him*? No, he wants nothing to do with me! He drove us out of New York when I started to come out in society. I *embarrassed* him—because he was married by then, and there were *two* Frances Montresors. Nobody was fooled by *Montusan*. I don't know why Mother thought they would be."

"She was wrong," Elizabeth said. "She was wrong about that, and I think she's very wrong about this. *Morally* wrong, and mistaken as to the necessity. You mustn't let her force you into it!" She looked me fiercely in the face. "Fanna, wake *up*! I don't understand! You're so spirited and independent, but all your mother has to do is frown and you just . . . *fold*. I respect my mother as much as anyone in this world, but I started thinking for myself at the age of eight!"

"I—" My voice croaked. My tongue felt as if it was made of cotton. "I think for myself."

"Thinking isn't doing. This is an absurd idea, and you're treating it as a commandment. 'I might have to get married!'" She threw my own words at me. "As if you were a child!"

I looked down at my feet. "I'm . . . not as old as you are."

"Yes!" she said forcefully. "Exactly my point. You're too young to be married, and you mustn't agree to it. I don't think they can force you. And you don't owe your mother your whole life's happiness."

But I did. Without Mother, my life would have been snuffed out like a candle-flame before I was two days old. I owed her *everything*.

We reached the springs, and about-faced like militia men on drill, if militiamen ever felt shaky from their soles all the way up to their armpits. Elizabeth's eyes glittered. She was furious at me, it seemed, and I couldn't bear it. "What will happen Monday?" I asked, hoping to shift the talk away from myself. "Will there be fighting?"

"No," she said flatly. "Our men won't be armed. They never are. Guns make it treason, but every Englishman has a right to carry a staff."

"Then . . . what *is* going to happen?" I tried to work it out in my mind. The judges planned to get to the Court House first. With them would come Sheriff Billy Paterson, Fa's staunch ally, who *did* carry a sword and pistols. If he and the judges went inside and locked the doors, and the Whigs had only sticks—then it was all over, wasn't it? No damage to Fa or New York government. No war, at least not here, not now. No reason to marry? Could it be as simple as that?

I suspected not. Behind Mother's talk of war lay something else, something I didn't want to mention to Elizabeth and could barely bring myself to even acknowledge. Mother had mentioned a family business. What business? What family? Fa had given me Cloud in part to cement his relationship with the rich and powerful DeLanceys. That had never been said in so many words, but his satisfaction with the purchase was out of proportion to the pleasure he'd had in giving her to me. He had dynastic ambitions, and only one pawn to deploy, his own daughter being far away in Ireland. That was behind this too. Mother wouldn't say that, even if I asked, and it seemed to me that I'd rather die than admit it to Elizabeth.

Which left us with nothing to say. We turned back onto the street, which seemed full of people now. I had a sense of news spreading, from Whig to Whig and Tory to Tory. Everybody seemed to be in the same mood, excited and trying to hide it: bright eyes, and firmly closed lips.

Elizabeth started to say something, then stopped herself. We'd always been direct with each other; it was the chief delight of this friendship. But now she was clearly thinking better of whatever it was she'd been about to say. *This is war,* I thought. Even friends can't speak candidly. I looked away to hide the tears prickling my eyes, and a moment later felt her small, work-roughened hand take mine. She squeezed it, almost too hard, and let it drop.

Chapter 7

Back in our kitchen, Mother was briskly grating nutmeg into her cheese cake mix, her face smooth and blank. I could see the moment I stepped in that she was behind her wall, with no intention of taking up the difficult topic between us. But there was no need to take it up. "Good news!" I said. "The judges—"

She met my eyes and shook her head slightly. I glanced around the kitchen. Isaac? I didn't see him, but Mother must think he was somewhere nearby.

But he wasn't, because a few minutes later I heard him clump up onto the back step. He came in and dropped another armload of oven wood on the hearth. "Thank you," Mother said. "Will you get the horses ready for when we finish baking?"

That surprised a question out of him. "Both of them?"

"Yes. Fanny and I want to ride out."

We did? Mother had ridden very seldom since winter set in. Isaac cleared off to the barn. I watched him disappear inside, but when I started to speak; she shook her head again. "Later, Fan."

"He's in the barn—"

"Later."

I shut my mouth, but not submissively. She wasn't worried about Isaac! She just didn't want to talk with me right now, and she was shushing me like a child. All right, I'd wait, but I had things to say to her, starting with why and ending with no. I listed them in my mind, as we baked off cheese cakes, pies, johnnycake, and bread. But my thoughts were tumultuous. I'd catch myself wondering: Would I make cheese cakes for *him*? Pies? Or would we have servants—but no, I wasn't marrying him. Was he handsome? Though that didn't matter either. Would I follow the drum? If war came . . . I'd only marry him if there was war, and I had to—and that was ridiculous! *Wars happen all the time without people rushing to get married! Honestly, is this necessary?*

Honestly?

I looked over at Mother, resolutely absorbed in her baking. We *would* talk about this. I would *not* fold, and the next time I'd see Elizabeth, I'd be able to look her in the eye, woman to woman. Mother had made a mistake pushing me out the door earlier, if she wanted me still shocked and compliant.

We finished our work by putting a dish of apples to cook in the waning heat of the oven, then sat down to a dinner of warmed-up venison stew, with a few of the cakes that had scorched or crumbled; only the most perfect ones would be set before the judges. Afterward Mother and I went upstairs to change.

It was my first moment alone since . . . *since*. And it wasn't real solitude. Even in this empty room, I could hear Mother stepping around her own chamber. It wouldn't be very many minutes before she'd be down in the hall waiting for me, tapping her foot.

I changed into a quilted petticoat and my riding skirt, arranged my cravat somewhat haphazardly, pinned on waistcoat and jacket, secured on my hat. With each layer, tie, and fastening, I felt myself become more fit for public viewing. The mannish cut of the joseph and the manly cravat were daring, ambiguous, controversial even.

The things girls said about this habit! Elizabeth had told me some of them. *It was unnatural!* From the waist up I looked like a young man—if a young man were prone to dressing in leaf-green twill. *Of all the impractical colors! That fabric would not wear well.* Etcetera. Some of it was social outrage, some was pure jealousy, because even these high-minded New England girls had an eye for fashion. It made me no friends, this joseph, but it was armor. When I checked myself in the mirror, I didn't see the portrait girl with those shocked, black eyes. A young woman looked back at me, her expression somewhere between composed and defiant. Not a simple creature, not a child. She was *somebody*. *I* was somebody, and not to be disposed of lightly. I smoothed one long green sleeve and looked the mirror girl in the eyes. *We'll see*, I thought at her. *We'll just see.*

I swept downstairs. Mother was already going out the door. She greeted Joost with a pat on the nose and a swift, assessing glance. "They look in prime condition, Isaac." It was rare that she praised him; I couldn't see that he seemed especially gratified. He helped her into the saddle, and I noticed his red, chilblained wrists. His arms were longer than his sleeves, and the cold had been nipping him. Someone should knit him a pair of cuffs. Whose responsibility was it to do that? Ours?

But he was holding his hands out now, ready for me to step into them. The moment I was in the saddle, before I'd even settled my skirts, Mother rode out of the yard, keeping ahead of me so I couldn't see her face. Joost was the slower horse, but she put energy into him, contriving to leave me trailing half a pace behind, all the way up the street to the Court House.

A surprising number of people were out on the gray, breezy afternoon, talking in pairs and small groups. Most went silent as we passed. A few with Tory leanings said hello, or nodded courteously, but many of our neighbors looked straight through us. After all, we were loathsome animals! Though what kind of animal wore fashionable habits, and rode fine, high-spirited horses? Perhaps the truth was the horses prancing and jigging and tossing their heads created the appearance that we were showing off. When I came up beside Mother, I saw the color burning in her cheeks. This was why she'd given up riding.

"What's your news?" she asked abruptly.

"*My* news? You're forcing me to marry!"

She didn't dignify that with a response. Anger flared in my chest. She couldn't have it both ways. I was either a child or a woman. A child couldn't marry. A woman must be treated as an equal. "That *is* my news," I said.

"You were going to tell me something," she said, in a voice of excessive patience. "When you came back from your walk."

For a moment I almost didn't remember. Impending public events paled next to what I was facing. But yes, there had been news. "Elizabeth says the judges are going to get here early and keep the Whigs out."

Mother looked scornful. "If true, where are they?" There was no sign of unusual activity from the Court House, just a wisp of smoke rising from the chimney to show that the jailer was keeping his prisoners warm and fed.

"They have three days," I said.

"No. It's Saturday, remember? Nobody will stir between sundown today and sunrise Monday, except to go to Meeting. The time for them to get here is now!"

Right again! Right, right, right. I hated that. Elizabeth loved to point out the times when Mother was wrong, but that was all too seldom in my view. But that didn't mean she was right about marriage, a question we would soon thresh out!

Cloud took all my attention for the moment, though, as she minced down the steep slope of Court House Hill fussing at the bit. She was anticipating her run, but Mother turned off the road immediately, onto the narrow track that led to the boat landing.

At the riverbank, she drew rein. I pulled up beside her, looking out over the broad expanse of ice. A stained and trampled trail crossed it, peppered with horse manure, some of it quite fresh. The ice was still sound, then, or people thought it was. Smoke drifted lazily from cabins on the other side, over in New Hampshire.

"Are we crossing?" I asked, suppressing a shudder. Under that opaque surface flowed black, hungry water. How strong was the ice, really? I always wondered, even in the depth of winter, and here we were at the beginning of spring.

"Not now," Mother said. "But if we need to—"

"Why would we need to? Mary Averill said—Mother, why do you look like that? She wasn't lying to me! Her whole family's in the militia! She must know their plan!"

"Plans change, Fan, and they fail. If I learned one thing being a soldier's daughter, I learned that."

"But—*when* would we leave? Where would we go?"

"We'll leave when we have to, if we have to, and we'll impose on Ben Bellows for a few days, until I find someone to escort us to New York."

Bellows was the leading man of Walpole, the town directly across the river in New Hampshire, and famous for his charity. He'd taken in Westminster settlers during the war when conditions in this area became dangerous. But there was a drawback. "He's a Whig."

"A friend." She turned back toward the road, taking up the center of the path so I had to follow half a pace behind like an aide-de-camp, watching her stiff, straight shoulders and yielding waist. This was no gentle ride to take the air; it was a military-style reconnoiter and not finished yet. When we reached the road and could ride abreast again, she forestalled all further questions by trotting briskly across to the Tory Tavern.

Out in the yard, we found John ushering a couple of boys with a keg through the taproom door while carrying on two simultaneous conversations, one with a stablehand, one with Silence Ranney. The herb doctress sat on her pony, stroking a cat that perched near her on one of the hitching posts. John's quick eyes caught sight of us, and he raised a hand in greeting. *Wait,* his face said.

Mrs. Ranney gave the cat a final scratch behind the ear and turned the pony toward us. "Fanna. Margaret." Though she was no older than Mother, her graying hair hung in strings beside her lean face. Her mouth was sunken; no amount of herbs could keep teeth in a woman's head through the births of thirteen children. Her nose was red with cold, her large, greenish eyes wide and apparently vague. I'd been fooled by that look before, though. Those eyes were more observant than they appeared. "You can save me a ride," she said. "Tell young Isaac he's to get this out to his mother soon." She held out a small deerskin pouch about the size of my hand.

I sidled Cloud close enough to take it. "Instructions?" The pouch gave off a sharp, resinous scent as I shoved it into my pocket.

"She knows."

"Mistress Ranney," Mother said. "What is your husband's thinking on this business?" Deacon Ranney, a staunch Yorker and pillar of town government, was one of those men whom Fa considered an ally. Not a friend, though, and his wife mulled Mother's question, her greenish eyes like stones in a cold brook, gleaming and impenetrable.

"This business?"

"The foolish promise Judge Chandler has made, to meet with the Whigs and talk about closing the court. The justices apparently mean to scotch it by getting to the Court House first and barring the door—but as everyone in Cumberland County seems to know that plan, I'd like to see our people secure the building today. Would the Deacon—"

"My husband won't involve himself," the herb doctress said. "If Judge Chandler made a promise, he should keep it. That's what we believe."

Ranneys always do what's right. How many times had I heard that said? Deacon Ranney might be one of us in politics, but he was New England to the marrow, all godliness and rectitude, and I wasn't in the least surprised by his wife's answer. Mother didn't seem to be either. She gave the other woman a moderately friendly nod, acknowledging the refusal, and bent down from the saddle to speak to John.

Silence Ranney shifted her gaze to me, and her cold eyes warmed a little. "Did you finish the drawing of the moss, Fanna? The Old Man's Beard?"

"Not yet. It's intricate."

She mouthed the word: *intricate.* Her lips folded oddly around it in the absence of teeth. She must have been a handsome woman before the ravages of childbirth, and clearly her health was unimpaired. Her grown daughters ran their father's tavern these days, while she rambled the roads and trails of Cumberland County with her bags of bark and roots. She was a true eccentric, and a free woman, and I suddenly wondered; would *she* help me? She liked me, I knew. I was a sort of student. She frequently set me these drawing tasks to refine my skills of observation.

She gathered her reins, preparing to ride away, and I felt an impulse to keep her near. "Tell me, Mistress Ranney, what is the moss good for? I meant to look it up in a botanical, but we've been so busy."

"Many ailments, more than you'll find in your books. It depends on the patient, and the illness."

I crushed down a spurt of irritation. It wasn't helpful when these doctresses made a mystery of things. If an herb helped a certain condition, that should be written down for everyone to read. "How do you know, then?"

"When I see the sick person, I see the herb too, standing between us, and the herb tells me how to use it."

"In *words*?"

"How else?" She pushed the hood of her cloak back. Her face was lit with interest, making her suddenly almost handsome. "You can't learn my method. It's given or it's not, and if given, the gift must be used in the Lord's service."

"And what is a person supposed to do who *doesn't* have this gift?"

"If dealing with a dangerous condition, consult someone like me. But every woman should know the powers of mint and ginger and mustard. And onions," she added, after a moment's reflection.

"Do you ever see an herb when a person isn't sick? When they're in danger in another way?"

A slight frown momentarily furrowed her brow. She studied me for a moment, made as if to speak, then checked herself, and turned as something Mother said caught her attention. The conversation with John was growing heated. "—secure it!" Mother said, and John shook his head vehemently.

"Exactly the wrong thing to do!" His voice had a sharp, carrying rap of anger. "Nobody's threatened violence yet. Let it not be our side doing that first!"

Near them, very near, the stablehand leaned into his work of boring a new hole in a harness strap, using the fence rail to steady the leather. Only that wasn't what he was really doing, I realized. I could almost see him tipping an ear toward John and Mother.

"Mother!" I called sharply. She turned her head, and I scrambled for something to say to justify the interruption. "We'd better go if we're going to keep our promise. Don't you think?"

She was quick, very quick. Only one moment of confusion; then she turned back to John, saying smoothly, "Fanny's right, we need to be going. But—" She looked into his face, and he looked back impassively. Whatever it was she'd asked, he was still refusing.

When we were out of earshot I said, "That stablehand was listening. Like Isaac does."

"He didn't learn much to the purpose! John won't stir himself. And to think that fifteen years ago he was a soldier."

"What did you ask him to do?"

"The same thing I asked Silence Ranney. It would only take a few men to hold that Court House until the sheriff gets here!"

"John would never do that," I said. "It would take him away from his tavern at a very busy and profitable time, for one thing."

"That's not his reason. This horse wants to run. Are you ready?"

I wrapped my knees securely around the two horns of the sidesaddle and nodded, and we unleashed them—and it was wonderful! Joost was of Dutch breeding, and they always galloped their horses up steep hills. Cloud was a Wildair, unwilling to let anything on four legs outrun her. Their hooves thundered and the snow flew up behind as they raced each other neck and neck. Didn't I vow I'd never gallop on the street again? Wasn't that only yesterday? Heaven help any child that strayed out in front of us now!

But none did. We burst up over the crest of the hill and the horses slowed abruptly, sides heaving. The steam of their breath gathered around us, along with a rich smell of horse sweat. The prisoners at the window of their cell cheered or jeered; I couldn't tell which, and I didn't care. The gallop had done miracles for my spirit.

"Could *we* do it?" I asked, when I'd caught my own breath.

"Do what?"

"Hold the Court House. If we had Fa's pistols?"

"No. We'd make ourselves ridiculous, and put ourselves in danger—"

"I *am* in danger!" She gave me a swift glance and gathered Joost's reins, ready to ride on. I kept pace with her this time, looking her straight in the face. "Is this marriage your plan? Or Fa's?"

"We'll ride down to look at Willard Landing," she said, "and see if they can be moved—"

"Mother, *answer* me! If I'm old enough to be married I'm old enough to be told the reason for it. The *real* reason!"

"Hush, Fan. Don't make a present of our affairs to everyone on the street."

"Nobody can hear us! You need to tell me! Why do you think there's going to be a war, and why am I the only girl in North America who needs to get married if war comes?"

"I don't know that there's going to be a war," she said. "Nobody does. Maybe the fever burned itself out over the winter. But if that's so, Fanny, why is General Gage fortifying the Neck? He expects to be attacked. I *very much* don't want an incident here, in our own county, to be the spark that ignites the conflict. That could ruin your fa, and it can be prevented, if somebody will only *do* something!"

"I don't care about that! Why have you suddenly decided that I need to be married?" The stubborn, closed look came over her face. "You have to tell me! You can't have it both ways! If I'm a child, you shouldn't be doing this; and if I'm not, then I should be told!"

Amazingly, that had an impact that she wasn't able to hide. She looked down at Joost's neck for several strides. "You're right, Fanny," she said finally. "Your situation is delicate."

"My situation."

"Your birth. If your mother had been—virtuous—"

"Why is *she* the one who lacks virtue? My father seduced a brother-officer's daughter and abandoned her. *He's* the one I'm ashamed of!" I was shocked to find angry tears running hot down my face. I brushed them away with my sleeve.

"They have nothing to do with you, either of them," she said quietly. "You started this world fresh, Fanny. Every baby does, no matter who its parents are. I knew that the moment I picked you up, and you opened your eyes."

"But you think I might be like her! That's why you keep watch over me! That's why you want me nailed down! Married to *anybody!*"

She shook her head. "I loved my sister, Fan. Loved the sparkle in her eyes when she was doing something naughty. She was like a colt, or a kitten. Playing. Playing at having a lover—and maybe he was playing too, but he broke his toy and threw it away. You are not her or him, but the world thinks otherwise. People who know your parentage won't expect you to be a woman of virtue, and that does put you in danger, especially during a time of upheaval. It also lessens your chances of making a good marriage—"

"And *this* is a good marriage? Someone I don't even know?" But in truth I wasn't thinking of myself primarily. My heart was breaking for that girl who had looked just like me, who was only playing and who lost her life. I bowed over Cloud's neck, trying to crush back my sobs.

"Fanny, Fanny," she said, and her voice was different now, the voice I heard when I was sick or terribly disappointed. "Oh Fanny. Hold your head up, don't let them see. We'll talk more when we get to the other landing."

Chapter 8

First, people weren't supposed to hear us. Now they mustn't see us—but in truth, the street was nearly empty now. The sinking sun, a white pearl in the gray sky down near the western ridgeline, had sent men to their barnyards, boys to the woodpiles, women and girls indoors, all doubly busy as they prepared for their day of rest and worship.

But not everyone was indoors. I spotted a scarlet cap crossing the backyards, Asa Averill glanced back at us as he went through the door of his cabin, a stray girl or two lingering near back fences watching some stray boy or other. I straightened in the saddle, sniffing—and if that was audible, people would just have to assume it was due to the cold!

At the south end of the street, the road dove sharply down Willard Hill to river level. It was a hill I seldom traveled on account of Billy, my unwelcome suitor, but it was a sightly one, with snow-covered meadows opening out to the east. This was the old part of Westminster. Forty years ago, settlers from Massachusetts built two cabins here, but before the town could grow any larger, New Hampshire split off from the Bay Colony, and the border was established south of here. The Massachusetts grants no longer held, and the settlers went home.

Years later the Averills, Carpenters, Phippens, and Goolds—married couples with children—canoed up the river to settle here under grants from New Hampshire. They stayed two years, until war resumed with the French and Indians and the place became too dangerous. For seven years the cabin stood empty, until 1760, the year I was born, when England defeated France, and it was finally safe for English settlers to return. That was when the town of Westminster got its start. That silvered log cabin, now the ell of the Willard farmhouse, was the oldest building in it.

53

A long, level track led out through the fields. We turned onto it, Mother giving the barest glance down the main road. She had no real expectation of seeing a posse coming. I paid more attention to the Willard house, having every expectation of being spotted by Billy. The house was sheltered against the side of the hill, but what a lonely place, set down away from the street! How much lonelier when they first came and there was no street, only a dozen or so settlers within fifty miles and the shadow of the bad old times lying over everything. A hundred years of war, and it wasn't done yet, apparently. No sooner had we defeated the French then we must turn and fight each other.

And before the settlers? Had it been peaceful then? That was a history out of reach to me. I knew only that this was Abenaqui land, but that they had nearly all died in a great pestilence. The remnant had retreated north into Québec, from whence they issued forth frequently with their French allies to kill and capture English settlers. Everyone in Westminster had stories of Indian attack in their background—everyone in New England! All that ended—or paused—around the time I was born. All the captives had come home, some speaking favorably of the Abenaquis and saving their wrath for the French, at whose behest these raids were made. Some former captives even blamed the British government. Who could tell right from wrong? War was normal in America, and left its long trail of debris and grief, palpable here on this stark white meadow where the graves of Abenaquis were often turned up by the plow.

The snow near the Willard landing was well packed down. Snowshoe trails led along the bank and out across the ice, which must be solid here as well. The surface looked granular and gray, like the skin of some enormous fish. This, too, was a possible escape route, and we wouldn't need to pass the Court House. Where, I reminded myself, nothing was going to happen. The judges and sheriff would arrive first and lock the doors, the unarmed protesters would arrive too late, and this crisis would pass.

But would that actually help me? Something else lay behind this marriage proposition. I hadn't gotten to the bottom of it yet.

"Why *now?*" I asked, breaking the silence. "Nothing's happened yet. Maybe it never will—or it might be a long time from how. A lot of things could be different."

Mother continued scanning the ice, and the opposite bank of the river. "One thing won't change," she said. "Your—background—is an obstacle for many. To the Buchanans, it matters little. Their interests are commercial. They see the possible advantage of land here on the river—"

"Who are the Buchanans?"

"The man your fa has chosen is Captain John Buchanan. A cousin of the shipping family."

I'd heard of the Buchanans. There was money there. But . . . "Just a cousin? How does that help?"

"He's well regarded within the family. He'll have a place in the firm whenever he chooses to leave the army."

"What is he like?"

"Your fa says there's nothing objectionable about his person."

"Nothing objectionable! How would *Fa* know? I don't need the Buchanans. Fa can protect me!"

"We both will, if we can. But if war comes, it's impossible to say what duties"—she hesitated—"and *opportunities* may call him away from us. You and I would have a claim on the Buchanans, especially if—"

Especially if I fell pregnant.

I could barely bring myself to think this, let alone say it. The sick feeling came back. I could only see this Captain Buchanan as Billy Willard in a scarlet coat. I'd fended off Billy for years, but John Buchanan would have a right to me.

On the other hand . . . on the other hand, it was in time of war that my mother was seduced and then abandoned when Captain Montresor went off with the army into Canada. An honorable man would have left her in someone's care; nonetheless, the story did tend to strengthen Mother's chaos-of-war argument.

"It's not everything I could wish for you, Fan," she was saying, her voice matter-of-fact again. "That's why I'm determined to do nothing rash. It would be regrettable to have you stuck in a marriage such as this when you might look higher."

I swallowed, and swallowed again. My mouth was almost too dry for speech. "I might look for love."

There was a pause. Then she said, "Love is dangerous when a woman's virtue is in doubt. Prudence is a better guide. The Buchanans are clear-sighted, Fan. They know as well as I do that no blame can attach to you for your birth—and what they think, others will think in time."

"Are you sure? Won't they look down on me in spite of themselves?"

"I think not. Once you're one of them, it will be in their interest to defend you, and they will. They have a reputation for sticking to their bargains."

It all had a smell of commerce to me. When I bought something at a shop—in the days when we lived where there were shops—I always defended it as good of its kind. I would never admit to making a bad choice. Was that the way I could expect to be valued?

"Is my—situation—the whole reason for this?" I asked.

She turned Joost and started back across the silent white field. I rode Cloud beside her, continuing to look her in the face, insisting on an answer. After a few moments it came. "It's *my* reason."

"What's Fa's?"

She sighed. A rising breeze stirred the stiff feather in her hat. "He . . . sees advantage. If he can gain your security and . . . create an alliance . . . it will help all of us, Fan. We'll prosper together."

"I should have been *asked*," I said. "Not told."

Another deep, swelling breath. "Having you secure, married into a wealthy family—gives him solidity. It did him no good, the association with—"

"With me?"

"With disgrace. We imperfectly concealed your origins, my dear. We failed to understand—well, who could have predicted we'd be constantly rubbing shoulders with the man when you came out in society? Who would have imagined his *discomfort*? If I had kept you quietly in Albany, or we'd lived in strict privacy in New York, all might have been well. We flew too high. We scorched our wings. Now your fa is soaring again, and I won't have him brought down. I doubt he could endure it."

I felt the cage closing around me. It was true, Fa was once again indispensable to people at the highest levels of government. He'd recovered his spirits, his financial prospects were good, and if he sought to better them, to increase his security, *our* security, could I blame him? Could I resist? I was the one who'd brought him low. It wasn't my fault, but it was due to me, nonetheless.

"Does he think I'd *like* John Buchanan?"

"I have to be honest, Fan—I don't know if he's given much thought to that. You know what he is when he's in one of his schemes. He thinks of almost everything, all at once, but it may be that his faith in you—how can I say this? You like *him!* Not many do. That may have given him a faith that you'd make the best of any man. But he would never ally you to someone with a bad reputation. He will have checked carefully. I'm sure he'll tell you that."

"I see." I did see. Too much. I'd always understood that Mother's first loyalty was to me, but that must have changed during those dark months after we left New York, when Fa was suffering. "What will happen if I refuse?" My voice grated out, harsh to my own ears. "Has he told people?"

"It hasn't been announced. He will have left himself a way out."

"Then what should I *do?*" I turned to her, pleading, and Cloud followed my turn, so that Joost was pushed off the packed trail into the deeper snow and had to flounder out of it. "What should I do for *me?* For my happiness?"

"You shouldn't ask me that," she said swiftly. "Don't put your happiness in the hands of anyone whose motives are mixed."

"*His* are! John Buchanan's!"

"Yes. Even if you wed him, keep your happiness in your own hands, Fan."

"Have *you?*"

But her attention had shifted to William and Billy Willard, walking out from the house to meet us. Billy, a few steps ahead of his father, was nearly as good-looking as he thought himself to be, but he marred it with his swagger, arms carried a trifle wide from his body, elbows cocked, fists squared. The Willards had been fighters as long as the family had been in America; during Queen Anne's War, every officer in Fort Dummer had been a Willard. Billy spent his childhood in the fort. It was how life was around here then, but he was the only person who swaggered about it.

"What's he trying to do?" I murmured. "Air out his underarms?"

Mother ignored that, lifting one gloved hand in salute. Billy's mother, watching us from the doorway, tilted her head in a frigid reply, showing off a snowy white cap with long strings. She'd put that on when she saw us cross the field, I was sure. Nobody wore a cap like that on Saturday afternoon!

William Willard greeted us. "Good day to you, Mistress Brush, Miss Fanna. What brings you to this end of town?"

Mother answered bluntly. "I'm trying to discover our plan for countering this nonsense about closing the court."

"Paterson's to gather a posse," Willard said, "and secure the Court House ahead of the session."

"When?" Mother asked. "Today? Tomorrow?"

His long face stiffened. "Tomorrow is the Sabbath."

"Our Lord might overlook a bit of Sabbath-breaking, if it was to defend the King's interests."

Willard's gray eyes congealed. "Fortunately, ma'am, Our Lord will condone Sabbath-breaking sooner than Azariah Wright will."

"Monday's soon enough!" Billy said. "Don't you worry, ma'am. Billy Paterson will bring the boys up in time." He tilted his chin up at us, showing off the strong column of his bare throat. He must have taken off his stock, I realized, to demonstrate his looks and manliness. *May he catch a cold!* I thought. *A* violent *cold!*

Mother said, "War doesn't keep the Sabbath, Mr. Willard. At least, the last war didn't."

His eyes flashed cold, unexpected fire. "You've no need to tell me that, madam! Me of all people."

Billy looked embarrassed. "The raid on Rutland was a Sunday. The Indians killed his father. But we were fighting papists and savages then. These are our own people—"

"Yes, *our* people!" his father said. "What call has 'Riah got to stir up this trouble? For *nothing!* For a *notion, a lie!* I've been at war my whole life long—we all have. *She!*" He gestured furiously at his wife. "It's only the last three years she's been able to sleep in her bed the whole night, without getting up to listen at the shutter. And now we've got express-riders running this way and that all night long, and she's at it again, and all for a bunch of made up nothing. *Rights!*" He spat into the snow.

Mother didn't say a word. The silence lengthened. A lazy snowflake drifted down, landing on the one of Cloud's slender, twitching ears. Then the air was full of them, as if someone had emptied a feather bed over our heads. Mother held out a gloved hand and caught one, looked closely at it, and said, "We'd best be going, sirs. I imagine we'll see you tomorrow at Meeting. Good day."

Chapter 9

"A complete waste of time!" That was every word Mother said, the whole length of the street. Her search for help, for men on our side willing to take action, had come to nothing. The conversation we'd had—or call it a running skirmish—had that also been a waste? For me it had been devastating. I'd been determined to discover the idea of marriage was simply absurd. It was not absurd, however; it might even be smart, and what *was* I to do? Run away from parents who loved me, and were afflicting me in part because of their love? I couldn't imagine it, not convincingly, but neither could I imagine defying them. But what could I do? Every alternative seemed impossible.

We reached home past sundown, the street empty, our defiance of the Sabbath highly obvious if anyone had chanced to observe it. There was no point in changing; we sat down in our riding habits to cheese and johnnycake, as if the kitchen were a tavern dining room.

I couldn't eat, though, crumbled johnnycake on my plate. I stared into the fire, got up unconsciously to pace, met Mother's eyes, sat back down. She didn't look at me again but sat methodically chewing the portion she'd served herself. I caught Isaac watching her, with something very near to a puzzled expression on his face. He must wonder why she'd ridden out this afternoon—

"Oh!" I reached into my pocket for the doeskin bag. "For your mother, Isaac. From Mistress Ranney. Get it to her soon, she said."

He took it without comment, placing it on the table beside his plate. He would give it to one of the family when he saw them at Meeting tomorrow, I supposed. Was his mother with child again? She hadn't been to Meeting in several weeks, often a sign that a woman was increasing—

My stomach lurched. Increasing. Marriage meant babies. There was no way around that. And babies could be the death of you. I had been for my own mother—

I was on my feet again. This time Mother forbore to notice. I lit a candle from the one on the table, carried it into the front parlor, and leaning my hot brow against the cold windowpane, looked out at the Court House through a screen of fat snowflakes. It would not be a deep snowfall. The clouds were already thin and fleecy. The fat, waxing moon shone through them, and I could see a candle gleam dimly in one window of the Court House. It was the visible symbol of Fa's power and influence, but if you need a fortress, it's a sign that you're in enemy territory—

"Fan?" Mother put her head through the door. I'd known she would. It was a few minutes sooner than I'd expected, though. Her level eyes assessed me, while pretending not to. "Good, you haven't gone to bed yet. Be sure to take a soapstone. That was a long, chilly ride. I feel it yet."

Checking on my whereabouts. Making sure I hadn't slipped out the front door into the night. "It didn't seem long to me," I said, in a voice that sounded hard to my ears. "I ride every day."

"So you do," she said. "But take a soapstone anyway." She turned away from the door, and I followed her back to the kitchen as I was meant to do. Isaac was banking the fire, yawning. Any other night he'd slip out after supper—probably to report to Captain Wright on what he'd overheard that day. But Saturday evenings even he stayed home and went to bed early in his blankets beside the kitchen hearth, warmer and snugger than either of us.

Mother got the warmed soapstones out of the fire, holding their iron handles with a heavy wool pad. When we had Anna, all this would have been done by her. Except in the very coldest depth of winter, we would have spent the evening in the parlor. A little ahead of bedtime, she would have gone up with a warming pan and the soapstone, so that even though the rooms were unheated, the beds themselves were at least tolerable by the time we went up. In our new life as loathsome animals without a hired girl, we must get our own soapstones, stepping around Isaac if he happened to have rolled up in his blanket by the hearth already. Would we have servants, John Buchanan and I? Though I wouldn't marry him . . .

We climbed the stairs with our soapstones and candles, said goodnight in the hallway without turning toward each other, went into our cold bedchambers and closed the doors. I set my candle down next to the mirror, parted the bed-hangings, pushed the soapstone down between the sheets. The bed was slightly repulsive to me, as if it were a stranger's bed. The girl who got out of it this morning would never get back in.

Time to undress now, but I couldn't and not for the usual reason. Every night came this struggle, to strip down to my shift, and submit shivering flesh to the icy sheets; every night I delayed until the cold of the room outweighed the chill of the sheets. But that was normal. Everyone in New England and New York experienced that.

Tonight undressing savored of indecency. John Buchanan—really, was I being asked to surrender myself, my very body, to him, a stranger, for the sake of safety and advantage? How was *that* safe? Nothing was safe, I concluded, pacing the room, hugging myself. Nothing was safe—and who was I to demand safety? I'd lived a sheltered life since Mother found me in that cold lodging by the river. I'd been cared for, I'd fared richly, I'd lived at peace, been educated and pampered—and was I weakened by that? I turned to my reflection: face dim and blurred in the light of the one candle, mouth small and tight, eyes glittering. How many girls like me, how many women like Mother, had been awakened by gunfire in the middle of the night, seen their men and sometimes their children slain before their eyes, and been dragged out into the snow to march to Canada? Some of them were with child. They gave birth and kept walking, the ones who could, the ones who weren't killed. They survived captivity and came back, lost a husband and married another and had more children—and I was saying 'I *can't*'? I could. Marrying was the easiest thing in the world. Everyone did it. I didn't know any adult in this town who was single. Oh, maybe widowed for a month or two, and most young people chose to wait till their early twenties to get started—

Chose. That was the important thing. When they were ready, they made their own decisions, wisely or unwisely, paired off according to their own inclinations. That was all I wanted, the simple privileges that even Anna could claim—a few more years to grow and learn, and then to make my own choice—

Just then my attention was caught by a sound out in the hall, a short rasp or scrape, repeated, and repeated again. What could it be? The spare bedroom was where we stored some of our winter supplies like corn and rye, that could be frozen without harm. Could a squirrel have gotten in?

Not a squirrel. This sounded almost like a small saw ripping through a board. I stepped to the door and put my ear to the crack, looking around the dim room for some sort of weapon. But I had nothing save the little knife I used to sharpen pencils, and I didn't really think this was an intruder. After a few moments I opened the door a crack, easing the latch so it didn't make the slightest clink.

The sound came from across the hall, from Mother's room—and once I realized that, I knew what it was. She was in her bed with her head buried under the covers and a pillow, her knuckles jammed into her mouth, and not even that could quiet her sobs.

Only once before had I heard her weep, in the weeks after we left New York. Then, as now, I'd stood paralyzed, my face hot with what felt like shame; I shouldn't be hearing this.

I should go to her.

I should go back into my own room and close the door and never let her know that I'd heard—and I stood listening, while the little scraping sound went on and on.

At last I did go back into my own bedchamber and quietly closed the door. I felt blank inside, all thought suspended. If . . . no.

But . . . no.

No.

Shouldn't—

I shouldn't. I shouldn't go to her because I shouldn't put my happiness in someone else's hands. She said so herself, and if I went in, I would hug her, and cry too, and goodness knew what promises I might make.

Also, I couldn't. It wasn't in me to cross that hall and open her door and face that sound. That was where the shame came in.

Slowly, feeling almost dizzy, I crossed to the window which overlooked the lane. The snow had stopped completely now. The village was smoothed over in an inch of fresh whiteness that clung to every twig and fence paling.

All the stains and smears of everyday living were erased. Even the cabins looked pretty in the moonlight. Nothing stirred—

But something *had* stirred. Right below my window, a crisp set of horse tracks went down our lane. No tracks came in, of man or beast. That was one of our horses, leaving. Had to be, and who else could have ridden out of here but Isaac?

Chapter 10

How *dare* he? Spy on us and lie to us and ride off on one of our horses! But did he? Maybe someone came in from the side of the yard, or had been hidden in the barn since before the fresh snowfall, and had stolen . . . which horse? Cloud? I had to know. Only one of them was gone. If it wasn't Isaac, then he could ride after the thief.

I snatched up my candle, eased open the door, and crept along the hall. Mother was quieter now. A few more minutes, and she'd have herself under control, and then, once I knew what was going on, it would be safe to knock on her door. I felt my way softly down the stairs crossed with bars of moonlight. There was no sound down here except the clock, and in the kitchen, a very faint hiss from the banked fire. Isaac's blankets were rolled in a shape that implied a sleeper inside, but I already knew before I poked them with my foot.

Empty. It *was* him! When Mother found out about this, there would be a bitter reckoning. I jammed my feet into my boots and let myself out the kitchen door.

The tale was written on the snow. Isaac's tracks strode to the stable door, and came out again beside a set of hoofprints, small, round, and clean. Cloud's tracks. He'd taken Cloud! Once she was clear of the door, his footmarks disappeared completely. He must have leaped onto her back without using the mounting block and ridden off down the lane—and not long since. He was in the kitchen when we got the soapstones, what, half an hour ago? No more than that. That was long enough to vanish completely, most nights. Not tonight! This line of tracks was easily read in the moonlight, and he was at the end of them.

I hurried down the path to the stable, slipping in the fresh snow. Joost turned his head when I opened the door; then, disappointed, he whuffled in the pile of hay in his manger. Isaac must have fed him to stop him from whinnying after Cloud. He wasn't completely settled, though. One ear kept tipping toward the door, and I wasn't the answer to the question he was asking.

"Don't worry, we'll find her," I told him, turning to the saddle rack. My saddle was missing; so Isaac was using that too? I girthed Mother's saddle onto Joost, then bridled him. He made it easy for me, holding his head low and opening his jaws for the bit. "Thank you," I whispered. I'd never ridden him before, never handled him, but he was justifying Fa's choice—the perfect ladies' mount, steady, calm, and kind.

I led him out into the yard where he paused, head high, testing the air and listening. I listened too, for any sound from inside the house. Impossible to believe all this was going on, and Mother didn't know a thing about it. But that appeared to be the case. I should tell her. But that would take time, with Cloud getting farther away every minute, and I knew she'd only tell me not to go.

But I *should* tell her. I couldn't just disappear. What if she discovered I was gone? What would she think?

Joost let out a short sigh and looked at me. I could almost hear his thought. *Are we going?*

We were going. I led him to the block. I'd never mounted Cloud by myself, never even tried, but Joost was different. He stood as still as if carved out of marble while I climbed onto the block, gathered my petticoats in my left hand, pulled them around in a smooth breadth, got reins and pommel firmly in my right hand, and stepped up, twisting to land almost exactly where I wanted to be in the saddle. Easier than I'd expected.

With a great whoosh of breath, as if to say *finally,* Joost set off, following Cloud's tracks down the lane, then south along the street through the sleeping village. Once past the Meeting-house I could see where the tracks turned up the side street, where Elizabeth and I walked this morning. I followed, past Reverend Bullen's cabin, dark under the white moon. Where Isaac had ridden at a walk, I did too. After the last cabin, though, he'd let

Cloud trot, no longer worried about waking anyone. Well, he knew best. He'd probably had a lot of experience!

Joost's hooves made a muffled sound on fresh snow. His heavy mane flowed over my cold hands. Gloves would have been a good idea—but none of this was planned. I'd just rushed out of the house—

—and no one in the entire world knew where I was.

As the realization hit home, I felt smaller, a dot crawling under the bright moon. The trees seemed exceptionally dark and dense, and I started remembering stories. Wolves had chased a few travelers home along this road. Catamounts had taken pigs and calves. *Painters*, people called them sometimes, meaning *panthers*. The big cats dropped on their prey from overhead branches, didn't they? The back of my neck crawled.

But Joost seemed to sense no danger. He carried me at a steady, energetic trot, as if he knew where he was going. Above the springs, Cloud had turned onto the road leading to the west part of town—a rough track, really, rising out of the valley in a long steady climb. The distance lengthened between me and Mother, and I began to feel quite odd—clearheaded yet dreamy, a little outside myself. It was a beautiful night, and a beautiful thing to be a lone traveler in the moonlight—something I'd never done before. Moonlight does strange things to the mind, they say, and mine had gone as flat as milk poured out onto a table. The only sounds were Joost's hooves and far off owls hooting. *Who-who-hu-who, who-who-hu-who-oo?*

Who indeed? Who was Isaac riding to meet? For whom might he be carrying a message? What if I caught up to him and he was with someone, or several someones?

Or what if I missed him? What if he turned off the road and I didn't notice, and Cloud's tracks disappeared?

But as I neared Robinson's gristmill, at the base of Rocky Hill, the simple line of hoofprints multiplied and braided. I pulled up, trying to figure out what had happened. In a moment I could see it; Cloud had gone down the lane to Robinson's and come back out again in the company of another, bigger horse with ragged, untrimmed hooves. The tracks went on together up the main road side by side, never crossing, the two riders probably talking as they went. I could almost see them, as if they'd left a trace of themselves in the air: Isaac in his red cap, perched in my sidesaddle, Cloud's coat the color of winter butter in the moonlight. The other horse? Probably that awkward-looking gray Nathaniel Robinson sometimes rode. The rider may have been the old man himself, but more likely it was one of his sons. He was kindly, Nathaniel Robinson—liked and respected, a leader in town affairs, and also, a leader among the Cumberland County Whigs.

What was going on here? Isaac had delivered a message, most likely from Captain Wright. The two riders would part somewhere up ahead, Isaac carrying word in one direction, Robinson in another. Everyone knew everyone else's business in Cumberland County; that couldn't be accomplished without a lot of riding. No wonder our horses were so fit!

Joost climbed steadily up the steepening road beside the Mill Brook, which gleamed darkly between pillowy banks of snow. In a few minutes, Cloud's tracks turned down the trail that led along a low-lying stretch of the brook and disappeared under the trees. This was the way to the farm where Isaac's family lived. The Robinson horse hadn't wanted to part from his friend. He'd balked and circled, and received a good thump in the ribs, no doubt, because he'd moved on at a faster pace, kicking up clumps of snow as he trotted up over the hill.

So Isaac had two errands, I surmised, one being to deliver Silence Ranney's bundle of herbs. It was a sufficient reason for Sunday traveling. If he had asked for permission to ride Cloud out here, Mother might even have said yes.

Joost tugged at the reins, gazing urgently down the shadowed trail. I held him still, my eyes drawn by the other set of tracks. A question rose to my awareness, and I watched in fascination as it revealed itself.

What if I kept going? West, and farther west, following this road to Crook's Mills and then over the hill to Brookline and beyond. Across the mountains. That was Ethan Allen country—but Fa's enemy would help, wouldn't he, if I said I was running away from that "busie Understrapper," that "Land Jockey"? With his help or without it, I'd make my way to Albany, to my grandfather, who commanded cannons during the European wars, and failed my young mother, and was always kind.

The idea took instant hold. I could smell the beeswax furniture polish in my grandmother's front parlor, hear the German sound of her English, recall the sheltering feeling of that house with its dark cupboards and leaded windows. I was a child there before Mother met Fa. I could claim a child's place again. Mother would guess where I'd gone, she'd follow me, but that would take time, and when she got there, she'd have a struggle on her hands. Partial deafness from years of artillery blasts gave Grandfa Schoolcraft the advantage in an argument. He heard only what he wanted to hear.

I thought of Indians. I thought of panthers. I thought of hunger, wolves, and getting lost, of children who strayed into the woods and were never found, or the ones who were found after many days, but who never really returned—wandering in their minds, people said. The woods weren't always good for a person's mind.

But could I do it? Just keep going?

The answer was yes. It might be foolish, it was certainly dangerous, but I could go. I'd most probably—well, fairly likely—make it to Albany, with a little luck and the kindness of strangers. Without a scrap of food, without a shilling? True, but I was more or less dressed for riding, and Joost was the very horse for the journey, kind and steady. By morning I could be miles away. And would Isaac reveal that he'd been out night riding, and had seen tracks going west? No. He couldn't betray me without betraying himself.

Joost sighed heavily, ending on a groan that was precursor to a whinny. He wanted Cloud. He was becoming distressed. I had not guessed he was such an emotional beast. "Hush." I stroked his neck, experiencing a most unwelcome vision: Mother's face, the look she'd have in her eyes when she discovered I was gone. Blind. Stunned. It would be a level of hurt she'd never be able to conceal or recover from.

The realization came over me like a cold fog. I couldn't do it.

No, *wouldn't* do it. I owed her everything, I really did. My little mother made a mistake in love; for her I was a consequence. For Mother I was a choice, made once in those cold lodgings when I was two days old, and made again every time she lied about having been a widow to account for having a daughter, when she left New York, setting aside her ambitions, when she sat watching Fa brood over his wine in the crooked house because he and she had given their adopted daughter an inadequate disguise. Now *I* must choose, and it wasn't a choice at all. I would not do to her what my own mother did—run off without a word and without looking back. I would stay and fight it out.

I felt the decision alter me, straighten me in the saddle. I remembered the sway of Mother's back as I followed her and Joost this afternoon, steely yet flexible, well-sheathed in her own fashionable riding habit—General Margaret, giving orders by day, sobbing fiercely under her pillow at night. My back felt like that. My heart ached like that. I swore under my breath. "*Damn!* Damn damn—"

Suddenly, down along the brook trail, a voice rang out—a girl's voice! I could tell that much, though whatever she said was lost to me. Another voice, male: Isaac. I heard the sound of a horse coming along through deep snow, sometimes breaking through a crust, and the girl laughing. Joost gave a breathy nicker.

Well now, I thought. *Now we're going to learn something!* Concealment was impossible. The tracks told the tale, and if we were going to have this out, it might as well be right here.

Chapter 11

B etween the tree trunks I saw movement. The girl said something and Isaac answered, and then they came out into the open about twenty yards from me, Isaac walking at Cloud's head. In the saddle—*my* saddle—was one of his sisters, the oldest one. I'd seen her at Meeting—around thirteen, plain as a pudding, with a freckled face and sandy hair and large pale eyes. At the moment she wore only the shift she'd gone to bed in, with a hooded cloak billowing loosely around her. Cloud, my high-strung Cloud, walked placidly as if quite used to this rider.

Suddenly the girl shrieked. "My *boot's* coming off! Isaac, grab it!"

That was too much for Joost. He let out a loud whinny. Cloud shied violently, Isaac stumbled in the snow, and the girl clung to the saddle. The shocked face she turned toward me was so much like Isaac's that I had to laugh—a rather shaky laugh, riding on the surface of other emotions, mainly anger.

"Hello!" I said, putting all the upper-class New York I'd ever learned into my voice as I rode toward them. "What an agreeable surprise! Isaac, will you introduce me to your sister?"

His expression went from shocked to truculent all in an instant. Amazing! He actually *had* expressions! He said not a word, just stood stroking Cloud's neck and glowering. It was the girl who answered. "He had to bring our mother her medicine. He hasn't done anything wrong."

"Of course not! Your brother is a great one for missions of charity. He delivered something to the Robinsons as well."

Her eyes flickered anxiously toward Isaac before she remembered that she should pretend not to understand. I felt guilty. One's comprehension is

71

so acute at that age, and one's self-control so lacking. I would have made just that slip.

"I'm on your horse," she said, making a valiant attempt to change the subject. "I'm sorry—but it doesn't hurt her. Isaac never even lets me touch the reins."

"Clara," Isaac said warningly.

"Never?" I said. "That's an interesting word. For instance, if I had a brother, I would *never* let him speak to me that way." It was a pleasure, and far from a paltry one, to see the chagrin on his face. He opened his mouth to speak, and then clamped it shut.

"Well, Clara," I said. "We need to get you back home. He doesn't usually make you walk back, does he? Oh, and your boot's there in the snow. Right beside Cloud's foot, Isaac. Put it back on for her. I'll follow you to your father's house, and then we can ride back to the village together." That would scotch any further plans he might have!

He glowered up at me from under frowning brows, his jaw jutting to one side. He looked like a bull about to charge. Possibly I'd gone too far—but I had thoroughly enjoyed it! After a moment, he turned and walked with Cloud back under the hemlocks. I let Joost follow—well, I couldn't have stopped him from following at this point—with my heart beating fast, looking down on Isaac's back, and on a set of shoulders that seemed broader than I'd noticed before. It crossed my mind that I might be trapping myself. My tongue had been a little bit sharper than my mind.

The trail along the Mill Brook was low and overhung with hemlocks, which shut out the moon. But ahead, a bright clearing beckoned, as well as the smell of smoke and livestock. In a few minutes we came out into the open, into the familiar pattern of a frontier farmyard—log house, log stock pens, log barn, a meager haystack, an impressive pile of firewood. The snow was rough and trampled, pocked with manure and other stains, the new coating too thin to mask the dirt of habitation.

Outside the cabin door, a large gray shape stirred. A woman stood there, wrapped in a blanket. She was immense, blocking the whole width of the doorway—Isaac's mother, big with child, and why hadn't I imagined she'd be awake? My heart dropped like a stone, and my mouth went dry.

"Miss . . . *Fanna*?" Her voice was incredulous, making me aware how out of place I must look in my fashionable habit, how entirely unexpected my presence was at this hour of the night.

"Is aught amiss?" she asked. "Does your mother have need of my husband? He's sleeping out tonight, setting up the sugar camp, but he could be fetched."

"No. No, no. I—" I *could* say I had ridden out to recover my stolen horse, but obviously, Isaac rode out here often. His mother must assume he had permission. He was waiting for me to expose his wrongdoing, I could feel it, and I couldn't find a single word to say. I sat gaping at his mother. After a few moments one corner of her mouth twisted up, as if she were holding back a smile. She said nothing; I said nothing; the girl said nothing. Isaac opened his mouth, and shut it again, and he said nothing.

"It's cold out here," I ventured, finally. "You should—I mean—don't let me keep you."

"Oh, I won't!" she said dryly. That corner of her mouth pressed deeply inward. She was definitely trying not to laugh; it made me feel as young as Clara, and remarkably foolish.

Isaac seemed to get his thoughts organized. "Clara, hop down," he said. "We need to get back to town."

Clara slid off Cloud's back, and I kicked free of the stirrups and dismounted too, surprising myself again. This was nothing I'd planned. "We'll switch horses first."

"You want to switch horses?" Isaac sounded dumbfounded—and he was right, it was foolish, amazingly foolish, to have dismounted here in the yard of someone who was likely a Whig, to have rendered myself vulnerable—to *care* which horse I rode the two miles back to the village. But it had been a long day, a very long day, and suddenly I discovered I was on the edge of tears.

"I'll hold the mare," Isaac's mother said, and went to Cloud's head. She was as wide as a horse herself in her current condition, though I remembered her as rather a lean woman ordinarily. She took Cloud's reins in one hand and laid her other palm on my wild mare's face, and Cloud let her. Clearly she was very familiar with this family. Isaac made a stirrup with his hands and tossed me up lightly. I organized my reins while he mounted Joost. It was almost comical to see him wrap his legs around the horns of the sidesaddle—just as I did mine, but without the covering of a skirt.

"Good night," his mother said, still humorously. "Mind what I said about Monday, Isaac. I don't want you anywhere near that Court House."

"I'll remember." He nudged Joost with his heel, sending him back along the dark trail by the brook. Cloud followed at his heels, feeling more earthbound than usual. I'd ridden her this afternoon, and the afternoon before, but how many nights had she been ridden? How far? And how had I failed to notice how remarkably fit she was?

Monday, though. Why did Isaac's mother warn him about *Monday*? That was when the judges would arrive in town with Sheriff Paterson and the posse. Mary Averill had reassured me about Tuesday, the day the Whigs planned to meet Judge Chandler in court.

Plans must have changed. The judges always arrived on Monday afternoon; the Whigs knew that as well as we did. It only made sense for them to try to get there first. Mother was right—and what a long time it seemed since I'd last thought of Mother!

Ahead of Isaac the path grew brighter. He reached the road, Joost turned toward home, and I brought Cloud up beside him. "So, Isaac." My voice shook with fury. "Are you an express-rider just for Captain Wright? Or do you also ride for the Green Mountain Boys?"

"The Boys are way over in Bennington."

"I know where they are! And I know what you do! You just carried a message to the Robinsons and they're going to carry it farther. Maybe just to the west part of town, maybe to Brookline. Maybe somebody's going to take it over the mountains, I don't know. But I know this. Everybody in Cumberland County finds out what everybody else is doing, and you're part of the reason why!"

He rode on looking straight ahead, his face as expressive as a turnip.

"What's Captain Wright's plan? Are the Whigs going to get to the Court House first?"

He smiled, mockingly. "Is that what you think?"

"It's obvious! They're going to meet the judges when they arrive on Monday. They aren't going to wait until the court opens, because they've heard the sheriff means to get there first." No answer. I could sense his stubborn fury starting to build. "That's it, isn't it? That's the plan."

"What's *your* plan?" he asked roughly.

"What do you mean, my plan?"

"You'll just marry whoever you're told to? *You?*"

The question hit me like a blow to the stomach. He *heard?* I didn't think he was even in the house when Mother told me that. What else did he know? It was none of his business, and probably an attempt at distraction, but I found myself answering anyway. "I may. Marry him. Or I may not."

"Clara wouldn't."

"*Clara* doesn't have to! If I do . . . it will only be if war comes. To keep us safe. It's how I can help Mother—don't you *snort!* You're doing the same thing! You have to live with us even though you hate us, so your parents don't lose that miserable farm! You're as much at their beck and call as I am at Mother's!"

"Ee-yup." The little word of agreement dropped like a stone in a pond; I knew it wasn't the first time he'd made the comparison.

"So we're just exactly alike, then! But not much longer, now that I've found out what you're up to."

He shrugged—easily, it seemed, not worried, but it was hard to be sure in the moonlight. "I won't tell if you won't."

"*You* don't have anything to tell!"

"Think the old lady'll be happy about this? You riding out at night?"

"The *old lady?* No, she'll be furious—at you! You're carrying messages for the Whigs. That makes you a traitor—"

"Shut up," he said abruptly. Both horses stopped in their tracks, staring off into the woods to our left. Cloud had gone hard and tight under me. She blasted out a loud breath. I could hear her heartbeat.

"Got her?" Isaac asked, in a completely different voice.

I sank myself deeper into the saddle and shortened the reins. "Mm."

"Then let's go home. Slowly. Stick with me." He let Joost take one step; Cloud matched him, trembling. Another. A third. Isaac halted Joost between each, then allowed him two steps between stops, then three, until he had eased the big horse into a steady walk. Cloud mirrored him like a dancer matching steps with her partner. I heard a sound now, like a bird squawking.

It seemed to be moving deeper into the woods, and in a few minutes, it was out of earshot.

"What was that?"

"Cat," he said. "A young one."

"Cat. You mean—catamount? Will it attack?"

"I ain't worried about the cat," he said. "It's the horses that'll kill us!"

A startled laugh burst out of me. Cloud jumped straight up, straight down, and plunged forward. Joost kept pace. But the horses weren't panicked, now, just taking advantage, eager to be home. With my newfound skill, I soon had Cloud under control, and Joost settled to a walk beside her. "Don't do that again," Isaac said. "It's moved off, I guess."

The back of my neck prickled. An hour ago, I'd imagined riding over the mountains alone—

Isaac snickered. For a moment I didn't understand. Then fury shot through me. "You're trying to scare me! That wasn't really a catamount!"

He shrugged. "Bears ain't awake yet. If it was wolves we'd have heard 'em. What else would scare horses that bad?"

"Anything! You can ride them through battle with death on every side, my grandfather says, and they never even shudder. Then they'll break your neck shying at a butterfly! It happened to someone he knew."

"That weren't no butterfly," he said, with a smile that roused me to unreasoning fury.

"You know, Isaac, you're the one who should be afraid! If the Whigs take up arms, that's sedition. You could be *hanged*!"

"That's why Captain Wright said no guns. You think we're fools?"

"Yes, I do, every one of you!" The words came quickly, as words always did with me. Understanding followed several seconds later. *No guns.* That's what Elizabeth told me this morning. Apparently it was true. "Does everyone know that?" I asked, watching him narrowly. If he'd let the information slip by mistake, he would try to make a recover.

He just shook his head. "Nobody would bring a gun to the Court House. We'd be asking for it."

No guns, then. *No* guns? "Then—why is everyone so *worried?* Judge Chandler promised not to bring arms against the Whigs—he gave his word and honor. So *no one* will have weapons! Nothing will happen!"

Isaac didn't answer that, and I couldn't read his face. We were almost at Reverend Bullen's house now, and it was past time for talking. We rode along the moonlit side of the Meeting-house, past the horse blocks and down our lane. The village was completely quiet and beautiful, with long black tree-shadows running across the surface of the snow.

But I was shivering, I discovered—cold, exhausted. The horses slouched to a stop in our yard and stood with their heads low, yawning and looking toward the stable door. I slid down and rested my forehead for a moment on Cloud's warm neck. Then Isaac led them away, and I let myself into the silent house.

Chapter 12

"Fan?"

I pulled the blankets tighter over my head. Last night it had taken me hours to get warm enough to sleep; the clock had kindly counted them off—*two*, and *three*, and *four* . . .

"Fan, we're going to Meeting this morning."

I groaned, turned over in bed, and freed my face from the covers. Sunbeams slanted through the bed hangings, and the room was cold and still. I thought back to that little log farm in the clearing, and that vast woman standing in front of her own door. Fa's door, actually. The family had to farm out Isaac's labor to pay for the place, and yet when she'd thought I need help, she'd offered it. Thinking of it made something twist in my chest. These people were good, even to loathsome animals—

"Fan? I don't hear you moving in there."

I laced my fingers together behind my head, gazing up at the canopy. She hadn't heard me last night, either, and then I *had* been moving. By the time I'd gotten home, she'd been sound asleep; I'd listened at her door again, and heard her deep, slow breathing. I'd learned some things last night. I would never have said it was possible to slip both out of the house and back in again without her knowing—yet I'd done it. I'd confronted myself, out there on the snowy road, and then I'd confronted Isaac, and . . . I stirred a bit uncomfortably. It couldn't be said that I'd confronted his mother. I'd sat there blankly with my mouth hanging open, and she'd laughed at me, seen me as a child. Which was true, but she had no idea—

Mother's steps paused at my door. Would she come in? I quelled the impulse to jump out of bed and manufactured a luxurious stretch, and a contented smile. But she went on down the hall and down the stairs. Now I could push back the covers and get out of bed.

It was cold, but not fearfully so—no ice in the pitcher when I went to wash my face and hands, so spring was on the way! I rushed through the bows and knots needed to undergird a properly dressed woman. *Innumerable*, I heard someone say once, so of course, I had counted them. There were nine this morning—enough to make you want to be a man!

I hesitated as to a gown. Warm, unobtrusive brown wool would have been my choice, but Mother would only send me back up to change. We were members of the Dutch Reformed Church in New York. Here we worshiped privately most Sundays. When we attended service, a few times a year, it was a political and a social act, meant to draw attention.

The gray silk, then. I pinned and tucked and scarved myself until all was smooth and seamless, then crossed to the frigid northeast bedchamber to look out at the Court House. It stood against its background of sky, crisp as an engraving. Lavender smoke curled gently out the chimney, catching the morning sun. No horses tied there, no activity, no garrison; no one had taken the least action overnight to secure it.

There was still time. The Whigs weren't coming until Monday, as I'd learned last night. I must find a way to tell someone without giving myself away.

That's what I'd decided in the night, shivering in my cold bed. The girl I was yesterday morning would have told Mother everything—with some trepidation, but she would have told. This morning I was determined to protect myself. Nobody need know how I'd come by my information. That meant protecting Isaac, too, but I didn't mind. It wouldn't hurt to have him beholden to me.

In the kitchen, Mother dished out bowls of hasty pudding from the kettle hung over the fire. I was ravenous this morning, and dug into the steaming bowl, rich with the scents of cornmeal, maple, and molasses. Isaac hunched over his breakfast as usual, expressive as a cabbage.

But then Mother turned away for a moment, and he glanced across at me, a smile denting one corner of his mouth—just like his mother's smile, but on him it was a smirk! He must have known I hadn't told Mother about last night, and he didn't look the least bit grateful or obligated. I lowered my gaze, allowing what I hoped was a mysterious and irritating smile to drift across my features, finished my pudding, held out my bowl again.

"You're as hungry as a young wolf this morning, Fan!" Mother commented. Her own face gave away nothing of last night's private anguish.

She ate her pudding standing, then leaned her fists on the table and issued her commands. "Isaac, bank the fire when you're done, and fill the foot warmers. Fan—" She looked me over. "That's good. You look fine. Quickly, Isaac. I don't want to be late this morning." She swept from the room, and I heard her feet on the stairs.

The stupidity slid off Isaac's face, leaving him suddenly—good-looking? Was that possible? He had a nice, square jaw and bright eyes. Hazel. I hadn't known that before. He looked at me directly and made a sound, a bird-like screech. My face went hot and I turned my back. Did catamounts really make a noise like that? I would have to find out.

Rat-tatta-tat-tatta-tat-tatta-tat! The militia drum sounded, warning worshipers of the hour. Mother came swiftly downstairs. We swirled on our cloaks and stepped into pattens, Mother slipped her arm through mine, and we started for the Meeting-house, with Isaac following behind. The snow in the lane was now heavily trampled. Isaac's boots had crisscrossed over the horse's tracks several times, obliterating the plain tale they told last night.

How many times had he done this? How often had I seen the evidence without recognizing it? Mother had missed it too—still didn't know—and that bothered me. We had been Isaac's dupes. We'd judged him by appearances, and if I didn't tell her what he was doing, it would be entirely up to me to keep an eye on him. And he would know I was doing it. Even now, I had to restrain myself from glancing over my shoulder. I might pretend to look past him at something else, but he would know. How cramped and complicated everything had become!

Was it that way for everyone else? All these families streaming toward the Meeting-house in bright skeins of red, blue, and green women's cloaks, shouts escaping from the children quickly hushed, the brown and black coats of the men and the hats ranging from tricorns to coonskins to knitted caps—so many people, so many views and questions, and glances darted around as everyone tried to guess what the situation was.

The Ranney team passed us and pulled up blowing and steaming at the Meeting-house door. Eight adults disembarked; then one of the sons, Daniel, drove the team to the horse-blocks, unhitched, and threw blankets over them. Daniel Ranney was worth looking at any day of the week! A rather silent youth, but I'd seen him laugh on occasion. *Ranneys do what's right.* Could he be galvanized into action?

"Fan," Mother murmured. "Eyes front." I complied, treasuring—I was a bit ashamed to notice—a certain relish at how much I knew that she did not. She did not have the Fan of yesterday—morning *or* afternoon.

Captain Wright stood near the Meeting-house steps, grim and inexpressive like an especially vibrant block of granite, watching the worshipers come in. He glanced at us indifferently, his pale eyes holding an almost feverish glitter. Was he just waiting for his wife and children, or passing a signal to some of his more far-flung militia-members? The doorway filled behind us. I made a show of managing my petticoats which allowed me to glance back, and my heart gave a double thump. *Everyone* looked that way. Their expressions were severe or pleasant, according to the habit of a lifetime, but their eyes were lit, wary, expectant, apprehensive. A chill prickled my skin. They all *knew* something. And not just the Whigs; our own sort were also brimming with secrets—all except the children, and fence-sitters like Joel Holton, who came up the steps behind us, glancing around curiously. He'd reportedly asked his friends and family on both sides to keep him out of this, and it looked like they had.

We followed the Ranneys into the great, dark barn of a Meeting-house. Oiled paper windows shut out two-thirds of the daylight. People's breath rose in smoky puffs, and a scorched smell came from the foot-warmers. Voices were hushed, yet the room was noisy because of the crowd, unusually large for March. The back benches were all full and the pews nearly so, each a high-walled square pen containing one family, sorted like buttons in a dry-goods store.

The pews up front were reserved for the most important families, church founders and the prosperous. We sat there with the Nortons when we attended. Usually Mother made a pre-arrangement with them; if she'd done so today, I wasn't aware of it. The noisy room stilled slightly as we passed up the aisle. Mother squeezed my arm and slowed her steps, drawing herself up regally. We swept past the blur of faces: Whig, Tory, Tory, Whig: Goold, Andros, Willard, Averill. Sperie's face brightened when she saw me, and she started to wave. Mary reached down to catch the child's hand but smiled her eyes at me. Billy Willard smiled too, in a way that made me want to clutch my cloak tighter around myself. But that would give him some kind of power. I straightened my shoulders so the cloak fell open, and the silk gown showed for all to see.

We reached the pew door. John and Anna, concealing any surprise, welcomed us with a few whispered words and rearranged the children, the smallest on her mother's lap, the next-smallest on a short-legged stool. Isaac handed in the metal foot-warmers, filled with coals from the hearth. I maneuvered mine under my petticoats so it would warm my feet and legs without scorching the fabric and looked around to see who else was here.

A spot of sky-blue homespun showed me Elizabeth in the Harlow pew, tending the child beside her. After a moment she lifted her head and saw me. Instinctively I raised my chin. I wanted her to see by my bearing that I hadn't *folded*. But it's hard to read a gesture across a crowded room. She just gave a friendly nod and turned her attention back to the child.

Movement in the gallery drew my eyes upward. That was where the boys sat jostling, snickering, and shoving each other, while the church sexton kept everything just under the boil, rapping the rowdiest with the long stick he carried. I saw Isaac slip in among them, stuffing his liberty cap into his pocket. Instantly he became younger, just one of the lads. How good he was at taking the color of his surroundings! Like one of those spiders one suddenly sees when one bends to sniff a flower, the kind with the big pincer-like front legs.

Reverend Bullen mounted the steps of the pulpit. The sniffles and stampings and whispers gradually quieted, and the eyes of the small children sitting beside their parents grew dimmer. Would they live through till dinner time, or die of boredom? Bullen was actually admired for his dullness. He's one who lets the Lord do the work, people said, without injecting any spark of his own. Perhaps he was afraid of sparks, standing as he did on top of all that gunpowder.

Composing an expression of pious attention and letting Bullen's voice fade to a drone, I scanned the pews. Who was the right person to tell what

I learned last night? All the obvious candidates—John Norton, Ephraim Ranney, the Willards—had ruled out action. Who was left?

Around me everyone stood, and I tardily followed suit. We lifted our voices in—well, not song! Lacking an instrument or even a strong voice to guide us, each person found his or her own way through the melody, mumbling half the words. The miserable off-key croaking straggled to an end, and we sat with a noise like a volley of gunfire as the seats rattled down on their iron hinges. I used the chance to slightly shift my position, so I could see the east side of the Meeting-house, lighting upon one particularly grim face: Dr. Bildad Andros, justice of the peace, energetic member of the court party. He'd been entertained at our house often and was an ally of Fa's. He even had a daughter my age. Not that I liked her much, or him; I didn't like many of the people on our side, to tell the truth.

Cumberland County *was* New York, the Assembly had very properly voted down the embargo, the King was the king, and he had every right to levy taxes; that was all stipulated, as Fa would say. But there was such a thing as being *too* right and caring too much about it. That was Bildad Andros. He burned hot, more like Captain Wright than John Norton, and that might make him the very man. He had more activity in him than most of our people. The trick would be to catch him after the service.

Chapter 13

By the time the morning service ended, my mind had slowed to nearly stopping, like a toad on a frosty morning. It took me a moment to revive, as Bullen descended the pulpit stairs, and everyone began moving toward the door. The hall filled with the low buzz of pious people *not* talking in the Meeting-house, just saying one quiet word to the person closest. My quarry, Bildad Andros, opened his pew door with more alacrity than most, ushering his family into the flow. He wasn't going far; there was still an afternoon sermon for the congregants to endure. But I wanted to speak with him before he settled down to his dinner—

"Fanna," Elizabeth said, at my elbow. "Will you be back this afternoon?" I shook my head. Morning Meeting was enough for Mother and me, more than enough. "Then let's talk outside."

"Yes, I'll catch up to you in a minute." I held back, and when Billy Willard tried to let me go ahead of him, I pretended that I'd left something in the pew. The Holtons passed—and there were a lot of Holtons—so by the time I reached the door, Mother and I were widely separated. Andros and his family angled off toward their sleigh and dinner. I followed as quickly as was compatible with dignity, caught up, and touched his sleeve. "Dr. Andros?"

He half-turned with an impatient glance, saw who it was, and adjusted his expression. "Yes, Miss Fanna?"

"Sir—sir, what will happen tomorrow?"

He frowned. "The judges will arrive, as they always do."

"And the sheriff? With a posse?"

"I believe so," he said stiffly.

"I've heard that the Whigs mean to get here Monday as well."

"Who told you that?"

I looked back at the crowd "I . . . overheard it." He raised his eyebrows, and his gaze shifted from one neighbor to another, making exactly the assumption I'd wanted him to—that I had just this moment gleaned the information from someone attending the service. "Suppose our men were to go into the Court House tonight," I said. "Then everything would be settled, wouldn't it? Everything would be safe."

His frown deepened. "Nobody will travel on Sunday except for Meeting. Paterson won't be able to gather a posse until sometime tomorrow."

"Westminster men don't have to travel. They're right here. They could go in after Meeting!"

"Nobody has their guns," he said, trying to conceal his impatience.

"They won't need—" I broke off as Asa Averill passed, carrying Sperie on his arm. Behind him Mary kept order among the older children, with a glance to spare for me. Everyone noticed with whom everyone else was talking today. Once they were out of earshot I said, "The Whigs won't be armed."

Bullen made a contemptuous face. "Don't believe that nonsense! 'Riah's been drilling those men for years. Nobody can tell me he'll come to a fight unarmed. I know him, I soldiered with him!"

"But—"

He swelled on a long, deep breath, trying to contain his impatience. "You're young, Miss Fanna, and you're a female. As I tell my own girl—you haven't seen much yet. You don't know men. I do." He glanced toward his waiting family, who would not start their noon meal without him.

I bit my lip to hold back a sharp retort. "I just . . . thought I should tell someone. While there's still time"

"Quite proper," he said, and turned away, not having listened any more than John Norton or William Willard did. *Useless!* They were useless, and without a man to put our urgency into action, Mother and I were also useless. I turned back toward the Meeting-house, and for a flash of time, less than a second, saw in the crowd the person most I wanted to see—Fa, dressed in his finest, standing with head tilted back as if listening to an argument he was about to skewer. Immediately he was gone, was never here—but if only he were! He'd understand all this. He'd know how to nip it in the bud.

Or maybe not. He'd been driven to the expedient of marrying me off; what did he see, beyond the outlines of this relatively insignificant local struggle? If only I could ask him.

But there was Elizabeth over near the Meeting-house. I picked my way toward her between ruts and horse manure. Sunshine warmed my face, and I smelled the food people were taking out of their baskets—pies, mostly; cheese; and squares of johnnycake. Some had brought cider, so there was a tang of alcohol on the air and color coming into faces that had grown pinched and pale during the long sermon. Azariah Wright's family perched with a group of hill-farm Whigs on the Meeting-house horse blocks. Wright continued to scan all who walked by. Some message was being passed. I could tell by the way men nodded—not a greeting, but an assent. *Yes. I will.* But how the message was being conveyed, and what it was, I couldn't see.

A different mix of families gathered around John Morse's cabin, close to our house, perching on his woodpile and mounting block. John Norton, a fat slice of pie in his hand, was deep in conversation with Deacon Ranney and Michael Gilson—three tavern keepers, one Tory, one Yorker, one Whig. The fourth, John Goold, had bustled back to his place of business the moment the service ended with a crowd of hungry worshipers at his heels. There'd been some relaxation of tension in all the groups, as if something had been decided. It disturbed me that I didn't know what, but maybe I'd get it out of Elizabeth.

She consigned the children to their mother's care as I approached, and stepped out of the crowd, taking my hand and looking deeply into my eyes. Her concerned expression gave way to surprise and dawning relief. "Your mother relented!"

"Why do you say that?"

"Yesterday you were half-collapsed, and now you're—" she hesitated, choosing her words. "Well, you're different. That's all I can say. Upright. *Did* she change her mind?"

"Not that she's told me!" I glanced away, made shy by her attention, and so grateful for it, for her noticing the change in me. What could I tell her? I'd thought of her at almost every turn last night. It was almost as if she'd been there. But of course, she hadn't, and I wasn't sure what I should reveal. Nothing here, certainly, with so many people around.

She gave my hand a squeeze, and let go, "What I wanted to say to you was, come over tomorrow afternoon. Come watch."

"Come *watch*?"

"Yes. Our men will gather at Captain Wright's and then march up to the Court House to meet the judges. I want you to see it, Fanna."

"Won't it be dangerous?"

"No, it's perfectly safe!" Her eyes and cheeks glowed. "Whigs everywhere are sworn to nonviolence. Everybody knows that! The whole village is planning to watch. This is important, Fanna. It's historic. You *should* see it, so you know what it's like. The dignity. The—the self-respect. I saw it in Worcester, and it was inspiring! It's how we human beings should comport ourselves."

She spoke often of the day when the Worcester Whigs forced the closure of their Court House, always in terms like this, and I'd always hidden a smile, because it couldn't have been as exalted an event as she described. Now I was going to have the chance to see for myself. "I could watch from our house," I said.

"You'll see much better from ours. You have a good line of sight, but we're next door. You'll be able to hear what they say. If one side lies about it later, you'll know. Why are you making me beg?" she asked, half-laughing, half-annoyed.

"You mean, instead of *folding*?"

"Yes! You're as stubborn as a goat this morning. I knew I'd offended you! Just *come*, Fanna. Everybody else will be watching. You don't want to be left out."

I didn't. "Very well, I'll come if I can."

"Good! When you see what it's like, you'll stop worrying about war, and so will your mother. This is an *argument*, not a fight! We intend to make our government treat us like British citizens, not like slaves. When your mother sees that, maybe she'll change her mind."

Tears prickled the backs of my eyes. To be thought of, to have my trouble remembered in the midst of all that mattered most to her, touched my heart. "Very well. What time?"

At that she hesitated—only for a second, but now I knew what message was being passed. The time of gathering had been changed. Wright was telling them all, by some means that I didn't see. But Elizabeth did, and that part *was* secret.

"Any time after dinner," she said, and I read a faint apology in her smile.

We parted. I spotted Mother near the Meeting-house, caught her eye, and then headed home. I'd no more than taken my cloak off when she came through the door. "It's going to be Monday," we both said. "Afternoon," I added.

"Who told you?" Mother asked.

"Everyone's saying it. The Whigs know the plan to keep them out of court, and they're going to get there first."

"As any fool would have anticipated! We can only hope our people decide to bustle themselves!"

Suddenly I had to laugh. "It's like that game the boys play, grabbing an ax handle! The one whose hand is on top at the end wins."

"That had better be us," Mother said grimly, and then Isaac arrived, and we said nothing more. After our cold dinner of pie and cheese, she sent him off to the afternoon service and stood at the front window, watching until he had quite definitely climbed the step and gone inside the Meeting-house. Then she said, "Come upstairs with me, Fan. I want to show you something."

I got up from the table with a little reluctance to be moved here and there like a pawn on a chessboard. But if she had something to show me that I didn't know about, I wanted to see it.

She led the way into her bedchamber, and reached into her pocket for the household keys, secured to her waist by a long piece of woven tape. Over her shoulder she said, "Webb has asked that the children be kept home tomorrow." Joshua Webb, a leader among the Whigs, was the teacher at the large log-cabin schoolhouse across from Captain Wright's.

"Who told you?" I asked.

Mother bent over the large chest at the foot of the bed and fit the key to the lock. "All women were told."

"But who told you? Because . . ."

"I know. Without a child in school, there was no real reason for me to be informed. Mary said something, and Mistress Goold, and Atherton Chaffee. It was kind of them." The lock stuck. She pulled the key partway out and turned it more delicately. Mostly focused on that, apparently, she said, "They anticipate a large gathering at Captain Wright's—and Mr. Webb, doubtless, will have his mind on things other than keeping children out from underfoot."

"Well, that makes sense, doesn't it? Or do you think it's a bad sign?"

Twist. *Click.* The latch sprang open, and she lifted the heavy arched lid, releasing an aroma of clove and southern-wood. "I don't know what kind of a sign it is. Here—this is something you should know about." She lifted out a linen haversack. "This holds food for a journey. Parched corn, pemmican. There's a purse with a useful amount of currency. And this—" She folded back the flap, reached inside with both hands, and drew out a long-nosed, gleaming pistol.

A force seemed to emanate from it. I found myself several paces farther away without any volition of my own, back in the doorway, glancing down the hall to be sure Isaac wasn't there. "That's Fa's. One of his dueling pistols."

"Yes. It isn't loaded, Fan. You needn't be afraid of it."

"I'm not." I was, though. Reluctantly I came forward again, fascinated. The pistol was beautiful, all polished wood and metal, and of a graceful shape. "May I?" Mother nodded and handed the gun to me.

I wrapped my hand around the smooth wood of the grip and hefted the weapon. I could feel how well-balanced it was—heavy, yet the weight invited my hand to level it, my arm to brace. Fa was proud of these pistols; he'd hinted once or twice that he fought a duel using them, in his young days. He must have the other with him in New York.

"I don't know how to fire a pistol."

"*I* do. In any case, men are terrified of firearms in the hands of a woman."

A number of scenarios flashed through my mind, all involving darkness, threat, and bad weather. My pulse began to race. Gingerly, I laid the thing on the bed. "So—you think we should leave?"

She bowed her head and pinched the bridge of her nose, taking a moment to answer. "I don't know. We need to be ready, but if we go, it might not be so easy to come back. It might be wisest to wait it out. By planting time this all may die down."

"It didn't in Massachusetts."

"Massachusetts is prone to an excess of democracy," she said dryly. "Here we have New York government, and New York has always understood how to put down rebellion."

"New York government, New England people. Like John says."

"Yes," Mother said. "That is, in part, the source of our discomfort. But now you know, so let's put this all away and sit down with our prayer books."

Monday afternoon, March 13, 1775
Westminster, shire town of Cumberland County, colony of New
York

Part Two:

The Liberty Cap

Chapter 14

"**W**as it hard?" Elizabeth asked, as I helped her put mittens on little Annis Harlow. Rhoda, Elizabeth's aunt, bent to stuff the child's feet into shoes. "Getting her to let you come?"

Was it hard? Living through Sunday afternoon and evening, that was hard. Pretending to read my prayer book and watching Mother pretend to read hers, with John Buchanan on my mind, and the possibility of needing to leave forever. Thinking about the haversack and the gun, and was upstairs the best place for them, and if something happened to Mother, how would I get the key. Hard.

Packing my trunk was hard. Mother had decided we should do that. "If we leave in a hurry we'll have just the haversack, but if Ben Bellows will take us in, we can bring more. Your smallest trunk, Fan. The bare necessities. What you need, not what you want."

I *wanted* my drawing implements; luckily, they were small. I *needed* decent wool gowns, petticoats and stockings, shoes, my joseph . . . but I'd be wearing my joseph if we fled, wouldn't I? I put it in, and took it out again, as it filled up the trunk too much: draped it across the trunk: *needed* it. I'd be wearing my joseph.

It was hard to live the whole day through with Isaac in the house, trying to act as if nothing had changed, and watching to see what had. Wondering if he knew about the haversack and pistol, and if he'd told anyone about the fate my parents had designed for me . . .

"Yes. It was hard."

Living through this morning was hard too, listening to the clock toll off the hours while nothing happened at the Court House and no one came riding from the south to secure it, and more hours passed. Watching

93

Mother's face tighten and her lips compress and seeing thoughts behind her eyes without knowing what they were. Watching Whig militiamen like the Goolds and Averills walk down the street in the early afternoon and disappear over Court House Hill. They did not carry guns. *Do you see that, Bildad Andros? They don't have guns!*

Elizabeth released Annis to her mother; the pair of them went out the door, and I said, "Do you want to know how I persuaded her? I said everyone would think we were afraid!"

"I can almost see her hackles rise!"

"And I said everyone else would be there."

Elizabeth laughed. "And she said—"

"'If everyone else was jumping off the Court House roof, would you do it too?'"

"We'll say that to our own children, I suppose," Elizabeth mused. "I wonder if we'll remember this day when we do."

"I hope not. I hope this turns out to be the dullest day of our lives!"

"Oh, it won't be that, whatever happens." She reached for her own cloak and started out the door. I had an impulse to hang back. A crowd had gathered around the Court House, just steps from the Harlow's front door, and they'd already gotten one good look at me. But she was halfway down the path already, and of course, I followed. The crowd was relatively small. Nobody from down on the Flats, no families from the hill farms; only the men had come—John Wells, Francis Holden, the three Crooks, the three Ides. Nice old Deacon Sessions ambled through; he wasn't in the militia but was involved with all the committees and proclamations. The militia wives like Mary Averill and Mrs. Phippen gathered at the edge of the bluff, talking animatedly, once in a while glancing down at Captain Wright's farm where we could see their husbands milling around, ant-sized.

Men continued to pass through, singly or in pairs, walking in long, ground-covering strides as they made for their rendezvous. The latecomers were from other towns: Leonard Spaulding, Solomon Harvey, groups from Fulham, Putney, and towns farther west. The out-of-towners carried knapsacks and haversacks, as if they planned to make a stay. I noticed that as they greeted the women, they sometimes glanced back over their shoulders.

Something was happening south of here. More friends coming along? I'd stopped believing we'd ever see a sheriff's posse.

Abruptly the flow stopped. There was a gap of several minutes before Atherton Chaffee sauntered through. He was one of the earliest settlers, now raising a brood of children with his second wife; he had a son the same age as his granddaughter Sperie. Chaffee was a friend of Fa's—a real friend, not a hanger-on, one who appreciated Fa's wit and the free flow of wine at our table. He winked at me in passing—or at Elizabeth? Both, probably. He did have an eye for a pretty girl—

And *he* would know what sound catamounts make! Impulsively I stepped forward and caught his arm. He turned and smiled, the same smile as his daughter Mary's, and the same warm brown eyes. "Miss Fanna. What can I do for you?"

How old he seemed! This was a town of children and their middle-aged parents; there were only five or six ancients like Chaffee in all Westminster. The wrinkles around his eyes were deep, his eyebrows white, with the long hairs springing forward in fantastic spikes and swirls. Yet he was tough and canny, and not easy to read. "I just wondered—" oh dear, what an absurd lead-in! *I just happened to be thinking about flora and fauna*! But I was committed now. "Can you tell me what sound catamounts make? *Young* catamounts?"

He didn't react at all, not visibly. "Well now, that's interesting," he said. "Because my boys saw the track of one yesterday, on our way in to Meeting. It's a little like a bird—funny sound."

He was watching me; I wondered what other tracks he and his sons had seen. Isaac and I didn't think of that, as we rode home down the snowy road quarreling. What story had our tracks told, to a canny man like Atherton Chaffee?

But he was still looking at me, with twinkling eyes. I had to say something. "Somebody told me they sound like a bird—but I wasn't sure I should believe it."

"Oh, it's so," he said. "It's so. They stray around calling sometimes, don't know why." Amusement gleamed deep in his eyes—also kindness, and he changed the subject. "Tell your mother now, if she needs anything I can do for her, she's to send young Isaac out. But don't fret about all this. We're just making sure we have our say." He touched the brim of his knit cap with one finger in a sort of salute, and continued on his way, leaving me confused, embarrassed, and not quite as sure of myself as I liked—but cared for. I did know that Mother and I were cared for.

He was the last Whig to pass. The minutes stretched and cold started to make itself felt. People began looking toward the south end of the street from whence Sheriff Paterson and the judges would come, but there was nothing to see in that direction either. "It's like war," I told Elizabeth. "My grandfather says it's 'Nothing, nothing, nothing . . . *BOOM*!'"

"Not just war," she said. "*Life*!"

Eleazer Harlow half-turned toward his barn, impatiently. "Hurry this along, 'Riah! Nobody's making supper, and the animals won't feed themselves!"

"My feet are cold!" Annis said.

"Come here." Elizabeth picked the child up and balanced her on one hip. "We'll get your toes out of the snow for a while."

"Pick me up too!" I stamped the blood into my feet, hugging myself as I turned in place. "Oh, there's Mother!" She came walking up the street toward the Court House, small and all alone and valiant-looking. My heart stirred with pity and admiration. And worry. Was she looking for me? Would this be embarrassing?

"There they come!" a little girl cried—Sperie Averill, perilously close to the edge of the bluff, pointed with her whole arm and looked back up at her mother, who snatched the nape of her cloak just as she seemed about to tip down the hill.

Voices erupted in the crowd. "I can't see!" "What are they doing?" "Can you see what they're doing?"

I closed my fist and squinted through the small aperture, a military trick of Grandfa Schoolcraft's. It turns one's hand into a spy-glass, in a minor way. Very minor; all I could make out was a dark stream of men crossing the King's Highway from the school to Captain Wright's front yard. Coming back out again, they formed a column with surprising quickness and began to move toward us, bristling like one of those fuzzy, stinging caterpillars, striding past the school, the cabins, the Tory Tavern. I began to hear the drum *rub-a-dub-dubbing,* and could pick out individual men—Captain Wright,

Webb the schoolmaster, Reuben Jones from Rockingham, our own Nathaniel and Reuben Robinson and Deacon Sessions, and then Obed and Asa Averill and Peter Lovejoy, Atherton Chaffee, and all the other Westminster militia men. Phil Safford, Captain Wright's brother-in-law, led a large group of Rockingham Whigs. They marched briskly up the steep hill toward us, almost as quickly as horses would. Each man carried a long, stout stick of wood, shouldered like a musket—

"*Dada!*" Sperie squealed, as the vanguard crested the hill. Several men turned their heads. The Averills and Chaffees smiled and poked each other, and a chuckle spread through the crowd.

I smiled, too, but I was aware of a tiny sense of letdown. Their resolution had talked about "discouraging all riotous, tumultuous, and unnecessary mobs," but I'd been expecting at least a whiff of tumultuousness. These men looked like they were heading to one of their conventions with glittering eyes, determined frowns, ongoing debates, and some shoving and joking among the younger men.

"An argument, not a fight," Elizabeth had called it. Well, it was an argument with *sticks*—but sticks weren't guns.

One young farmer caught my eye, marching with the group from Fulham. Not especially handsome; in fact, his face was rather like Isaac's. But something in how he carried his head, the flash of his eye, the set of his shoulders, and the same exalted expression Elizabeth wore when talking politics made me want to look at him, if only to figure out why I wanted to look at him.

"Who's that?" I asked.

"Who's who?"

"Right behind Leonard Spaulding."

"He's from Brattleboro," Elizabeth said, as if that answered my question.

"And what's his name?"

"French. William French."

"Another Billa!" I teased.

"Not Billa. He's called William."

She did know him, then. I wanted to press harder. Elizabeth was always so cool and well-defended, but I'd found out something. She liked him. Did he like her? I hoped so, but I couldn't see that he was searching the crowd for one particular face, as a lover should.

"He's quite good-looking," I ventured.

"Annis, you're heavy," Elizabeth said, setting the little girl down. "Ask your father to hold you for a while." She was a trifle pinker in the cheeks, and I felt a sudden pang of bitter panic. Elizabeth could choose and pine and blush and hope, and if this William French did like her, she might even marry for love. My left hand clenched in a fist, and I pressed it to my lips. *Me too, dear Lord, me too.*

The head of the column disappeared behind the Court House, and in a moment came the sound of many boots clumping upstairs. The other end of the street was still empty. This was it, then. The Whigs were in. We were nowhere. That would shape whatever was going to happen next.

Elizabeth was counting, folding down the fingers of one hand and then the other as the men continued to pass. Already there was more sky than shoulders at the back of the column, and then it was all sky as the last marchers topped the hill. "How many?" I asked.

"Only about a hundred."

"*Only?* How many people live in Westminster? Four hundred, maybe, and most of them are women and children!"

"In Worcester there were six thousand men. They choked the—ow! *Fanna!*"

"Sorry." I'd gripped her arm hard. "I didn't mean—but will you *look* at him?" Striding along at the very tail of the column under his red cap and carrying what could only be called a club, came Isaac.

Chapter 15

"Y̶ou knew what the red cap meant," Elizabeth said. "You must have!"

"Yes, but he's not supposed to be anywhere near the Court House today!"

She smiled satirically. "You Loyalists are very fond of being obeyed."

"It's not *my* mother he's disobeying, it's his!"

I shouldn't have said that. I knew that instantly, and my hand flew up to my mouth as if to catch the words. But Elizabeth wasn't paying attention.

The last of the protesters disappeared behind the Court House; the Harlows consulted each other with their eyes, each scooped up a child, then stepped outside their own fenced yard and headed around the other side of the building. We followed. Rounding the corner, I saw Isaac and several other boys standing on the step, contriving to look important rather than left out. The road near the Court House was full of women and children, with a few men who hadn't taken sides yet, all watching, talking, waiting for what would happen next.

A peaceful scene, but Elizabeth frowned. "A hundred isn't enough."

"What did you expect? This county is half-Loyalist."

"Not half! Cumberland County divides in thirds—Whigs, Tories, and the 'I-Don't-Care-Leave-Me-Alone Party.'"

Or 'Keep-Quiet-and-Hope-For-the-Best?'" I suggested. "That's my party!"

"Really?" she asked. "Not Tory? Then I've talked you around to our way of thinking! You've an independent temperament, Fanna."

"It's not that. But—"

"I'm sorry," she said suddenly, reaching for my hand. "I forgot. Stop *worrying!* Did you ever see anything less like war?"

99

"I don't know what war looks like. The last one ended the year I was born."

"I remember, a little. Being afraid, and when I understood that my parents were afraid, too, that was the most—"

She broke off. Suddenly half the crowd was looking over their shoulders toward the south end of the street. A rider was coming fast—one of the Goold boys, bareback on a thin, shaggy horse. He pulled up short in front of the Court House and leaped off, plunging through the door. Isaac grabbed the horse's reins, and it whirled as if it were ready to race back home again. Agitated voices from within; several men came to the doorway and stood, frowning down the King's Highway. Their view was blocked, as was ours, by the Meeting-house, standing gray as a wasp nest in the middle of the road.

But we on the ground had only to take a few steps to one side, and we could see all the way down the street. "*There!*" someone shouted, and then I saw it—a dark smudge at the crest of Willard Hill that turned into horses, riders, men marching on foot. A broad surge of them filled the whole width of the road. Poking high above the men's shoulders I saw—

"Guns," Elizabeth said, in an odd, choked voice. Her face had gone white. All around us people looked suddenly sober, uneasy.

The posse swung around the east side of the Meeting-house at a quick march, the men striding long and fast, approaching us rapidly. Sheriff Paterson was in the lead on his prancing black horse. His jaw was stubbled, his face red; the late sun glinted off his saddle fittings and the hilt of his saber. He wore his officer's gorget, a quarter-moon of metal hung around his neck to remind everyone that he was a military man, a person of authority. I'd always thought gorgets looked silly, as if a child had hung a piece of broken kettle around his neck and called it armor. But today that slice of metal had a sullen gleam of threat to it, a swagger that reminded me that I'd never liked Billy Paterson, however much Fa's ally he might be.

Sam Gale, the handsome young Englishman who'd succeeded Fa as clerk of the court, rode beside Paterson, a set of dragoon pistols in his belt, handles pointed forward. His usually pleasant, open face hardened as he surveyed the Whigs on the Court House steps. Sam Gale I did like—English, but not superior about it. He'd even deigned to marry Judge Wells's daughter, a colonial girl. But now he looked the complete Briton, stiff with outraged haughtiness.

And the rest of them: old Judge Sabin from Putney, the court's great intellectual, frumping along on his easy-gaited horse, assistant justices Greenleaf and Butterfield, and Bildad Andros. The court officials were resplendent in their richly frogged coats, their powdered wigs, their best beaver hats; but today in place of the usual bland superiority, their faces were suffused with rage.

The posse behind them, some seventy farmers and artisans, carried sticks, cutlasses, muskets. The Willards—William, Billy, and young Joseph—fairly bristled with weapons. They'd only traveled from the far end of the street and seemed quite fresh. The others looked hot from their long march, tired, and furious. Somehow, though the sun was near to setting, they must have imagined they'd be in time. Instead they were met by a Court House filled with Whigs, and Azariah Wright and Joshua Webb waiting shoulder to shoulder out on the step.

All around me now, I heard a name on everyone's lips. "'Chandler.' I told him!" "All he could say was, 'Chandler promised—'" "Where *is* Chandler?" "He gave his word and honor." "That's what *I* was told! His *word* and *honor*."

"But *our* men don't have guns!" someone said, in a clear, indignant voice, and others hushed her as the posse drew near. People drew closer together; straying children were collared by the nearest adult, and we all stood facing the men like a flock of sheep facing the herding dog. But there was a hardening in the faces around me—that stubborn, close-mouthed New England look that you could mistake for submissiveness, until experience taught you otherwise.

Paterson rode straight at the east door, as if about to take his horse right up the step. More Whigs had crowded there, and others leaned out the upstairs windows. Isaac and the other boys had been brushed aside by grim-looking men with cudgels in their hands, and stood off to one side, silent for once, intent.

About fifteen feet from the door, Paterson raised his hand to halt the column behind him and reined in the black horse. "In the name of the King, I command you to disperse." His voice was thick and deep, a field-officer's bellow.

"*You* disperse!" somebody yelled out an upstairs window, but Captain Wright said not a word. A short man on the ground, facing a man on horseback, he refused to acknowledge the height difference, lifting his eyes only, not tilting his head. It gave him the look of a bull about to charge.

Paterson waited a moment. Then he opened his saddlebag and brought out a scroll of vellum. The words of the Riot Act rolled out like cannons roaring, certain words blaring louder than the rest as Paterson gave them emphasis.

"Our sovereign lord the KING chargeth and commandeth all persons, being assembled, IMMEDIATELY to disperse themselves, and peaceably to DEPART to their habitations, or to their lawful business, UPON THE PAINS contained in the act made in the first year of King George, for preventing TUMULTS and RIOTOUS assemblies. GOD SAVE THE KING!"

Upon the pains . . . Under the law that Fa had drafted in his first few months in the Assembly, it was a felony for more than four people to riotously gather—a felony punishable by death.

Suddenly the color drained from the scene, and everything went a sort of purple-gray, as the sun dipped below the ridge. I raised my head and found my gaze pulled toward the back of the crowd. Mother's face, wild and fierce, seemed to rise above everyone else's. They were watching the Court House. She was looking straight at me. I lifted my chin, acknowledging that I'd seen her, and then my attention was dragged back to the Court House steps.

Captain Wright said something I didn't catch. All I could hear was Paterson's response. "If you don't disperse in fifteen minutes, by God, I'll blow a lane through you!"

"You c'n come in," someone said from behind Wright, in that high, nasal New England twang. "Long as you disarm first. And if you don't, you can't."

The Brattleboro men in the posse stirred and grumbled. "We got to take this?" "I *said* we should hurry!" "If we'da hurried, there'd only be 'bout fifteen of us—and no damn guns!"

I was shaking suddenly, tiny tremors chasing themselves all down my body. Elizabeth's arm was hooked fiercely through mine; when did that happen? I felt a movement in the crowd near me—the Harlows, steering their little girls around the back of the Court House, toward home. Mary

Averill gathered Sperie in her arms and half-turned but couldn't seem to tear her gaze away from the building her husband, father, and brother-in-law had entered just twenty minutes ago.

Dr. Jones from Rockingham stepped forward now. I swallowed the hard lump in my throat. Jones was as zealous a Whig as Azariah Wright but known to be a balanced man. His voice was deep and loud, but steady. "Are you come for war? We're come for peace, and we'd be glad to hold a parley with you."

"Damn the parley with such damn rascals as you are!" Was that *Sam Gale*? I'd never once heard him raise his voice; now he was shouting and brandishing a pistol. "I'll hold no parley with such damn rascals except by this."

A tangle of angry shouts from the Whigs. Someone in the posse yelled back, "You'll be in hell before morning!"

One of the Fulham men retorted: "You try to take this Court House, we'll send you and all your men to hell in fifteen minutes!"

Judge Sabin urged his horse toward the front and spoke to the sheriff, who listened with a look of intense irritation, then turned on his own men with a snarl. "Quiet, all of you! We'll give them their hour."

Of course. By law, rioters had an hour to disperse. Fa had explained it to me once. "That's the King's justice, the King's mercy. The law prevents him from acting like a rattlesnake, that warns just as it strikes." So there was time. The Whigs could go away and pay no penalty—but they wouldn't. I knew that.

The groups consulted among themselves for a few minutes. Then two of the men on the Court House steps walked across the open ground toward the sheriff and judges. They all talked heatedly, arms waving, men leaning into each other's faces, but all the words I could make out now were "damned rascals!" After a few minutes the Whigs turned back to the court house. The armed members of the posse stacked their muskets against a tree-trunk, then squatted to stretch their backs, or stood grumbling, kicking the snow—

"Come home, Fanny. *Now.*"

Chapter 16

Mother was at my side, her face bleached of color, the skin stretched tight. Other women hurried away with their children, looking back over their shoulders.

"Elizabeth, you too!" Mother said. "Get off the street before something happens."

Did Elizabeth even hear? She stood shaking her head, dazed. "*Elizabeth!*" I gave her arm a little squeeze, and she turned her face toward me, but her eyes looked blind.

"It isn't supposed to be this way," she half-whispered.

"It *is* this way!" I said. But Mother had me by the wrist, as she might lead a reluctant child. I twisted free at the cost of a fingernail scratch on the arm, but followed her up the street, looking back over my shoulder like everyone else. Elizabeth just stood there, with people hurrying all around her. When I looked a second time, she was walking toward the cabin, and I could turn my head away.

"*Outrageous!*" Mother said, when were free of the crowd. "All this puffing and blowing and strutting, when all they had to do was get up a little earlier in the morning!"

"They have guns," I said. "Judge Chandler promised they wouldn't, but they *do.*"

"I daresay the mob has guns too!"

"No. We saw them come up the hill and go into the Court House. They have *sticks!*"

"Then we'll drive them out all the sooner," Mother said grimly.

Drive them out? I turned around to look back again. The Court House doors were firmly shut. The upstairs windows seethed with motion; faces pressed to the glass and were nudged aside, replaced by other faces. *Could the posse drive out a hundred men?* Only by violence, but Asa Averill was in there, and Atherton Chaffee, and nice old Deacon Sessions, and it was wrong!

"He gave his *word* he wouldn't bring arms against them!"

"My dearest girl, don't be naive!" Mother said. "Do you suppose he meant that? Even if he did, it's something only a fool would say. Come *along*, Fan!" She reached for my arm again and paused. "Oh, merciful heavens! *Now* what?"

A group of men had peeled off from the main posse and rode slouching toward us: Sheriff Paterson, Sam Gale, the three justices, and old Judge Sabin—all the most important members of the Court party, but they didn't look particularly important just now. Even the horses had stopped prancing and just plodded wearily. The men exchanged remarks, but in asides, never meeting each other's eyes. They were ashamed. All that bluff and bluster and they were still out in the street, with the dusk drawing down around them.

"I suppose they're coming to make their excuses," Mother said, with a bitter twist to her mouth. "Let's go inside, so we can open the door when they knock."

I followed her in the kitchen door and went immediately through the house to the front window. The men were tying their horses at the Meeting-house blocks. Paterson refreshed himself from a small flask and offered it to Sam Gale. I shuddered. Gale was the only eligible Loyalist I'd met in here Cumberland County, and his marriage had been a blow to my ideas of the future. Occasionally I imagined him widowed, a few years hence when I'd be in my twenties, and conjured up a fine romance. But the Sam Gale of my imaginings was not this dangerous brute, wiping his lips now on the back of his hand and giving Sheriff Paterson back his flask.

Boots crunched toward us across the snow. I withdrew to the kitchen, where Mother was poking up the fire. But the knock came on the front door, the one leading into the parlor we'd spent so many days making clean and elegant for these people.

Mother waited until the knock came again before she made her way to that seldom-used door. I followed, stationing myself beside Fa's armchair where John Norton had sat only three nights ago. That chair was the nearest thing we had to a man in the house. In a sedate and dignified swish of skirts, Mother opened the door and stood back.

Our allies poured in on a reek of sweat and spirits, filling the room as they doffed their hats and looked around for a place to put them, for all the world as if they expected to stay. But they weren't invited until tomorrow evening. Did we have to rush around and find food and drink for them? One look at Mother answered the question. She took up position near the cold hearth and stood poised, hands lightly clasped in front of her—no bustling about, no whiff of hospitality.

"Good evening, sirs. Have you come to explain your plan?"

"There is no damned plan!" Paterson said. "The rioters have the building."

"The damned rascals!" Sam Gale sounded contemptuous. "They actually imagined that we'd stand out there and parley with them! I soon put paid to that notion!"

"Of course you're not going to *talk* with them," Mother said. "I assume you intend to drive them out!"

They glanced at one another. Gale said, "We'd do that gladly, ma'am, but none of us wants to get his damned head shot off!"

"I'll thank you, sirs, to refrain from profanity in this house! None of you stands in the least danger of being shot. The Whigs are not armed."

I felt the pulse beat in my throat. Paterson straightened. "Of course they're armed!"

"I watched them pass through the village, and Fanny saw them come up the hill. They had no weapons."

Paterson mulled it over, working his stubbled jaw from side to side. "Seems unlikely," he said finally. "'Riah to hole up without the means to defend himself? I don't see it."

"Are you doubting my word, sir?" Mother asked sharply. They all looked at each other again. Nothing was said, but I sensed an unbudgingness. They didn't care to take the risk. Mother said, "Judge Wells and my husband will find this very interesting."

"If they were here," Gale said, "they'd see it as we do."

Mother's cheeks flamed. "If Mr. Brush were here, sir, none of this would have happened! He would have protected the Court House on Friday afternoon when all this started, and the Whigs would never have had the chance to enter! If you weren't women in men's clothing, you'd give orders to drive them out at once, and bring the leaders to trial for treason!"

The room went dead silent. Paterson's face darkened with rage, and I saw the quickly checked twitch of his arm. If Mother had been someone else, he would have backhanded her. But she was Assemblyman Crean Brush's wife, and he had to take it; they all did. Fa was the conduit to New York government, New York power, New York wealth. Paterson and Gale owed their positions to him, and the others had their hopes.

"You have the authority," Mother said. "You have the arms, and you have only to contend with traitors who'll run at the sound of their own voices!"

"No, they won't," I said, to my own complete surprise. The words came without forethought, but I didn't need to think. Mother was wrong, terribly wrong. "They won't run. And . . . I think they have a just cause."

The men rounded on me, Judge Sabin slightly pop-eyed, Paterson's face congested and purple with the effort to contain his fury. Whatever I'd been about to say about the rebel's cause flew straight out of my head. It didn't matter. Nothing mattered except to stop them, stop Mother, from making everything worse. I must frighten them if I could—and I thought that was quite possible. "Remember, there are Green Mountain Boys on the other side of the mountains, and Ethan Allen will come to help them!"

Mother's eyes snapped. "I wouldn't be more surprised to see you sneaking after Ethan Allen than I am to hear you say that!"

My mouth fell open. *What* did she just say?

But she turned her back on me. "Don't listen to her. The girl is crazy! Sheriff, the King expects you to do your duty."

She said "the King," but she meant Fa. Paterson's cheeks sucked into ominous hollows. "And I *will* do my duty, ma'am," he growled, between clenched teeth. "We are obliged to give the mob a certain amount of time, and then they will be dealt with."

"In my considered judgment," Judge Sabin interposed, more to the sheriff than to Mother, "our first duty is to wait for the chief justice before deciding on a course of action. Things have not proceeded as he may have expected."

Paterson bowed stiffly. "Very well," he said. "Having paid our respects to you, ma'am, we will return to our post." He turned on his heel and stalked out the door, followed by the others with varying degrees of apology. Bildad Andros took particular care never to meet my eyes. He must have some regrets just now!

Judge Sabin lingered a moment. "This was badly done," he told Mother. "The sheriff wisely sought to augment his force as he came up from Brattleboro, but the men had to put things in order at home before they could join the posse, and that delayed us. This will be harder to put right than it would have been to prevent. But we are no minutemen, ma'am, to leave our oxen yoked in the furrow and our house doors ajar."

"Believe me, sir," Mother said, "you have no need to tell me that!"

Sabin gave a gracious nod, as if he'd just received a compliment. "Perhaps you did well to light a fire under the sheriff's tail. The chief justice is most apt to leave things as they stand, without a little urging. I believe he'll receive that now. Good night, ladies." A stiff little New England bob of the head, and he was out the door after the rest of them. Mother closed it firmly behind him and twisted the key in the latch. She turned, and our eyes met.

"I was shocked at you, Fan," she said quietly.

"And *I* was shocked at *you!* How can you say I would *run after* Ethan Allen?"

"Better they think you attracted to the man than to his politics!"

"*Attracted?* He's almost as old as Fa! And he's married! Anyway, is *that* what you were trying to say? Because it didn't sound like it!"

"Oh, for goodness' sake!" she said impatiently. "Don't we all have something more important to think about than Ethan Allen?"

"I don't know, *do* we? Maybe he and the Boys are on their way over right now!"

"In all likelihood they don't know a thing about it! But what really matters, Fan—how could you say the rebels have a just cause? How *could* you?"

"They're not rebels!" I said. "It's a protest! They just want to be treated like British citizens, with the rights we'd have if we lived in England."

"*We?*" Mother said.

"Yes. We're Americans, you and I! We were born here. Americans *are* British! We should all have the same rights. The King and parliament shouldn't be able to do whatever they want to us. *They* should obey the law, and *we* should have a right to help make it! Fa got Cumberland County seats in the Assembly, and everybody thought *that* was right. Well, New York should have seats in Parliament! All the colonies should! Maybe then the government would actually know something about America, and they'd stop being such fools!"

Mother stared at me without speaking for a long moment. "Elizabeth has an apt pupil," she said finally, and turned and walked out of the room.

Chapter 17

I shut my eyes. There was a tremble deep inside me, near to the bone. Everything had gone awry this afternoon in the space of twenty minutes. Up until then it had been a chess game. Who would block whom? Who would capture the castle? But this was real, and it wasn't the threats and the shouting that had sealed it for me. It was Elizabeth saying, *It isn't supposed to be this way.*

Then what way was it supposed to be? There should have been thousands of Whigs on the street, as there'd been in Massachusetts, but that was an impossibility in sparsely-populated Cumberland County. It was easy for a Massachusetts protest, even a nonviolent one, to succeed with such overwhelming numbers, and with the Regulars penned up in Boston. But here, political sentiment was much more divided. The Whigs had no choice but to outwit our side—which regrettably, hadn't been difficult! Now they were in the building, trapped by their own stubbornness, and the posse, clotted near the Court House, talking irritably to each other, were also trapped by a situation that should never have been allowed to happen.

I watched from the window until the men on the street were just dark blurs, and the aroma of warming venison stew penetrated the room. I followed it into the kitchen. Isaac was already there, and Mother was dishing him out a bowlful. She didn't look up when I entered. Had she even been going to call me? I hadn't an idea in the world what to say to her. What had just happened between us? A rebellion, or a protest?

At least this was one conversation Isaac had *not* overheard. He'd only just come in; his face was red with cold, and he smelled like fresh air. "What's happening over there?" I asked him, sitting down at the table. "Is Judge Chandler here yet?"

They both looked startled, alerting me to my mistake. I'd never talked to Isaac before, other than to ask him to do something. Our quarrel on Saturday night was more than we'd said to each other in the whole year that he'd worked for us—and my question was much, much too casual.

He considered his answer and settled on brevity. "Yes."

"And what happened?"

His jaw set. I didn't think he was going to speak, but after a moment, he drew a long breath and looked up. The expression on his face was the one I'd seen last night—no resemblance to any root vegetable whatsoever. That corner of his mouth dented in, just like his mother's did, and his eyes were level and direct. "Captain Wright told him to his face that he'd broken his word to us."

"What did Judge Chandler say to that?" I asked.

Isaac looked contemptuous. "Said it wasn't *his* fault! *He* hadn't agreed to them being armed. He said the Whigs could stay in the Court House overnight and nobody would bother us, and he promised to go take the guns away."

"And did he?" I asked. "Take the guns?"

"Not that I saw! He went out and talked with the sheriff and the judges and they all went off down to the Tory Tavern, guns and all."

The guns were still out there, then. "What are the Whigs doing now?"

"They wrote up their demands, and then the Westminster men went home to supper. They've set a watch, though. There won't be any more surprises!"

"So you think they'll try to drive the Whigs out?"

Mother stirred. "Isaac has no more idea of that than you do, Fan. Anything he has to say is mere speculation."

Isaac looked her full in the face. "They won't try anything," he said. "You saw. They're cowards! They wouldn't say boo to a goose!" He pushed back from the table and went out, leaving half a bowl of venison stew cooling on the table.

He didn't return, though we sat up waiting for news long into the evening. Nothing happened that we could see or hear, and we spoke hardly a word to one another. No words could compete with the echo of what we'd said earlier. *Chasing after Ethan Allen. I think they have a just cause.* After statements like that, it seemed safest to trust to silence.

At last Mother banked the fire and lit our candles. She handed me my hot soapstone, still without saying a word, and I followed her up the stairs, feeling truly resentful by this time. My opinion wasn't *that* extreme! Many Loyalists said similar things; we adhered to our government, and we wanted it to be more fair and competent. Even Fa said that—but *I* wasn't allowed to? I wanted to protest, but the silence was like something physical that I couldn't push through.

At her chamber door, Mother reached for the latch. I thought she was about to go to bed without another word, but she paused, turned, and looked me up and down as if seeing me for the first time all day. "Sleep in what you're wearing tonight, Fan," she said. Her voice was neutral, a command that she never doubted would be obeyed. But thank goodness! She was speaking to me again!

"Then you think they'll try to drive the Whigs out?"

"I don't. They've gone off to the tavern, if Isaac's right. They'll drink six or eight bowls of punch and talk about the great things they'll do, and we won't see them again until morning."

"Then Isaac's right? They're cowards?"

"Not cowards. Fools! At every step they've done precisely the wrong thing, and I have no expectation that will change. But we should be ready. Good night."

Her chamber door closed firmly behind her, creating a puff of wind that made my candle flame shudder. Cupping my hand around it, I let myself into my own chamber, feeling rattled. Ready for what?

The candle slid a gleam of light over my green joseph, draped across the small trunk. If we fled, would I go in what I was wearing? A wool work gown and quilted petticoat, warm and sturdy clothing chosen for standing around outdoors this afternoon with Elizabeth; I couldn't imagine getting on Cloud in anything so clumsy and bulky. I needed every advantage that a well-cut riding habit could provide.

But did I believe in the threat enough to undo every pin and petticoat string that held me together, and get myself into the joseph? Was this real? It didn't seem as if it could be. But I remembered the passion in all those voices, even Sam Gale's, and Sheriff Paterson's darkly flushed cheeks, his dangerous look, and I set my jaw, feeling as mulish as Isaac. If we were leaving, I was going in my joseph, and that was simply that.

So I changed, pausing often to look at myself in the dim and murky glass. I was as green as spring itself when fully dressed, as new and shining as a daffodil leaf. Perhaps that wasn't wise. If they caught us, wouldn't it be better to look like an ordinary, humble New England girl? My fashionable joseph seemed calculated to inflame a rebellious mob. On the other hand, everybody in Westminster knew exactly who I was, and had seen me wearing this garment dozens of times. Being well-dressed would keep up my courage. If nothing happened overnight—which seemed most likely—I could change again before breakfast.

I got into bed and sat leaning forward with the covers pulled up to my chin, hugging my soapstone. It was easy enough to *say* "sleep in your clothes," but not so easy to do if you happened to be a woman. The farthingale pad gave shape to my skirts, but a most uncomfortable arch to my back when I tried to lie down. I could take it off—*ha!* If I wanted to start untying petticoat strings, I could! It was deep down under a number of layers and staying where it was.

I put my head down on my knees. Surely there was no need for all this! Our men were at the tavern drowning their sorrows in John's excellent rum and rendering themselves completely unfit for storming up Court House Hill. It was the morning that was in question. Would the judges try to enter the court at the appointed hour? Would the Whigs let them? And then what? Whatever happened, the consequences would play out over weeks—months, even.

Meanwhile I had to get through tonight, which was already long and uncomfortable. I sat up and rubbed my neck. Would sleep be possible? I could curl up on my side, maybe. It seemed worth trying—and it proved fairly comfortable, but sleep was as far off as ever.

The clock downstairs tolled ten, and then ten-thirty, and I began to entertain a certain amount of ill-will toward the thing. Nobody else in this town had a clock. If others lay awake—and they surely did—they must be estimating time by the sinking moon. It was waxing, gibbous, a little fatter than half. *Pay attention to the moon, child,* I remembered Cadwallader

Colden telling me in his dry, cultivated voice; our current acting governor was a scientist who had educated his own daughters decades earlier and took an interest in me. *A naturalist should always have in mind what phase the moon is in,* he told me, and I always did. Waxing. Gibbous. Sinking.

Now, right *now*, was my last chance of seeing what was happening. I shoved the covers back. I'd go to the spare room. That window looked out on the Court House like a box at the theater. I'd be able to see whatever there was to see—hear it, too, if I could ease the window open without waking Mother.

My candle had been snuffed an hour ago, but there was no need of light with that moon. I opened my door cautiously. No sound from Mother's room, not even the usual gentle snore. I imagined her lying in there, eyes wide, staring at the ceiling. Holding my breath, I slipped past her door and along the upper hallway to the door of the spare room, my train looped up and my stockinged feet making no sound. The iron thumb-latch made only the tiniest scrape when I pressed it. The door opened noiselessly.

A puff of cold air met my face—*outdoor* air, and a dark shape blocked the window. Moonlight picked out the lines of a chair, a blanket wrapped shawl-wise around a woman's figure, smooth-brushed hair parted in the middle and braided for bed—

"Hello, Fanny." Her voice was dry. She didn't even turn her head. She had crept out of her room as silently as I did, and opened the window without alerting me, though I'd lain wide awake just a few feet down the hall. My heart contracted in a spasm of love and irritation. We were too alike. I could never get the better of her.

"It's perfectly quiet out there," she said. "They've all just gone to bed."

I came to stand behind her chair, postponing the moment when she would notice what I was wearing. The Court House was dark. I heard no voices, no footsteps. After all that fury, the unexpected peace of the scene was almost—

"*Shh!*" Mother stiffened and leaned forward. Now I heard it too, something moving near the Court House—a muffled trampling, the clink of metal. Were horses tied there? Or—

"*Man the doors! Man the doors!*" a startled voice rang out. Confused shouts answered from inside the building; feet pounded down the stairs. I heard the east door fling open, and the voices were suddenly louder, as if many men had crowded out onto the step.

"Take *aim*! *FIRE*!"

BangbangBAM!

I felt the sound in my body and heard the musket balls thud into something solid, and outraged shouts. Louder than all was Sheriff Paterson's roar: "*FIRE*, God damn ye! *FIRE*! Send them to *HELL*!"

Many more guns this time in a ragged volley that lit the east end of the Court House red. Then I heard blows, grunts, curses, wood splintering, and a man screaming wordlessly, in utter, deep-throated disbelief. The sound turned me cold all over, and it didn't stop.

Over the ugly sounds a clear voice called, "Don't run, boys, don't run! We'll go out the same way we came in!" The south door burst open, and the west. Dark figures poured out. "Head for 'Riah's!" a voice bellowed. "Everybody head for 'Riah's!"

More men came racing around the east corner of the Court House, one in the rear half-carrying another. "Help me with Phil! He's all cut up!" Two of his comrades turned back and threaded their arms under the injured man's shoulders. They sped after the rest, angling through the graveyard as fast as they could run.

Now other men loped past us, heading toward the Court House. They carried muskets. I couldn't see the faces, but I could put names to them. Averill, Goold, Phippen, Lovejoy—the village members of Captain Wright's militia, running toward the sound of battle. One of them even had a nightcap on his head. They didn't pause at the Court House but followed the others through the graveyard and on down the hill.

In a moment the street was empty again, but not quiet. The Court House was lit with many candles, loud with raucous voices and wooden benches scraping across the floor, and under it all, that terrible groaning, bubbling shriek.

I was leaning out the open window with no memory of getting there, but Mother's grip on my shoulder, strong as the bite of a horse, pulled me back inside the dark room. My mouth was parched. "Somebody's—" I could hardly form the word. "Somebody's hurt. We should—"

"That's no place for us, Fan. Listen!"

They were laughing now—oh dear Lord, someone was imitating the hurt man! *That* was what amused them! My knees buckled; I almost fell. Mother's arm caught me around the waist and held me up. I was shaking and she was too. "Isaac," I said. "What about Isaac?"

"I pray the poor fool is safe out of the way! He must have been. They weren't letting boys inside—Your hands are freezing, Fanny. I'll close the window—"

But she didn't, because we needed to hear what was happening. Instead she opened the blanket she was using as a shawl and drew me into it with her. We stood there together in the dark, shuddering, listening.

The cries of the injured man grew much quieter all at once, "They've taken him inside," Mother said.

With that sound lessened, we could hear more, though nothing was understandable. The voices were slurred, profane, filled with drunken hilarity. Nothing made them laugh more than their own imitations of their victim. I felt physically ill.

In a few minutes we heard horses galloping. A rider crested Court House Hill without any hindrance from the men around the building. As he passed our lane, I saw the horse was carrying double. The passenger in back sprang off, landing on all fours in the snow as agile as a cat. The other rider continued straight down the King's Highway, out of sight and in a moment out of hearing, as the steep slope of Willard Hill cut off the sound of hoofbeats—one of Captain Wright's express riders, off to raise the alarm in Putney, Fulham, and points south. The posse had driven the Whigs from the Court House, but now they were out there in the night.

There are Green Mountain Boys on the other side of the mountains, and Ethan Allen will come to help them.

Chapter 18

The man who'd jumped off the horse slipped behind one of the cabins, and I lost sight of him. At the Court House, all the doors stood wide open, and men reeled in and out, sharing jugs and flasks, laughing, congratulating each other. All their noise could not drown out the moans of the wounded man. But their exultant relief made me ask, "Is it over?" A childish question; I wanted to be a child, and be reassured as a child, because Elizabeth was over there in the dark and shuttered cabin next door, and so were the little girls, Annis and her sister. It must be terrifying. It *must* be over.

But Mother said, "Shh. Listen."

And then I heard what she heard, someone staggering down our lane. The person who'd jumped off the horse? But that rider had landed lightly. I'd seen him dart behind the nearest cabin, obviously unhurt. I leaned forward, still within the blanket and Mother's embrace, and saw someone in a tricorn hat, carrying a musket, lurch toward the back of our house. In a moment came a thunderous knock on the kitchen door.

We didn't say a word.

"You're safe now, ladies!" I recognized Billy Willard, his voice loose and slurred. "We've got the Court House! Paterson said he'd blow a lane through 'em, and by God, we did!" He stepped back, peering at the downstairs windows. Swayed. Hiccupped. His hand flew to his mouth as if to stuff the little squeak back in, and he hiccupped again, and giggled. How I hated a man who giggled! "Mistress Brush? Miss Fanna? You in there?" He knocked again, harder, as if he would batter the door down.

"We're here," Mother said, in a calm, dry voice, without stepping nearer to the window. "What has happened?"

He tilted his head to look up at us. "Oh. There you are! Well. I'll tell you what happened. We all went down to the Tavern, see, the sheriff and Judge Chandler and me and Dad—and the rest—and we had a little somethin' to drink, and we laid our plans. I was one that come up to catch Whigs. They went home to supper, see, only didn't all of 'em make it. Oh no! Quite some few are stashed in a room down to Norton's.

"Then 'round eleven"—he made a broad gesture that nearly unbalanced him—"up the hill comes Billy Paterson and the rest of his boys. Dad was with 'em and I joined too, right in the front row with ol' Brown Bess here." He patted his musket fondly. "We got about a rod from the door, and they'd heard us, or seen us, and the steps was crowded. Ol' Billy hollers, 'Fire!' and three men did, but the shots went high. You could hear 'em burrow into the wood above the door. First shots always go high, but Billy was mad. He yells, 'Fire, God damn ye! Fire! Send 'em to hell!' He wasn't any too steady on his feet, but he was in good voice, by the Jesus! So we did fire. Some of 'em went down, and we went over the top of them into the Court House, and it was a pretty good fight for a minute or two. But they seen how it was going, and they run like rats out of a burning barn—"

Mother interrupted. "Are there dead?"

"One. But there'll be more. Y'hear that? It's that French from Brattleboro—"

"*No!*" The protest was torn from me. For a moment I wasn't here in this room. I was at Elizabeth's side, seeing that young man march up the hill in the sunshine, so alive and good to look at.

"I say yes!" Billy said. "It *is* French, and I'm the one knocked him down. He was standing there on the steps just like a straw target, and I raised old Bess and put a ball right in his face. He's been pretty loud against New York, but he's singin' a different tune—"

"Billy?" Someone else was walking briskly along the lane—William Willard, also carrying a musket. He put a hand on his son's shoulder. "I told you I'd come with you, didn't I? Now hush. Mrs. Brush? You there? You can tell your husband, ma'am—we got him his court house back."

His bland self-satisfaction ignited something inside me. "And should we tell him *how* you got it back?" I asked, in a shaking voice. "Everybody knows the Whigs didn't have arms. It was a *massacre!*"

"Fanny," Mother murmured, in a cautioning voice.

Willard said, "You're wrong, Miss Fanna. There was shots from inside the Court House—"

"There can't have been! They had only sticks. They were proud of it—" My voice almost choked off. I swallowed. "Anyway, *when* did they shoot? Billy says you all ran right in. I haven't heard that any of *you* were shot! But if they'd had guns, they couldn't have missed you!"

"Easy to see you've never been in a fight, Miss Fanna. There's a damn sight more missing than hitting!"

"'Course they had guns!" Billy was leaning on his own musket, eyes wide and unfocused. "Who goes into a fight without a weapon?"

"You're wrong. I saw it. The whole town did—"

"Fanny," Mother said again. "They've been drinking—"

"And they're *lying!*"

"They were there. You weren't. Someone may have brought guns in later—"

"No. No, they *wouldn't* have! They knew that would put them in danger. It was all planned!" I was arguing in part to drown out poor French's voice. Only it wasn't a voice anymore, just a sound. Our side did that to him and turned this from an argument into something ugly and brutal. *We* were the mob, as tyrannical as they'd been saying we were.

"They was warned," William Willard said. "The Proclamation was read to them—I heard it myself. That court is Justice, Miss Fanna. Without it we're at the mercy of any mob that can whip up a grievance. A man won't be able to call his life or property his own, and as for liberty—*pfft!* Where's liberty, if we're to be ruled by 'Riah's pet militia and some committee proclamations? We'd better all stand up for the rule of law while we still have it!"

He sounded like Elizabeth. Everyone was for liberty, everyone was for law, and yet somehow a man lay over there moaning in uncontrollable agony while others laughed and gloated. I shuddered, pressing both hands to my face. I wanted to block my ears, but it didn't seem right. We couldn't do anything for French, nothing at all. The least we owed him was to listen.

"Best close the window, ma'am," Willard said, his voice softening. "A sound like that ain't good for the mind."

Mother's arm tightened around me. "No, it isn't, sir. What's been done with the wounded? Has a doctor been called?"

Billy snorted. "Andros is some kind of doctor, but all he's nursing right now is a jug!"

"Not much a doctor can do," his father said. "French took three or four shots to the head."

My hands dropped to my sides. To the head. Three or four shots . . .

"Mine was the one knocked him down!" Billy said.

His father's eyes flared coldly. "We both did our part. As to who knocked him down—we were in the front, so likely 'twas one of us." He looked directly at Mother as he said this. He wanted her to mention this to Fa! He and Billy had come to us fresh from murdering a man, and they expected some sort of reward!

Mother said, "Mr. Willard, a doctor should be brought to see to this young man."

"He's a damned traitor!" Billy said.

"We are a civilized country," Mother answered. "Even those we plan to execute, we first restore to health. The government in New York will expect you to bear that in mind."

"If you say so!" The older Willard sounded skeptical. "I say the government ain't obliged to look after damned fools. But we'll send for Dr. Hill. No, not you, Billa. We want somebody that can stay on a horse!" He nodded to us. "Good night, ladies. And Miss Fanna, you remember now. We're fighting for our country here. This is what it takes. You understand that?"

"If this is what it takes"—my voice quavered so badly I could hardly get the words out—"then I don't want to win."

His face didn't change. He took Billy by the sleeve. "Pick up your gun, boy—no, not like that!" Billy fumbled the long musket into position against his shoulder, and his father steered him down the lane.

The moment they were out of sight, someone stepped from behind the maple tree at the edge of the yard, rushing toward the stable. *"Isaac!"* We both said his name aloud.

For a moment it looked like he was going to just keep going, but then he stopped and came toward us, white-faced, eyes glittering, so changed, I hardly recognized him. "You were there," I said.

"You're not hurt?" Mother asked quickly.

He ignored that. "They're laughing. They dragged him into the cell like a dog and they're *laughing*."

"Who did it? Billy said—"

"They *all* did it. The judges, the sheriff . . . I have to go," he said, speaking to me directly. "I need to get out to Crook's before I lose the light. The moon's almost down over here, but it won't be on the west side of the hill. I'll start for Holden's at dawn and be back here by sun-up. Don't worry, I've made that trip six or eight times already, and you rode her the next day and never noticed a thing. She'll be fine. Captain told us, 'Don't kill any horses. We got 'em right where we want 'em.'"

He turned toward the stable. Mother stepped forward out of the blanket. "Isaac," she said, in a voice not loud, but ringing. "That mare stays right where she is!" And something heavy landed on the windowsill, with a metallic rap.

The pistol! She'd had it all this time, concealed under the blanket, and I'd never suspected. Now the long, wicked barrel pointed straight at Isaac.

He turned, and his whole body jolted. He must be able to see the gun, even in the growing darkness. "You won't need her tonight," he said, urgently. "Nothing more's going to happen, not till morning."

"She stays," Mother said.

I saw Isaac weighing his chances.

Then another sound came from French, not a scream or a groan, but something between the two, followed by two or three imitations, and wild laughter. Unendurable. I put both hands over Mother's, turning the barrel of gun aside. She went still, her grip loosened, and in a moment, I had the weapon in my hands. I pulled it back into the room.

The moment Isaac saw that, he broke for the barn. I heard Joost nicker at him, some quick scuffling sounds. "Fanny," Mother whispered. I heard the tremor in her voice and turned back to her. I could feel her breath on my face.

"I'm sorry. But if he doesn't take Cloud, he'll get another horse. And you wouldn't have shot him. You know you wouldn't!" I was crying outright now, hot tears pouring down my cold face. Her hands came around mine on the gun barrel. She took it from me and laid it carefully on the chair, and wrapped her arms around me, rocking back and forth. No words. In a few minutes I heard Cloud being led out into the yard, and the soft sound of Isaac leaping into the saddle. Pressed against Mother's warmth, I heard hooves galloping down the street and turning up the west road. All around us I knew there must be more riders, racing to spread the word.

Chapter 19

I woke in bed beside Mother. She lay still, head turned toward the gray rectangle of the window. The bed was warm, almost too warm. I felt lazy and comfortable, with a sense that something terrible had been averted or solved, that I was safe . . . and then the events of last night flooded back into my mind.

Mother shifted on the pillow to look at me, alerted by some change in my breathing. Her face was a pale oval, her eyes dark. She studied me searchingly.

"Is anything happening?" I asked.

"I don't hear anything."

"Isaac?"

"I don't think he's back yet."

"He'll take good care of her. . . . You don't hear *anything*?"

"Your ears are as good as mine, my dear."

Last night they were better. After we had gotten into bed, I could still hear the sounds from the Court House; at least I thought I could. Mother said no, she hadn't heard a thing, and she might have been right, because they had continued even after I buried my head under the pillow.

"You do look like me," she remarked, startling me. "I'm glad of that. Though you have a great look of your mother too."

Who would my children look like? I wondered. And who would be their father? Did I even have to worry about that anymore? Here in bed in the tender half-light, I dared ask. "Do I need to marry now? We . . . won, didn't we?"

Her eyes closed. A deep breath stirred the bedclothes. "This is a small place. War and peace don't hinge on it."

"But yesterday you said—"

"Yesterday I said many things, some of which I bitterly regret. After all, I think John was right. Patience would have been a better way. As my father says, when you fire a big gun, expect a big recoil."

"That's what *I* said. What I meant, anyway."

"I know." She gave me a deep look. "Has someone been . . . *indoctrinating* you, Fanny? You seem very sympathetic to the other side, all of a sudden."

Was she really worried about that? "No. I've just been arguing with Elizabeth. The Whigs say the same things we do. Liberty, property, rule of law . . . William Willard last night sounded just like them. But they can't all be right, can they?"

"Oh, *right*!" Mother said. "Is that what it's all about?"

"Isn't it?"

I felt her shrug under the covers. "It's about power. Who leads. Who rules. We make up all kinds of principled arguments to buttress our position, but it comes down to that."

"They think we should rule ourselves. I mean—that *they* should rule *them*selves."

"That's just treason," she said. "We're one people with one king. We can't give this small group more rights than everyone else has." She sat up, letting cold air into the bedding, crossed her arms and hugged herself.

"Do you suppose he's dead?" I asked. The sounds were gone from my ears. The air felt empty.

"We must hope so."

"That's awful." This morning I was able to speak of it. Absent the sound, it seemed distant, the kind of thing one has read about with a pang of pity, whereas yesterday it seemed like to ream the heart out of my body.

"All of this is awful," Mother said. "That's what the fools don't understand, when they start ranting about how this or that is unjust and unbearable and amounts to slavery. The alternative is *war*."

"Or the government could listen to them. We're the ones who fired guns."

She turned her eyes toward me for a long moment, then lay back down, hauled the covers up to her chin, and stared at the ceiling. "Yes," she said eventually. "We fired first, and I don't know what will happen now, but if it looks like war, I think you do need to marry. I know it's not what you want, and I'm sorry for that, but when you're a soldier's daughter, you learn the truth about war and what happens to women. Think about last night—Billy Willard, drunk and ripe for anything. And all of them coming into our parlor reeking of sweat and fury. And that was *our* side."

"They could have harmed us whether I was married or not. I don't see how it helps."

"The Buchanans have wealth, and status with both sides. It will be in everyone's interest to take care of their family. Most important, they have ships. If you need to escape to England or Canada, that should be possible."

The image—and smell—of New York Harbor entered my mind. I had been on anchored ships a few times, but never sailed; my grandparents' stories of their journey to American shores had quelled all desire to do so. But that wasn't the only reason Mother's words made me uneasy. "So you think we'll lose? But we're the greatest empire in the world!"

"Only if we hold together. British strength is cut by exactly as many American men as sympathize with the Whig cause. You know what happened in Massachusetts during the Powder Alarm. A hundred thousand men marched on Boston! If we *had* been so foolish as to shell the city, they could have walked into the harbor and drowned there, and the rearguard marching on the dead corpses would have been enough to take all our ships. It's impossible to even fathom how vastly the Regulars are outnumbered."

"But many Americans are loyal."

"Yes, but we seem to lack drive. Had positions been reversed, the Whigs would have been inside the Court House on Friday afternoon, and everything in Cumberland County would be quite, quite different this morning."

How different would things be by this afternoon? Instead of voicing the thought, I sat up and pushed back the covers. Time to face the day, whatever it might bring. At least it had already brought reconciliation with Mother, which seemed to be the thing I most needed.

We hadn't slept in our clothes after all. It had seemed clear that nothing more would happen overnight, with the posse firmly in possession of the Court House, and so we'd stripped down to our shifts and tumbled in together for warmth and comfort. My joseph lay across Mother's trunk with all my petticoats, my pocket, my farthingale pad. After a peek out Mother's window—much too dark to see anything yet—I picked the whole pile up and crossed the hall to my own chamber, where I dressed in what I'd worn yesterday. It might not prove to be exactly what I needed, but I had lost all faith in thinking ahead. Thus far, none of us had predicted the future with any accuracy.

Clothed again, I went to the spare room to look out that window. The room had a great freshness from all the air that had flowed in last night, and it was even colder than our chambers.

By now it was beginning to be light out. The scene outside was calm, perfectly ordinary except for all the extra horses tied here and there. Smoke puffed from one or two chimneys, including the Court House. The snow outside the doors was heavily trampled, stained, and littered with debris. What had happened to the sticks the Whigs carried? They'd been taken from Captain Wright's woodpile; maybe they were even now burning in the Court House fireplace.

No sign of Isaac. No sign of Cloud.

We went downstairs. Mother wakened the fire and swung the kettle over the hottest coals. "I'm going to give Joost some hay," I told her. "While nobody's stirring."

"No, wait. You can't know that someone hasn't taken shelter in the barn. We'll go out together, after breakfast."

I hadn't thought of that. I'd lived at peace my whole life; it seemed I had a lot to learn about war time.

While breakfast warmed, I went to my window in the front room, glad of the pane of glass between me and any sounds. To my indoor ears the street was quiet, and that was how I wanted it. Poor French. If not dead, I prayed he was in a painless stupor and drifting toward eternal peace. And yesterday he'd been so all-alive! Thinking of it brought a crushed feeling to my throat and chest, that did away with my early morning comfort. Elizabeth had been much closer to the Court House. I shuddered to think of her over there in the cabin, trying to comfort the little girls and listening to that awful, piteous sound. Did she know who it was? That was the worst thought of all.

I was turning away from the window when I glimpsed what I'd been waiting for—Cloud coming down the street at her springy walk with Isaac on her back. She'd already worked hard this morning and stretched her neck long and low: no prancing now, just steady, powerful strides. The sun rimming the eastern hills caught her gold coat and Isaac's scarlet cap, brilliant among the brown cabins and dirty snow.

Passing our lane, she glanced toward home and breakfast. Isaac did too. I doubted he could see me, but he lifted one hand, and rode on toward the Court House, passed it by the graveyard side, and disappeared down over the hill. He'd be reporting to Captain Wright; perhaps there would be more messages. But he was back! Cloud was back, and she was fine. I went out to the kitchen to tell Mother.

In half an hour, Isaac came through the kitchen door, bareheaded, carrying an armful of wood. He dropped it beside the hearth and slid into his place at the table. Mother gave him a large bowl of hasty pudding and handed over the butter and maple sugar. "Thank you," he said, meeting her eyes, then mine. Everything was out in the open now. He'd done as he said he would. We must move forward on a new basis.

And still, we didn't know what to say to each other. What was the message, I wanted to ask, and how far would it be carried? What might he want to ask us? In the end, we just ate and parted ways. He brought in more wood, and water, and I saw him at his usual work in the stable. It all seemed very strange—the bright morning, the quiet, the odd little bubble of calm we seemed to be in—

Then came a knock at the kitchen door, and the bubble shattered.

Sam Gale stood on the step: Fa's hand-picked successor as county clerk, son-in-law to Judge Wells, ever polite, always polished in his dress. He was an ambitious man whom people liked to see succeed because he was so pleasant, an Englishman who didn't set American bristles on end, and he was enough a friend of the house that he always came to the back door. This morning, though, his face was greenish, his hands unsteady, and it was palpable that he was suffering a blinding headache. His clothes had been slept in, and something had been spilled on his breeches and not wiped off. After our talk about men and war, I felt a moment's unease, but if Sam Gale came at either of us in his present condition, I was confident we could take him. The fireplace implements would be a very present help.

"That fellow is dead," he said abruptly. "Dr. Hill came about three in the morning, but it was too late. Their Honors wanted you to know. But the one we thought a corpse has woken up, so—only one dead."

I'd almost known it, but still I felt the truth like a stab. "I'm sorry," I whispered, to whom I didn't know. My thoughts flew to Elizabeth. Did she know? Horrible!

"Where are *our* wounded?" Mother asked. "You may bring them here—"

"We have no wounded."

"*No* wounded?" she repeated. Gale started to shake his head, and squeezed his eyes shut.

"Because the Whigs were unarmed!" My voice was matter-of-fact, but his eyes popped open.

"I'm sure they were armed. Andros took a bullet through the sleeve—"

"You probably shot him yourselves," I said. "Did any of the men you put in the cells have weapons?"

"No," he said, looking surprised. "The ones with firearms must have all escaped."

"That's not very plausible! They *had* no firearms, Mr. Gale. We all saw that."

"Fanny," Mother's voice held a great deal of reserve. "Mr. Gale isn't quite himself this morning. His memory of events may be somewhat . . . compromised. Did you spend the night in the Court House, sir?"

"We all did."

"I imagine there was more rum there, yes? The jailer keeps enough on hand for a tavern, I've been told. Perhaps it was unwise, though, to keep on drinking. You will need clear heads today. What do their honors plan to do this morning?"

"We'll open court, but—I don't think we'll take up any cases. The first order of"—he turned even paler, and pressed his trembling fingers against his mouth, gulped, and went on—"business, is to write up a true account of—what happened, and attest to it. It's our"—he gulped again—"our duty to relate—the true facts—exactly as they happened. It may be rep—represented very differently in coming days."

"Yes," I said. "Someone might say that the Whigs had guns!"

Mother ignored that. In ordinary times she would have invited Sam to sit down to breakfast with us. Other days, other ways; now she only thanked him for bringing the news and marshaled him out of the kitchen. She paused a moment on the step, looking off toward the Court House, then shut the door firmly and unambiguously behind Sam Gale.

"Of course, that's where Isaac's cap is," she said. "On top of the Liberty Pole!"

Chapter 20

I would have spent the morning at the window, but Mother wanted the kitchen tidied, and an inventory taken of the pewter and glassware. She didn't say why; I knew why. If we left, it would be useful to have a list of what should be here when we returned. It was also a distraction.

Therefore, I missed seeing Captain Wright arrive. He was there the next time I looked out, crouching in the middle of the King's Highway near the Meeting-house steps, almost at the end of our lane—doing what? A wisp of smoke rose in front of him from a small mound of tinder. Beyond the fire, four muskets stood leaning against each other like beanpoles.

A tiny flame licked at the pyramid of birch bark and dried mushrooms. Three militiamen come around the back side of the Meeting-house, carrying firewood. They wore powder horns and cartridge cases slung outside their coats.

"Mother?" I called, softly. I didn't think they could hear me, but they weren't so very far from the house. She came into the room. "They've got their guns *now!*"

She came to the window as more village men arrived: the Averills, Peter Lovejoy, a couple of the Goolds, all striding up the street with muskets on their shoulders. Joining the first group, they stacked arms and crouched around the fire. One fashioned a tripod and swung a small kettle over it.

"Running bullets," Mother said, "right out in the open."

I glanced up the street. There were people going in and out of the Court House, but I saw faces at the upstairs windows. "Isn't it dangerous to be out there? Couldn't they be shot?"

"I believe they're out of range. Accurate range, anyway, especially this morning! You saw how Sam's hands shook!"

"Then—" The question was too childish to ask, but it was the only thing I wanted to know. What was going to happen?

"Don't fret, Fanny," Mother said, seeing my face. "There isn't the least chance they can take back the Court House. Our side *has* guns."

"So you admit—"

"I'm not *admitting* anything. I saw what you saw, but neither of us knows what happened after dark." Then, as if compelled, she added, "Though if the Whigs had been armed, last night would have gone differently."

I shuddered. How bitter to think that if the Whigs hadn't been so noble and principled, if they hadn't foresworn violence, French would be alive, and his Westminster friends would be inside the Court House, instead of out in the snow, few and small under the broad sky.

A drum rattled on the west road. I rushed to Fa's study and pushed the shutter back. I saw musket-barrels as close together as the teeth of a comb, coming fast by Reverend Bullen's house. They turned the corner onto the King's Highway and marched past the Meeting-house, a few on horseback, the rest on foot. I knew them all: the two Holden brothers who farmed the westernmost ridge, the three Crooks, William, Andrew, and Robert, with young Billy Crook, who was my age. Old Atherton Chaffee, Atherton Jr., and two of the other Chaffee sons. All the men carried muskets, and I saw pistols and sabers in a few belts. Jonathan Fuller, the drummer, with his wavy, mouse-colored hair caught loosely at the back of his neck, provided them a brisk marching rhythm; his normally dull and babyish face was flushed and all-alive.

They swung past the house looking very martial, and I picked out more men I knew by sight: David Daley, Robert Miller, the three Ides, John Wells. With them were others, not in the militia, and they looked as angry and determined as the rest. Every man up there in the hills seemed to have finished his chores and his breakfast and come down here with his gun. They marched up fast to the fire. Captain Wright stood to greet them, not surprised or relieved, or anything except satisfied. All was going as planned.

"Let's work, Fan," Mother said. "I don't mean to swell their audience!"

I picked up my list, about to return to the glassware, but here came another band of men marching past the Court House, which offered no reaction. At the front of the group was Phil Safford, Captain Wright's brother-in-law, carried on a litter; walking beside Safford was Stephen Sergeant, captain of the Rockingham militia. Safford's head was heavily bandaged. He looked very ill, but when they brought him to Captain Wright, he stood up. The two clasped hands and turned to survey the men around them. Color came to Safford's face. His stiff movements loosened as he talked and forgot his pain.

"Fan?" Mother said, turning from the table.

"I'm sorry, I *have* to watch! This is something we'll—" My voice broke, as I remembered what Elizabeth and I had imagined telling our children.

"I suppose we must," Mother said. "I don't like feeling helpless, but we are, and that must be faced. Let's be comfortable, anyway." She drew a chair up to the window. I stood until my feet were tired, and then I got one too.

Men kept arriving by twos and by fives until I couldn't see the fire, could only tell where Captain Wright was by the way the men were facing. He was the magnet, they the iron filings.

"No women," Mother commented. True. Yesterday we'd all been out on the street. This morning the women and girls watched from their cabin doorways, shawls drawn tight around their shoulders, but they came no closer. Even the boys were back behind the fences or up in the trees.

Another drum heralded a large militia group, marching up fast from the south. I counted forty men at least, faces I knew from Putney and Fulham, sweating, red-faced, furious—and now, surely, the crowd outside outnumbered the posse inside.

Jonathon Fuller beat a rattling rhythm on his drum. It seemed to tell everybody something, and they began shifting into formation. A bareheaded boy—Isaac, of course it was Isaac—hopped onto one of the officer's horses, gathered the reins of all the others, and led them down the street toward Goold's Tavern. Something in that sight made me even more aware of how alone we were. Even our hired boy was on the other side.

"Should we go?" I asked.

"Yes, two hours ago! It's too late now."

Indeed. There was no way to leave this house without being under the direct gaze of all those men. Would they harm us? I thought not, but they could if they wanted to. I had a moment of strong regret. If we'd gone the minute Isaac returned this morning, we'd have been across the river hours ago, comfortably settled at Colonel Bellows's house, patting dogs and holding cats in our laps, and drinking cider. But here we were: penned in, mere watchers—and something dreadful was about to happen.

But in a few minutes, Fuller tapped out a different tattoo, and the formation loosened and came apart. That happened three more times through the rest of the morning, and nothing came of it. Still, I couldn't look away, as men kept arriving. The sound of their angry voices was a constant drone, like flies on carrion, reaching even through the closed windows. Twice as many men were in the street now as inside the Court House. More than twice . . .

The Court House stood dark against a creamy, cloudy sky, its main doors firmly shut, but I did see some activity near the back and the cells. It was impossible to tell what was going on, but I had the impression it was a different group of people than the militia—more mixed, more casual.

Near noon Isaac returned to the house, bringing in more wood. "What are they saying out there?" I asked him. "What are they planning to do?"

He shrugged, eyes sliding away from mine in the old way.

"*Isaac!* We're trapped in here! We can't tell anybody anything! What's happening?"

He shrugged again, seeming to agree that we were harmless. "Captain's waiting. He thinks we'll have more men come in. And . . . the jailer's letting people in to see French. He's still there on the cell floor, and they're . . . pressing their handkerchiefs into his blood."

My pulse leaped in my throat. "Did you?"

For answer he took something out of his pocket—a square of linen, not very clean. If it was meant to be a handkerchief it had done other things too, including napkinning and tying things up in bundles. He opened it. In the center of the dirty, crumpled cloth was a smudge of dark red, like the deep color at the center of a pansy. My stomach fluttered queasily.

"What does he look like?" I almost whispered; it seemed horrible to be curious.

Isaac's face turned the color of unfired clay. He clamped his jaw shut and bundled the handkerchief away.

"Fanny," Mother said, a sort of generalized reproof. "This is war—"

"It's *not* war!"

"It is. It's taking normal disagreements past the point when you can argue about them. You can see what that leads to. If a few people had only born that in mind—"

Like you! I wanted to say, and didn't, and she heard me anyway. She went to the table and began slicing cold meat for our noonday meal. Isaac made an odd sound in his throat and rushed out the door, as if he suddenly needed fresh air. As it closed behind him, Mother lifted her head.

"What's that?"

I opened the door again. Now I heard it too, the shrill clear piping of a fife, and the rattle of yet another drum. It seemed to be coming from the north. I ran to the front room. In a moment a fifer, a drummer, and a tall, straight-backed man on horseback appeared over the rim of the hill. A phalanx of militia men marched behind, each with a musket on his shoulder.

"It's Ben Bellows, Mother! Young Benjamin! With the Walpole militia!" The hope was so fierce it almost hurt. Though they were thorough Whigs, the Bellows's were our friends. Could the younger Ben possibly be coming to our rescue?

The large column continued to pour past the Court House, orderly, bristling with weapons, and far too numerous to be just the Walpole men. There must be units from other New Hampshire towns.

Bellows rode up to Captain Wright and lifted his hat in salute. He didn't even look toward this house. All the leaders turned toward the Court House, talking with great seriousness. The trickle of early arrivers had swollen to a massive sea of deerskin and homespun and broadcloth, hats of all varieties above flint-hard, furious faces. Musket barrels tossed above the crowd like antlers. The men seemed to get angrier by the minute. I saw them touching their foreheads, their mouths, behind their ears. Those must be places where French was shot. Oh, dear God, the *mouth*? I couldn't even imagine that—but Isaac had seen it. Automatically I looked for his red cap, and then up to where it blazed bright against the sky next to the Court House.

Men would die today. The truth of it sank into my very marrow. Guns would be fired and men would die. The only thing we didn't know yet was who, and how many.

Suddenly I was aware of the house, empty of anyone except us. How it stood out among the log cabins and barns—a real house, a spacious house, with so many glass windows. This room, all the rooms, were full of expensive luxuries—books, wine, glassware and china, the slowly ticking clock, the portraits on the wall—the expensive wife and expensive daughter of a rich and powerful man. It was all an outward sign of Fa's connections and abilities, and it all could be so easily smashed. A snowball or gunshot through one of the windows, and the men would be inside and everything ripped apart.

And what would happen to us? Could we make it even as far as the stable, if we ran? I didn't see how. If the mob turned . . .

I went back to the kitchen. We picked at our dinners. My mouth was too dry to eat, really, and my stomach knotted around every bite I swallowed.

Afterward Mother said, "Why don't we go upstairs, Fan? We can watch from the spare room and probably see better."

And not *be* seen, I thought, glancing at the door. Would she lock it? I wanted her to, but didn't suggest it. Fear was creeping in around the edges, and I was afraid of it, afraid that if I gave in, it would only grow.

From the window of the back bedchamber, we had a much better view—a mixed blessing! We'd always called the Whigs *the mob*, but they weren't until we made them one. Mother stood with her arms crossed, frowning down on the scene. Abruptly she said, "Even if your fa were here, there's nothing anyone could do."

No. This was beyond individual action. May as well try to turn back the tide, or scold a thunderstorm into submission, as go out there and attempt to change what was about to happen. Only one person could, and I didn't see Ethan Allen's hemlock-green coat anywhere.

Chapter 21

B y two o'clock, matters seemed to be building to a pitch of anger and determination. The mass of men heaved and stirred, with some officers seeming to urge them on, others standing helplessly and watching. Fifes skirled; drums rattled. Here and there hands began flipping open cartridge cases. My mouth went dry, and my heart pattered in my parched throat.

Now a large skein of men separated from the main group, moving toward the Court House—the New Hampshire militia men, with Ben Bellows towering above them on his horse. They surrounded the Court House on three sides, and turned their backs to it, facing their fellow militias across a small gap. Their muskets were no longer shouldered, but ready to load.

"He's *guarding* it!" I exclaimed. "But—he's a Whig too!"

"He's a Bellows," Mother said with a smile that trembled on the edge of tears, and I understood. Our old friend Ben was a large person in every way—prosperous, generous, and hospitable, a man who stood for order and justice, a friend to all, including those inside the Court House. His son was made in the same mold. He would resist wrong conduct, even from his own side, and he was so liked and respected that his militiamen would go against their own judgment to obey him. His character was the only safeguard those men inside the Court House could count on—but they *could* count on it, as long as the New Hampshire men stayed with him, as long as there were more of his men than of the others.

How long would that be? The balance shifted steadily over the long afternoon, as more and more militia groups and individual men poured into the village. Mother and I watched as long as we could stand the cold, went down to the kitchen to warm ourselves and eat bits of johnnycake, carried cups of tea upstairs, and watched some more. The angrier the mob seemed, the more resolute the New Hampshire men looked, but could that last? My back ached from standing so long at the window. My toes were frozen lumps inside my shoes. And the sun was sinking low. I didn't want the sun to go down, I really didn't.

When something finally happened, it was in the smallest way. Two men walked up to Ben Bellows—Captain Wright and someone else, Dr. Jones, maybe, or Joshua Webb, the schoolmaster. Neither carried a musket. They spoke with Bellows for several minutes while the crowd quieted, watching. Then Wright and the other man walked up the steps and knocked on the Court House door.

After a long time, the door opened a crack, then wider. The two stepped inside, and the door shut behind them.

Out on the street the crowd went still, everyone craning their necks to see.

Nothing happened. The sun sank. Shadows stretched long. The clock mentioned that it was now 4:30. Twenty-four hours ago, the sheriff had promised to blow a lane through the Whigs, and he had done so. Where would that lane lead us?

A minute or two later, Captain Wright came out onto the Court House step and said something to Bellows. Those in the crowd near enough to hear began cheering, and the roar spread. Bellows told off a few of his men, who followed Wright inside. The crowd surged toward the building, and the New Hampshire militia parted to let them through.

"What's happening? I don't understand."

"The judges must have surrendered," Mother said. "Now we must hope the Whigs will use them honorably."

I remembered Elizabeth telling about the officials in Worcester, paraded in front of the crowd and forced to apologize. Humiliating! I would hate to see that happen even to Sheriff Paterson and Sam Gale. But they killed a man, and now they were caught. Being forced to apologize was far from the worst thing that might happen to them.

A figure popped out the west door of the Court House, like a weasel out of its hole. The New Hampshire militiamen seized him by the upper arms and the scruff of his coat. No one else followed him, but an impossible number of men crowded in at the front. A few minutes later, the same men began emerging from around from the back of the building. They were passing through, no doubt viewing French's body, and they were much angrier than when they went in.

Now the crowd before the south door gave way to let three men out—disheveled, with torn clothes. They must be Whigs who'd spent the night imprisoned. One had his arm thrown around another's shoulders and was being helped to walk. They stopped short, staring first at the crowd, then at something on the stone step beneath their feet. My stomach churned, remembering the smudge of blood on Isaac's handkerchief.

But the mob was elated. A loud cheer went up, then another, and hats flew in the air, as other men came out, perhaps twenty in all. A woman made her way through the crowd outside, the men all giving her room, helping her along, until she reached one of the freed men and threw her arms around him. He put an arm around her in turn, but didn't look down. He was talking, all the freed prisoners were. I could almost see the story flow, like a ripple across a beaver pond, repeated by the first hearers to the men behind them and so on, until they lapped up against our own front fence.

I didn't need to hear it. I knew it. French, shot in the face, dragged into the cell like a dog, mocked as he lay dying, with his friends so packed in around him that they were unable to help. The sheriff and his men did this. Court officials did this.

A new, ugly rumble swelled through the crowd like far-off thunder. The New Hampshire militiamen squared their shoulders, and Ben Bellows sat impassive on his horse before the Court House door. Mother's knuckles whitened on the windowsill. I felt a thin thready pulse in my throat, a cold buzz all around my body. It wasn't over. This might be the most dangerous moment.

At last Captain Wright stepped out again. A roar rose up from the assembled Whigs. Musket barrels bristled. They *knew* now, they knew exactly what had happened, and here was their leader. What would they do? What would he?

Ignoring them, he stood next to the horse's shoulder consulting with Bellows, then strode off cross-lots toward the Harlow cabin, the home nearest the Court House. The roar died to a frustrated snarl, and men turned to each other angrily.

Eleazer Harlow met the captain at the front fence. They talked calmly; then Wright returned to the Court House. He picked several men and led them inside. They came back out bearing another man on a stretcher made of coats and muskets. Below us, all the necks craned, and the mutter stilled. Everyone watched as the stretcher-bearers with great care maneuvered their burden through the gate and up the icy path. Elizabeth, a flash of sky-blue homespun, held the cabin door open, and followed the stretcher inside.

"Is that—*him?*" I asked.

"No, that man's alive," said Mother. "I saw him lift his hand—Fan, you're shivering! Let's go down by the fire."

"Yes." I stood hugging myself, not moving. I couldn't tear myself away. Mother put a hand on my arm, and we both stood there, poised between going and staying.

"Oh, look!" Mother said suddenly. Here came Elizabeth, hurrying toward us along the edge of the burial ground. She looked small and slim and young, and my heart beat faster as several men approached her. But it was safe for her. She was one of them. She paused to speak for a moment, then continued down the street. Now I saw that she had a basket on her arm. She was not the only female out there, suddenly, and there were a few children as well, all keeping to the fringe of things, out of the knot of angry men. Elizabeth skirted around them, too, and turned into our lane.

"She's coming *here!* I'll be right down!" I called, descending the stairs in a rush and opening the kitchen door. It let in the cool, moist, late-afternoon air and a rumble of many voices, like a vast flock of sheep.

Elizabeth looked thinner, older, than yesterday. There were dark smudges under her eyes, like soot. "We need—" she said. "We have—" Her voice seemed to dry up and whither. She swallowed and started again. "We have a wounded man in our house, and not enough material for bandages. Would your mother—Aunt Rhoda said your mother would have what we need."

"Mother?" I turned as she came through the kitchen door. "Bandaging? Do we have some?"

"Of course," she answered calmly. Of course we did! It was part of running a great house, to be always prepared to dispense hospitality or healing remedies, and while this house was no Hudson River mansion,

Mother had done her best to live up to that ideal. But first, the news. "Elizabeth, what have you heard. What's happening in the Court House?"

Elizabeth repressed a shudder. "They're paying their respects. He's still on the cell floor, and they—walk past."

"Where are the judges?" Mother asked. "Where is the sheriff?"

Elizabeth's face changed, becoming dull and implacable. "They're holding them. In the courtroom. They may bring them out to face the people or lock them in the cells. Some of the men want to burn the Court House down around them. I heard that said. But up until now they haven't been harmed. All the benches in the courtroom are tipped over, and the rafters are splintered by bullets. There are pools of"—she swallowed—"of stiffened blood. On the front steps. On the stairs."

"And you need bandaging," Mother said. "Just a minute." She left us alone in the kitchen.

It felt like a moment we would remember all our lives. So much had happened since yesterday afternoon. We had all, *all*, been wrong, about everything. In this I was Mother's equal, and Elizabeth's, and I knew beyond doubt there was no point in speculating about what might happen next. Only the past had any surety about it.

"Did you know?" I asked. "Last night—did you know who it was?"

Her face quivered. "Pretty quickly we did."

"Oh *Elizabeth!*" I reached my hands out for hers, and she took them, looking down.

"Don't think . . . I didn't love him, Fanna. I didn't know him, really. I'd only . . . picked him out, sort of, as the one I'd like to know, if I got the chance—" She ducked her head suddenly, trying to force back tears.

I put my arms around her. A place in my chest hurt. Poets write of heartache; I never understood before how literal that is.

Elizabeth stirred, putting me a little away from her, but gently, as if that was somehow the kindest thing to do. "Well," she said. Her voice grated, as if she had to force it out. "It looks as if I was wrong. There was violence. War may follow. So what will you do? Let them marry you off?"

I understood what she was saying. We both had our sorrows, but we'd discuss them as women, not fall on each other's necks, weeping like girls. "Everyone was wrong," I said. "Everyone thought things would go differently.

So maybe I will marry him. Maybe we'll be happy. No one can say for sure that we won't."

She smiled at that, faintly. "I suppose not."

"First we have to get away from here, though."

"I think you do. Westminster will be no place for you—"

"Or you! This can't stand. The government won't allow it. They'll send troops, there'll be more fighting—"

She smiled grimly. "If there is, the Regulars will lose. A hundred thousand Minutemen marched to Boston during the Powder Alarm. That will happen again—"

"*Maybe!*" I said.

She looked down. "You're right. But I think the Minutemen will come out in force. Nothing about this has made it less likely!"

"Do you still care," I asked, "about all this liberty business?"

"It was wrong," she said. "They gave their word and they broke it. They attacked their own countrymen. Such men are not fit to govern us."

"I know! But do we have to tear *everything* down? I want the government we've always had, only . . . better. Different—"

"What's to *make* it different? That's what this is about! We didn't want war, Fanna. I hope you remember that. It's they who've made war, not us."

I was grateful that she'd said *they*, not *you*, but I couldn't leave it there. "I'm pretty sure it's always that way. It's always the other side's fault."

Her eyes flashed. "In this case it *is* their fault! Who brought guns? Who broke their word? It's not a matter of opinion. There's an objective truth. You *saw* it."

I didn't see quite everything, but enough to know she was right. "Yes. I know. I'm just . . . do you think Ethan Allen will come?"

"Why should he? We don't need Ethan Allen! We don't need to set up another king to rule over us! The men out there right now, ordinary men, our neighbors—*they* brought this to an end without violence, and without some *great man* riding in to save the day. That's the point. We can govern ourselves."

"But *is* it at an end? They have prisoners. What will they do with them?"

She stared at me, almost blankly. I knew how she felt. I felt that way myself—buzzing with exhaustion, like a bee trapped against a window pane, lightheaded, and somehow off to one side of my ordinary self. "I don't know what they'll do," she said. "But I trust them. Don't you? Haven't they shown that they deserve your trust?"

That was beyond where I could follow her. Trust that seething throng out there? I might trust some of them, individually, but right now they weren't individuals. They'd fused into one vast creature. Did it have a mind, or a conscience? Was it answerable to anyone? "Before, they hadn't seen him," I said. "Now they have."

Then how I wished, *how* I wished I hadn't said that. Elizabeth's face went white and rigid. And after all, did anything else matter in the face of so much pain? The dead, the wounded, the shock, the grief—at that moment, Mother came in, a pile of soft cloths on her arm and a flask in her hand. Her gaze swept across our faces, taking note of this serious moment. But there was no time to acknowledge it.

"This is a tonic wine my father swears by for wounds. Give your man a large spoonful every two hours. It will bring down a fever. How badly is he wounded?"

Elizabeth shook her head. "I can't tell. They were getting ready to cut his clothes away—and I'd better get back. They'll be needing these."

"If you need anything else—"

"Wait!" I rushed to the pantry, and brought out several of the crumbling, savory-smelling cheese cakes, wrapped them in a cloth, and nestled them in Elizabeth's basket. "Give him these, if he can eat. We make them every session, for the judges."

"Thank you," she said, and without another word, slipped out the door.

Chapter 22

By now it was nearly dark, making it hard to follow the little figure in blue with the world gone dusky around her. But we both stood at the window, watching anyway. Mother's breath was the only sound in the house other than my own. Outside, though, the rumbles were louder, becoming rhythmic, welding into a chant we could hear even through the walls of the house.

"Bring them *out*! Bring them *out*!"

My heart turned over. Bring who out? Us?

Elizabeth, skirting the front of the graveyard, paused. Turned? I couldn't tell; she was too far away in the gathering twilight.

"*Bring them out! Bring them out! Bring them out!*" The glass before my face trembled with the reverberation. But nobody was looking our way. The faces, now just blurs in the dusk, were all turned toward the Court House.

"They mustn't do that!" Mother's voice wavered, and I rushed to reassure her.

"In Worcester—Elizabeth says—they made the Loyalists walk in front of the crowd and recant. Over and over until everyone had a chance to hear. But they didn't *hurt* them."

"Nobody had been killed in Worcester."

True. No one was killed in Worcester. No one had ever been killed, in all this year of disturbance, until now.

BRING THEM OUT! BRING THEM OUT! BRING THEM OUT! BRING THEM OUT! It was one mighty voice now, with a high yip and trill of other voices ranging around the edges. A drum began to beat, an urgent rhythm, *ba-rum-bada-rum-bada-rum-bada-rum*. Mother reached for my hand.

"I can't *see* anything!" I pressed my forehead against the cold glass.

Suddenly the chant broke up in a great howl and went quiet. Minutes passed. The mottled darkness that was the crowd seethed against the grainy gray snow.

Now came a low rumble—like sheep again, distant sheep. That was hundreds of men all talking at once, in an indignant, cheated tone. The mob seemed to break apart slightly. I could see patches of snowy ground between groups.

"What happened? Why did they give it up?" But there was no point in asking Mother. Neither of us knew, and there was nobody to tell us.

Still, it seemed that the mood outdoors had changed and stayed changed. I could notice my cold feet again, my aching shoulders, my hunger. It was finally possible for us to turn away from the kitchen window.

"Light the candles, Fan," Mother said. I found the box of spills on the mantle and bent over the hearth, touching the tiny twist of paper against a glowing coal. In a moment it flared clear yellow, and I held it to the candle wick.

Now we could see each other. Mother rubbed the back of her neck and sighed. "Was there ever such a day? I'm going to heat supper."

"Goodness!" I said, suddenly struck with a thought. "They must be terribly hungry! They left home as soon as it was light. How many men do you think are out there?"

"Four hundred, maybe."

"And the horses! How are all those horses to be fed? Nobody has much hay left. They're all trying to hold out until spring."

Mother said, "Either an army has a supply train, or it lives off the country."

"You mean . . . by looting. *We* have hay. We have food."

"The door is locked."

"Not the stable door!" I reminded her.

"No, it's not. That's true." Her calmness was maddening.

"Everybody out there knows this is Crean Brush's house!" I said. "Aren't you *worried*?"

"Fanny," Mother said, turning from the hearth to look at me. "If we get through the next few hours without this house being ransacked, I'll consider us lucky. You remember what happened to Governor Hutchinson's house."

"That was years ago, in Massachusetts—"

"Isn't that Massachusetts out there in the street? Everything about it follows the Massachusetts pattern."

I was about to agree, but then it struck me. "No, *yesterday* was Massachusetts! It was exactly the kind of protest they held last year. Today is new."

She didn't respond to that, but I sensed it had gone home, and not reassuringly. She brought the kettle in from the pantry and hung it on its crane over the fire. But any appetite I'd thought I had was gone. I made my way through the dark front parlor to the window again. No candle. What if they saw it, a candle at the window, my face peering out? I stood there in the shadows, breathing in the scent of linseed oil and beeswax furniture polish.

Four or five small fires had been kindled on the street. The orange flames winked in the darkness as men crossed back and forth in front of them. The scene had a settled look, not particularly menacing—except that the fires meant the militias were not going away. How often had Grandfa Schoolcraft been part of a scene like this, as an army settled down to encamp?

Another fire blossomed at the end of our lane. The flames, tiny at first, rapidly climbed the dry twigs placed on top of them. Dark shapes obscured the blaze as men crouched to warm their hands. I saw the outline of legs, backsides, a cartridge case, powder horns. Right out there at the edge of our yard. We were bottled up in this house like General Gage in Boston!

I crossed my arms, tucking my fingers into my underarms to warm them, watching. As the fire grew, so did something in me, a stubborn hard defiance. How *dare* they pen us in? Who did they think they were? Everything was liberty, liberty, liberty, but only for them and their point of view. Like Ethan Allen, calling Fa a *land jockey* when he was the biggest land speculator in the Grants! They weren't any better than us, these Whigs, with their high-sounding talk. They were just like everybody else!

I crossed the room and felt along the mantel until I found the box of spills, took one out, and crouched over the cold hearth. Deep behind the back log, a few embers glowed. There was a slight hiss as the spill lit. I lifted it to the wick, and in a moment soft golden light surrounded me. Those outside would see it. Let them! Obviously they knew we were here. What was the point of pretending otherwise?

I lifted the candle. In the rising light, everything in this room seemed to gleam—woven carpet, polished table, shining glass and pewter, silk gowns in the oil paintings on the wall. *Toc,* said the tall clock, its perpetual comment. *Toc. Toc.*

If the thin shell surrounding this was broken, it would all spill out. Our belongings, touched and tended daily by our hands. Our shelter, lined with soft things. This room was New York. It was everything we were or wanted to be.

At their mercy?

Damn their mercy! We had a right to be free, too. We had a right to be here.

Mother's quick steps came down the hall from the kitchen. I knew the light would fetch her! She stopped in the doorway, looking across the room at the window, and the campfire outside, pressed her lips firmly together for a moment, then said in a neutral voice, "You didn't even draw the curtains, child."

"Hiding scares me."

Another pause. "Well. There's something to that." She crossed to the window and twitched the curtains shut, with only the briefest glance out. "We won't cower, then. But we needn't be reckless, either. This is no time to give way to impulse."

With that, she returned briskly to the kitchen, every footfall proclaiming: *This is a normal evening. I am doing my normal work.* She couldn't expect me to believe that. She meant to signal—possibly—that she believed in my discretion. I stood a moment more in that now-blind room, listening to the voices not very far from me. Then I blew out my candle and followed her.

The kitchen was still cold, the fire neglected all afternoon, but she'd found the warm spot in the coals, and I could begin to smell the stew. I went to the pantry for the johnnycake and nearly dropped it at a sudden thump on the door.

"It's me! Let me in!"

Isaac.

I opened the door, balancing the pan of johnnycake against my hip. He came in on a gust of fresh air, bearing an armload of wood, which he dropped rattling at the hearth. Mother looked up, apparently unsurprised. "I'm afraid supper will take a little time. We've neglected the fires sadly."

"Here." I handed him a piece of cold johnnycake, and took one for myself, suddenly ravenous. "What's *happened* out there? Where are the sheriff, and the judges?"

He'd taken a bite already and answered thickly. "In the cells."

Mother turned from her fire. "All of them? The chief justice as well?"

"Everybody. Even the Willards." He turned toward the door.

"No, wait! We heard them shouting. 'Bring them out, bring them out.' So why . . ."

"Damned if I know!" he said roughly. "They should face us for what they done, but *Bellows*"—he almost spat the name—"wouldn't hear of it. So the bigwigs decided to pack 'em in the cells, with the New Hampshire men sitting outside. Much *they* care! They didn't know French!" He gulped down the rest of his johnnycake. "I've a message for you, ma'am. Captain Wright says if you lack anything, send word. They're right out there at the end of the lane."

"Those are *our* men?" I asked.

He gave me an odd look. "Yes. Captain Wright's militia."

"What do they have to eat?" Mother asked. "All those men out there—what are they eating?"

"I don't know. Folks are giving them food. Bellows sent home for a big kettle or two and something to put in it. I think the captain did the same."

"And the horses?" I asked. "Is there enough hay in town to feed all those horses?"

"Bellows's men are bringing a load. Our hay's safe; don't worry. I bolted the barn door from inside after I finished feeding."

Our hay? We both made mistakes with that word! "How did you get out of the barn, with the door bolted?" I asked. "And how are we supposed to get to the horses if we need to?"

"Well—you can't go anywhere right now anyway, but I'll open it, since our own militia's here. Now I can stand here talking, ma'am, or I can get the rest of the wood!" Without waiting for her to make a choice he went out, slamming the door behind him.

"How interesting," Mother said after a moment. "All that seething resentment! What an effort it must have taken the boy to be such a perfect lump all these months!"

The fire was brisking up now, as if in answer to the energy Isaac brought into the room. I placed slices of johnnycake on the toaster and stood it on the hearth. "He had no sleep, remember. And he's been out there all day in the cold."

"Yes. And I suppose they don't need him anymore, with every Whig in Cumberland County right here on the street. If Captain Wright wants to give someone a message, all he needs to do is raise his voice! I'm glad the boy's back, though."

"Do you think the Westminster militia are there to protect us?"

"Protect us, keep us here . . . something like that."

Atherton Chaffee, I was thinking. The Averills and the Phippens. William Crook. Captain Wright, even—middle-aged men, old men, fathers and grandfathers. Many had homes, wives, children, right here on the street, beds they could sleep in and tables to sit down to; yet they were bivouacked out there in the snow just beyond our gate. Whatever their reason, I felt better than I had in many hours, knowing they were there.

Chapter 23

I went to bed with Mother again. Usually I slept wonderfully well when I shared a bed with her. This night, I seemed to feel the press of all the furious minds outdoors, a kind of low, continuous mutter that wasn't really there when I made myself listen, really listen, with my ears.

Then Fa was here, on the Court House steps. He clapped twice. The militiamen faded into the fog as he stood there, turning his hands over to examine his fingernails—a dandy, daring and dangerous. But he wasn't there when I opened my eyes.

This Wednesday morning was pearly-white with fog. Peering through the spare-room window, I couldn't even see the Court House, only the Westminster militia stirring around their fire. It was as if they were alone, but that couldn't be true. Wasn't true, I realized, when a familiar Putney man stepped through the white mist. He'd been invisible until he was right beside the fire. Who else was out there? And what were they doing? The almost-peaceful look of the scene, with the rising sun beginning to glow through the fog, hid something—probably more of the same, the quiet stirring-awake of a military encampment where no such thing belonged.

I carried my bowl of porridge to the front window and stood watching. The Westminster men were quiet, thoughtful, some a little stiff from a night spent sleeping on the ground. One stepped away from the fire to relieve his bladder, and someone else made a joking comment. He threw a startled look at our house and hastened off in the opposite direction.

As my spoon reached the bottom of the bowl, Leonard Spaulding, the Fulham blowhard, emerged from the thinning mist with two other men I didn't recognize. They dragged a younger, smaller man by the elbows between them. Spaulding and Captain Wright seemed to be questioning

149

him. I read *No* in the man's face—no, and no, and no, to every question. Eventually they released him. He hurried away, directly toward this house. His face was unfamiliar, yet I felt I'd seen him before somewhere. I drew back from the window, but not quickly enough. He was right outside the window, and our eyes met.

Let me in, he mouthed.

My heart thumped. I shook my head. He glanced back over his shoulder at the men watching, and kept coming, around the side of the house. I rushed to the kitchen, not surprised to hear a knocking. Isaac and Mother were still at the table.

"It's somebody Leonard Spaulding had outside," I told Mother. "But the militia let him go. He wanted me to let him in the front door."

Mother got up heavily and walked toward the sound of knocking. Something about the sway of her petticoats made me wonder if she had the pistol.

Out on the stoop was the young man I'd seen, and coming up behind him, looking formidable—and old!—was Atherton Chaffee. Their two voices: "Is this the home of Crean Brush?" and "Do you know this man, Mrs. Brush?"—mingled with the background rumble from the street.

Mother glanced at me. "Is this the one?"

I nodded.

"I believe he has a message for us, Mr. Chaffee. You look cold, sir! The tea is hot, if you'd like some."

The wrinkles around Chaffee's eyes deepened. "Like as not the boys'll smell it on my breath, but yes, I'll drink a cup of tea."

And in a moment, we were all around the table, Isaac the spy, Atherton Chaffee the Whig militiaman, we Loyalists, and this person in the brown coat whose name we didn't even know.

Chaffee provided an introduction of sorts. "Says he's Robert Hancock—I get that right? Robert Hancock, shoemaker from the Bay. Says he come up from Brattleboro this morning, but *not* to reinforce the court party . . . but when we asked was he carrying a message to anybody, he said no."

"Then I was wrong," Mother said smoothly, pouring the tea. "I was hoping for a message. Mr. Hancock, will you?"

"No-no!" he said, shaking his head rapidly.

"If you can't drink tea with an old Whig, I don't know when you can drink it, Hancock!" Chaffee twinkled his eyes over the steaming cup. "Young Isaac, you too! Nothing puts heart in a man like hot tea. No? Suit yourselves. Now, Mrs. Brush." He looked Mother squarely in the face. "Is there anything you need? Anything at all? You know I speak as a friend."

"A running start?" Mother said, with a little laugh.

He smiled but shook his head. "No call for that. Nobody means you any harm. You're Westminster. If your good man were here—but he ain't. Miss Fanna, I'll wager that mare of yours is itching for a run, but I wouldn't. Not yet."

"What's going to happen?" My perpetual childish question! But Chaffee had seen war first-hand. He must have a better sense of things than we did.

"Don't know. We'll hold an inquest, I guess, and bury young French, and then . . . there's different opinions. I thought things would settle down, but there's more men coming up from Fulham today, I hear, and Fulham's mad, damned mad. They liked young French. We all did." He drained the tea and stood up, tall and slope-shouldered against the rafters. "You want this man taken away? If so, just say the word."

"No," Mother said. "I'll hear what he has to say. But thank you." With a nod to us, a wink at Isaac, and a smooth, considering glance at Hancock that sent a warning chill down my spine, the old man let himself out the door.

"Now then, Mr. Hancock," Mother said. "What does bring you to us?"

"I was told this was the home of Crean Brush, the assemblyman. And that he had a daughter. Not a son." He looked at Isaac.

"This is our hired boy."

"Is he loyal?"

"Not at all," Mother said. "At least not to the Crown, though I must say he's done his duty by us through all this. Isaac, do you want to go or stay?"

"Oh, have your secrets!" Isaac said roughly. "I got to water the horses." He shrugged on his coat. Mother handed him a wool hat that our previous hired boy left—gray, not red. He pulled it on and stomped out the door.

"*Were* you coming up as reinforcement?" I asked Hancock.

"Yes. I was inside the Court House when those men came in—"

"And you tried to escape!" I said, remembering the figure popping out the side door.

"Yes. They let me go, but now they're catching everyone, coming or going. I thank you for taking me in, ma'am."

"Yes. Well," Mother said, and I knew what she wasn't voicing. We hadn't opened the door with idea of housing Hancock forever, and like me, she was probably eager to see the back of him. He was just exactly the kind of man neither of us took to. His little quick eyes darted around the kitchen, glanced through the door to the next room—as if he were taking inventory! Why was it so often the case that the men on our side were unpleasant?

Be that as it might, Mother served him tea, which he was willing to drink, now that he was alone with us. Afterward we returned to the front room window, in time to see yet another militia group, very large, march up from the south—a couple of hundred men at least, with the radical Fulham doctor Solomon Harvey at their head. They had four prisoners in their midst.

When Hancock saw them, he exclaimed. "They were with the posse! They're rounding up anybody who was there!"

The larger crowd parted, and Harvey led his men through, toward the Court House. They disappeared, and the familiar scene closed in, a blur of shoulders, buckskin, broadcloth, tricorns, guns—ominous in its shifts and swelling voices, and yet almost becoming dull. Was I actually bored with revolution? My hands wanted to be busy again, to stitch a seam or scrub a pot or—

"Someone's knocking," Hancock said. "Don't you hear that?" He looked toward the kitchen.

Mother stood up from her chair. "Come with me. Yes, both of you."

Hancock followed her and I followed Hancock, stifling a laugh at how easily he was managed by General Margaret. She went straight to the back door and opened it, to the startlement of the young woman who stood there, hand half-raised to knock again.

"Mrs. Brush!"

"Rebecca. Come in." Rebecca Gale, wife of Sam, daughter of Judge Wells who served with Fa in the New York Assembly—a pretty, darkhaired girl a few years older than me, whom I never could like. Why should I? I'd harbored some girlish imaginings about polite, cultivated, English Sam Gale, the most eligible bachelor in Cumberland County, but those imaginings depended on me growing up, and in the meantime Rebecca Wells had nabbed him. I wouldn't have him now for anything in the world, but the habit of dislike lingered.

She nipped through the door, shutting it quickly behind her. "Oh, thank goodness! I'm so glad to be in this house! So *many* of them! We'd heard—but I had no idea!"

"You'd heard about this?" Mother asked. "Yet you came."

"Yes." She looked past us at Robert Hancock. "Can I—is it safe to speak freely?"

"I believe so," Mother said. "This is Mr. Robert Hancock from the Bay, who came up this morning as reinforcement and was captured."

"So was my brother Oliver," said Rebecca. "We set out together, but we met a contingent of the Fulham militia and they took him."

"Why didn't they catch *you*?" I asked, and instantly wished I could erase the sharp edge from my voice.

"I had the horse," she said. "When they overtook us, I galloped away." In answer to some look on my face her cheeks flushed. "I came to help Sam! Oliver can't be of any use to him now, but maybe I can help them both. There must be some way—mustn't there, ma'am?" She turned appealingly to Mother. "Don't you think there must be something I could do?"

Mother evaded the question. "Where is your horse?"

"I left him at the Willards. Billa's there, very unwell. He's as pale as winter milk, just dragging himself around. Something he ate, his mother said."

"No, something he *drank*!" I clapped my hand to my mouth, preventing myself from mentioning Sam Gale's condition yesterday morning.

"His mother is *militant*," Rebecca said. "She had Billa's rifle to hand and a pot of venison stewing to feed the men. She offered to come with me—because Joseph's in the Court House, you know, her younger boy, and her husband too. I said no. I'm not well-known in Westminster. I might not be recognized."

"You'll be recognized," Mother said. "This isn't a Westminster affair anymore, if it ever was. May I ask what you hope to accomplish?"

"I'll see Sam and do whatever he wants. And I brought him some cheese and biscuit. Who knows if they're even feeding them!" Her voice broke. "And now he'll have to share it with Oliver, and whoever else they've captured. Why did they let you go, Mr. Hancock?"

He blinked rapidly. "I—I'm from the Bay. I convinced them that I couldn't be involved."

"But Rebecca, how will you get in?" I asked. "You won't be able to slip past them unnoticed." Though she had slipped past us; how had we failed to see a woman in that crowd of men? It just showed the truth of things. It was a man's world, and men were the ones we looked at.

She turned a bit milk-faced herself, and said quietly, "Yes, I see that. I shall just ask them to let me see my husband. They can't deny me that right."

"They can do anything they want!"

"But they won't."

Her self-assurance pricked my temper. "You don't know how angry they are," I said. "Our people killed William French! Sam was outside the Court House waving a pistol. He might even be the one who did it."

Her eyes flashed angrily. "Don't be ridiculous! Of course Sam didn't do it!"

She didn't know him. That thought and a dozen others possessed me in the space of a second: She didn't know her own husband. She wouldn't believe me if I told how he was that night, or Tuesday morning, and maybe she'd be right to disbelieve me. Sam had been far, far outside his usual self. In future years, even he might look back and disbelieve his own memories. Maybe I would too.

And what would I think about this moment? Rebecca Gale—how would she seem to me once a few years unfolded, once whatever was to happen next was in the past?

She was still talking. "I know exactly how angry they are, Fanna! I just walked among them. Do you want to know what I heard them say? They're talking about firing their guns into the building, to kill everyone inside. One of them said—" she shuddered. "He said, '*My flesh crawls to be tomahawking them.*'"

My flesh crawled, too, when I heard that, but the threat wasn't something to be taken seriously. "It's easy to *say* that. They can say whatever they want, with Ben Bellows and his militia standing there—"

Her face brightened. "*Ben Bellows!* Oh, thank goodness! He'll let me in." She whirled toward the door.

Mother caught her arm. "Are you sure this is the time, Rebecca? Shouldn't you wait to see how the day develops?"

"No," She shook her head, so all her dark ringlets bobbed. "That's exactly what I shouldn't do. I'm brave enough for it now, and if I'm to help Sam, I must act!"

And she was out the door.

Chapter 24

A puff of fresh air filled the kitchen, filling me with envy, longing, irritation. I made for my window in time to see Rebecca hurrying down the lane. When she reached the Westminster militia, standing around the remains of their fire, she went straight to Jabez Perry, the second in command, throwing back her hood and raising her head to show her face. Unbearably theatrical! But it worked. She and Perry spoke briefly, Atherton Chaffee sauntered over to join them, and then all three began making their way through the crowd toward the Court House.

"A spirited girl!" Hancock commented, setting my teeth on edge. I turned to Mother.

"Why don't *we* do something? Why don't we go out there?"

"Whatever for, Fan? The moment I see something we can do, I'll do it. Until then we wait, and watch."

"But that's all we do, wait and watch! You and me and all of us! Why is our side so *hapless*?" I should have shut my mouth, but suddenly that wasn't possible. Everything I hadn't been saying spilled out in a rush. "When we *do* do anything, it's wrong! The Whigs weren't even armed! All we had to do was push through the doors. All four of them at once—how could they have resisted? Instead we've killed a man, and can *we* turn out an enormous crowd to defend ourselves? No! We straggle up by ones and twos and get picked off—"

Mother was in front of me, thrusting one hand toward my face. The biting aroma of smelling salts flooded my nose and mouth. I gasped, choking, trying to push her away, but her firm hands, one still holding the bottle, caught mine. "Fan," she said. "Fan. It's understandable that you should be overset, but bear in mind Mr. Hancock."

Mr. Hancock? I had forgotten his existence. My last sob rasped off. Tears still flowed down my face, and I saw him blurred, his little black eyes darting away, refusing to meet mine.

"I'm not hysterical! I wasn't—"

"You were, a little," Mother said calmly, with another quick squeeze of the hands. "We've had a long siege of it here the past two days, Mr. Hancock, with no end in sight. I'm sure you'll forgive my daughter for speaking a little too freely."

"No, no, nothing of the kind," he stammered. "Though even if—I mean—that's a force out there, ma'am! Five hundred or more—even the Regulars wouldn't attack them lightly."

"Of course not. We must accept defeat for now and bide our time until the moment for action comes. Meanwhile, Fan, please help me prepare dinner. It appears we'll have guests. Mr. Hancock, if you'll join us? That room is considerably warmer than this." Thus keeping him under her eye; he couldn't withstand her invitation, even though the front room windows were far better for watching.

Addressing a large turnip with a sharp knife, slicing half-frozen mutton, wiping away onion-tears, I felt my nerves settle, as Mother had doubtless intended. It was impossible not to hear the sounds outside, impossible not to wonder what the shouts were about. Had Rebecca gotten in? What was happening? But it was a relief not to watch. The queasiness brought on by that heaving sea of shoulders, heads, and guns passed off. I listened to Mother probe Hancock—little, casual questions that had more meaning behind them than perhaps he realized: where he came from in the Bay, his opinion of events there, the odd coincidence of his having the same last name as the Whig leader John Hancock.

"Everyone has cousins they blush for," he said. A good answer. I took note of it, being the cousin for whom some people blushed.

"And your general opinion of all this foolishness?" Mother asked. "The idea that Parliament breached the Constitution with the Stamp Act, that it's violating our rights as British citizens. Is there any merit to that?"

Not feeling all agog to hear Hancock's political views, I finished my task and drifted unobtrusively to the front window again. Such a relief to be alone! If one could be said to be alone with such a throng in view! All heads strained toward the Court House; I started to get a gnawing feeling in the pit of my stomach.

But in a moment, a sight diverted my attention. Breasting the tide, a lone woman rode slowly past the Court House and on up the street—Silence Ranney on her pony. Was her husband in the cells? He was a known Yorker and active in county affairs, but I hadn't heard of him being involved in this, and she seemed to ride serenely above it all, the men making way for her. Everyone knew Mrs. Ranney, the best herbal doctress in the county. She'd brought many of these men's children into the world.

Someone struggled through the crowd to intercept her. It took me a minute to recognize Isaac; I was used to picking him out by his red cap. They spoke, and I saw her nod. She must be going to his mother. Isaac came toward the house with his shoulders hunched up near his ears, as if the goings-on on the street were of no further interest. I couldn't help myself. I unlatched the front door and poked my head out. "Is everything all right?" I called.

A score of heads turned. Two-score. Four-score. I didn't let myself shrink back behind the doorframe but lifted my chin and stood my ground. Isaac waited until he was close to answer. "I don't know. They didn't send for her, but Mistress Ranney's going."

"She has ways of knowing when she's needed."

"Ma didn't need her last time." Isaac frowned. "She's *never* needed help." I couldn't think what to say. At least his mother wasn't alone, like mine. She was in her own respectable home, surrounded by her family. But there was peril in every birthing, and Mrs. Ranney must be heading there for a reason. "I hope . . . I *pray* all goes well," I managed. He flushed and went on around the corner of the house.

"Miss Fanna?" Asa Averill, Sperie's father, had come down the lane while we were speaking. "Captain says better not show yourself. These men are pretty riled up."

Captain Wright's actual words were probably something like, *Tell that damned fool girl to get back indoors!* He was right, but I wouldn't let them make me cower. "How is Sperie?" I asked, managing a tone of calm. "And all the children?"

"Like you, Miss," he said, a rare smile twisting his grim mouth. "Cooped up and causing their mothers trouble! Good morning, ma'am." He lifted his hat slightly as Mother came up behind me. "Just sending Miss Fanna back indoors. Oh, and I have this for you." He handed me a small, dirty piece of paper, folded in a triangle.

Mother's hand was on my arm, drawing me inside. The heavy door closed out the noise and sizzling anger. "Fanny, honestly! What were you thinking?"

"I was talking to Isaac. Mrs. Ranney just rode through—on her way to his mother."

"I suppose her time must be near," Mother said. "Is that for me?" *Mrs. B* was scrawled in dull pencil on the outside of the triangle. I handed it to her, and she unfolded it, scanning rapidly. I couldn't read her expression. After a moment she passed it to me.

Sit tite. Will bring you hom with me wh affairs settled here. B Bellows.

I turned it over. That was the whole of it. "Well. That's good." Mother looked out the window. "I can't even see him anymore." That was how big this crowd was now. Even someone as tall as Ben Bellows disappeared in it.

"He's here. He must be, because nobody's tomahawking anybody. At least he's thinking of us."

"He has many things to think of," Mother said. "More every minute, by the look of it. Still, I'm glad to get word from him, and I confess I'd be even gladder to be already across the river in New Hampshire. Though I hate to abandon this house."

"Just for a while," I said.

She didn't answer, only stood looking out the window—not at the scene, but through it and a long way beyond: thinking. Planning? Finally with a sigh she turned. "Come help me in the kitchen, please."

Isaac was there already, seated in his place at the table. Hancock took my spot, and rather than correct him, I slipped in beside Isaac on the bench. "Did they let Rebecca in?" I asked him.

He shook his head, puzzled. "Who's Rebecca?"

"Sam Gale's wife. Atherton Chaffee and Jabez Perry took her over there.

He shrugged. "I didn't see. Too many men out there. There's some from the Bay that just got here." He looked across at Robert Hancock, measuringly. "Wonder if they know about you?"

Mother said, "Mr. Hancock has done nothing to merit the attention of the mob. If he could convince Leonard Spaulding of that, surely it must be true!"

Isaac gave a little snort of laughter, and I repressed a smile.

"You may not know, Mr. Hancock," Mother said, "that Leonard Spaulding, the man who detained you, is a frothing, radical Whig who was jailed for sedition a few weeks ago. His friends broke him out, and he's had the freedom of the county ever since—yet they call us tyrannical! Fan, the pudding. Will you tend it, please?"

Reluctantly I went to the hearth and stood stirring.

"I hear the Boys are coming," Hancock said. "But how would Allen get wind of this? Down in the Bay the Whigs have Committees of Correspondence, express riders. But you people hardly even have roads up here!"

"There are roads," Mother said. "If you're willing to lower your standards. And Captain Wright is Allen's cousin. I imagine they have ways of getting word to each other."

Isaac ducked his head. I saw his ears turn red from holding in his laughter. How many times had *he* been the link, sending word on to Allen? He and Cloud—

Then I saw it.

When the moment for action comes . . .

The only meaningful action we could take was to get word to Fa and the government in New York. We had Hancock, a Loyalist, right here in this kitchen whom we could send on that errand.

And we could send him on a very fast horse.

Chapter 25

The fire seemed too bright suddenly, dazzling. My heart beat so hard I was afraid Mother might hear it. All I could think of was my Cloud—the tender gray skin of her muzzle that I loved to kiss when no one was looking, the wicked ears needling back at me when I did something clumsy in the saddle.

The breathtaking speed.

Don't kill any horses, Captain Wright told his riders after the Massacre. It was an expression of confidence. He knew he had the court party bottled up. But Hancock wouldn't be confident, and messengers routinely rode horses to death. I saw one of the poor creatures once in the Bowery, an ugly huddle, hair stiff with dried sweat, blue tongue lolling out. What was the message? Nobody ever said. The man was much admired for his determination and endurance, and the horse was dragged away somewhere. Or left to be consumed by the hogs that roamed the New York streets; I didn't know. I avoided that corner ever after—

"Don't let that scorch, Fan."

But this was the one thing we might be able to do. If Hancock could get past that crowd on Cloud, no horse in Cumberland County would be able to catch him. He could ride straight to Fa, tell him and the Assembly and Cadwallader Colden about this emergency. They would send help.

Had Mother thought of this? I dared not so much as glance at her. How often had she picked up my thoughts the instant they arrived? I did the same with her, so I knew—she'd think of this, and soon. It was the obvious thing. But I didn't hear it in her voice yet. . . .

So. I'd lived my whole life in the shadow of this clever woman, reacting, not initiating, in all areas of real importance. *Folding.* Just this once, the future opened like a broad, untrodden road, mine to make or mar.

And no.

A thousand times no.

Not my Cloud. She was Fa's best gift to me, the gift that said, *I see you. Your spirit. Your quality.* I loved her, not the way I would love another person, but as a part of me, the small clear spark in the center of myself that was free and always had been. I loved that spark the way the Whigs loved liberty; it *was* liberty, and I wouldn't let Cloud, its living embodiment, be used up, wasted, because Mother spoke too sharply, and the sheriff's men were drunk. William French chose to be where he was. Cloud couldn't, but I would choose for her—

"You've stopped again!" Mother brushed me aside and swung the pudding off the heat, giving it another stir. A few dark, scorched streaks swirled across the surface. She made a little tongue-click. "Well, that won't kill anyone. Tip it out into the dish, Fan, and put in the butter."

The pudding slopped into the earthenware dish, and a scorching, molten drop splashed onto my thumb. I let the pain feed my wits, carried the dish to the table, and flicked knobs of butter over the top, head down so Mother couldn't see my face. My pulse was loud in my ears. When I finished, I sat beside Isaac, who slumped there fiddling with his knife.

"How—" It came out in a little breathless puff. I cleared my throat and said in a casual voice, meant to be heard, "How are the horses? Do they need exercise?"

He shrugged. "*She* does. He's all right."

"Then take her for a gallop, please."

Mother looked up, alert; the word no was halfway to her lips.

"A short one. What good is she, Mother, if she's too fresh for me to stay on?"

Isaac said, "She'll be—"

I dug my fingernails into his leg under the table. It was the first time I'd ever touched him. To his credit, he didn't show the startlement he must be feeling. "That horse almost trampled a child on the street a few days ago," I told Robert Hancock. "A *Whig* child. It could have been very bad."

"All right, I'll take her out," Isaac said abruptly, getting up. "I ain't hungry anyway." Ideas were circulating behind his eyes; I could tell by their very blankness. He headed for the door, and I looked around for some pretext to follow him. Thank goodness! The hat, the common gray knit hat Mother had made him take yesterday, lay abandoned on the table. Maybe he left it there for this very reason. I snatched it up and handed it to him at the door.

"Go home," I whispered. His eyes widened. "Go see your mother. Stay as long as you can."

He frowned over my shoulder at Mother and Hancock, then nodded, shoved the hat onto his head, and departed, quicker than he'd ever obeyed before. Did he understand? I didn't know. I just hoped Mother didn't.

Willing my legs to steadiness, I went to the front window to watch them leave. Mother followed me. "Fanny?" she said, and stopped herself as Hancock joined us. She was frowning, puzzled. I was still a little bit ahead of her.

Hurry, Isaac! Get out of here!

In a moment, they appeared, Cloud practically dragging Isaac. She wore only a bridle, and I knew why. Isaac was perfectly happy using a sidesaddle at night, but he wasn't willing to appear in one before the assembled militia of Cumberland County and surrounds.

"That's a fine animal!" Hancock said, in the most sincere voice I'd yet heard him use. And she was, such a fine animal—deep chest, sloping shoulder, and strong short back, warm-gold in the sunshine, flowing mane and tail, springy step, expressive head—

"Wildair breeding." My voice sounded airless and thin.

"I'll say she's wild!" Hancock said. "You ride that horse?" I nodded, thinking the same thing. *I ride that horse?*

Mother said, "Wil*dair*, not 'wild.' They're a strain of English racehorse. But she's a ladies' mount, Mr. Hancock, perfectly biddable most of the time. The crowd and the noise have made her nervous."

That was certainly true. Isaac didn't even try to use the mounting block, just ran alongside her for a few steps and then leaped at her back. It was a slippery scramble before he was able to pull himself up.

As soon as he was aboard, Cloud went still, head high, gazing across the sea of men. I sensed her taking it all in, yet attuned to Isaac's hand on her neck. How noble she looked! How pure, how free. Many faces were turned toward her. She was a familiar sight here in Westminster, but the men from other towns could seldom have seen so fine a horse.

Go! Go!

Isaac edged her, mincing tightly, down the lane. The Westminster militia let out a cheer, and she half-reared. She came down plunging, shaking her head and kicking out behind. I'd never seen her behave so badly. But Isaac laughed, wheeled her around, and aimed her for the space between the houses.

I rushed into Fa's study to watch her go—belly deep in snow one moment, leaping a rail fence the next, a glinting arc of gold crossing the back yards. When they reached the solid surface of the west road, her white tail flagged up behind her and she took off at a gallop, Isaac clinging to her neck. I felt a painful stirring in my chest as they disappeared.

"That boy can *ride*!" Hancock said. He'd come into the room behind me, which I found I didn't care for. I believed him to be honestly on our side, but he didn't belong in here among all Fa's secrets.

I took a moment to compose myself, to put on what I hoped was a formidable smile, then turned. He was very close to me but took a step back the moment our eyes met, and another, and I was able to shoo him out as if he were a barnyard fowl. Mother put her hand over her mouth, but I saw her eyes dance.

"Come into the kitchen," she said. "Rebecca's on her way back."

"Already?" I stood on tiptoe to look over her shoulder. There they were, coming along the front of the cemetery. The frail, shrinking way Rebecca clung to Lt. Perry's arm set my teeth on edge. Didn't she ride all the way from Brattleboro to rescue her husband! That kind of courage should hold its head high, not creep and meech.

But she was pale as parchment when she sank onto the settle beside our fire, her eyes wide and dark. She stared into the flames blankly, swallowing, pressing one hand against the base of her throat. Mother, after a business-like glance, poured tea, added several lumps of sugar, and pressed the cup into Rebecca's hand. "Drink."

"Yes, Ma—oh!" A sob caught in her throat. "Sorry. You sounded like my mother."

"Drink," Mother repeated, and I saw Rebecca's inclination to collapse in tears recede and dry up. She sipped at the tea, and a little color came into her face.

"What are they doing over there?" I asked, as soon as seemed decent.

"Sam's not hurt. He said they've given them bread—"

"But what are the *Whigs* doing?"

"Getting ready to hold an inquest. I knew him, you know," she said. "William French. We played together as children . . ." Her lower lip trembled, and this time I believed the emotion. She looked the way Isaac did after he'd seen the body. "Poor boy," she whispered. "Poor boy."

"So they're holding an inquest?" Mother repeated. "How . . . prosaic. And presumptuous!"

"The county coroner's there," Rebecca said. "They're seating the jury now. It's all being done just as it should. Even my father would admit that."

"But how dare they?" Mother said. "*They* aren't the government!"

"Well," I said. "The coroner is the coroner. It's Timothy Olcott, Rebecca, isn't it?"

"Yes. He's the only county official who hasn't been locked up or gone into hiding."

Mother asked, "Were you able to speak to your husband?"

"Yes. He says—" Rebecca glanced at Hancock and drew a deep breath. "He says get word to Ma, down in Brattleboro. Have her send a messenger to New York, to my father and Mr. Brush—"

My heart gave a big *ga-thump*. Here it was, right out in the open. Well, fine. Cloud was safe for the moment—

Rebecca said. "You have horses, don't you, ma'am? And here's a messenger. He could start at once." She gestured at Hancock, who stirred, flushed, swallowed, and was silent.

Mother's face went still. She didn't even glance at me, but I knew she understood what I'd done. She took a moment before she answered. "We're down to one horse at the moment." Her voice was calm and quiet; I had to admire her self-control. "If I let him go, we'll have none, and I can't consider that."

"What about Fanna's mare? I just saw her—"

"Our hired boy has taken her out for exercise."

"But he'll be back soon," Rebecca said, "won't he?"

Maybe he would, or maybe he wouldn't. I wished I could be sure he'd understood the hint. I turned to our prospective courier. "Are you a rider, Mr. Hancock?"

He looked uneasy. "I have ridden, of course, miss. Though it's a fair distance to New York."

"And have you ridden blood stock? The Wildair line are very spirited, as you saw."

Mother said, "As I have told you, Mr. Hancock, Cloud is a ladies' mount. You will have no trouble."

"Isaac did!" I said. "But I expect she'll be calmer after her run."

Mother looked me full in the face for one calm, clear-eyed moment. She'd never been more in command of her expression. Thinking; that was all I could tell.

"In any event, the point is moot," she said. "Rebecca, Sam was right. It's your mother who must send the messenger. What, a known Loyalist to set out from this of all houses, on the best horse in Cumberland County? They wouldn't let him get halfway down the lane! No, you must walk to the Willard's farm, sir. Rebecca's horse is stabled there. Ride to Brattleboro, get a fresh mount, and you can leave without being suspected."

We were all disposing of him as if he were ours to command. I saw his hackles rise at that, but then he glanced around the room at the gleaming pewter and china, the fine candleholders, all the little details that told of prosperity. He had a chance to be of service to two wealthy Assemblymen at once, Fa and Judge Wells. That would undoubtedly be good for Mr. Robert Hancock.

"Where is the Willard farm?" he asked.

"Bottom of the hill, at the south end of this street."

"Oh! Well then, you're right, ma'am. That's the way to do it. I'll start at once—"

"Not quite at once," Mother said. "Wait while I get you some money. You'll need it for your journey."

The moment she left the room, Rebecca said, "I'll walk down the street with you, Mr. Hancock, to make sure they let you have the horse. And—I'll wait with them. I can't bear looking at those men out there."

I was tired of looking at them too, but her theatrical shudder was too much for me. "Better look at them than Billy Willard!" I said. "He was the one bragging he'd killed your friend French!"

Rebecca flushed. "Was he?" Her eyes filled with tears, but she bit her lip hard and forced them back. "I can't care about that right now. I have to think of Sam, and our family."

I respected her for that. I had to. When real trouble comes, your thinking clarifies. I'd learned that, and so had she, and she was brave.

But irritating. The little gasp with which she uttered her next thought had me clenching my teeth again. "Is any Loyalist *safe* in this county anymore? What will become of us? Will we have to leave? Mrs. Brush?" She turned in her seat as Mother came back into the room. "What will become of us all? What will become of our *property*?"

"I've no idea," Mother said calmly. "I have never lived through anything like this before. Mr. Hancock, please accept this to cover your expenses." She handed him some folded papers. "I'm sure Mrs. Wells will supplement it. Give my husband this letter, if you please, and remember, he and Judge Wells must receive an *accurate* report of what has gone on here. They need to understand the truth. What they do with the information is up to them. Godspeed, sir."

He bundled it into his pocket, with a slightly dazed look. How his day had turned upside down! He seemed willing to go, though. Eager, in fact. He'd be a hero without having to do anything dangerous. It seemed ideal.

Then he'd be gone, though, and Rebecca would be gone, and I'd be alone with Mother.

"Rebecca, stay," I urged. "She's going down to Willard's, Mother, but don't you think she's better off here?"

"I think she should suit herself," Mother said. "You're welcome to stay, Rebecca, but if you prefer to be out of earshot of all this, who can blame you?"

Of course, Rebecca preferred that, especially after the timely reminder. Mother shut the door behind them, latched it, and turned.

"Well, Fanny?"

Chapter 26

I had dreaded this my whole life and avoided it. Oh, I could be spirited enough with Mother and kick up my heels. I could speak with complete freedom. I had no physical fear. But to directly confront her, coolly and quietly, to test my power? Never. An icy drip seemed to slide down my spine. I repressed a shiver.

But as I looked back at her, eye meeting eye, I suddenly noticed—I was as tall as she was. When did that happen? I thought of myself as shorter, but it was no longer true.

"Am I to understand that your allegiance has changed?" she asked. Not the question I'd expected. I hardly comprehended it at first, and when I did, felt the impulse to rush into speech. But no, this was no time for gabbling. I shook my head.

"Then . . ." She hesitated, and spoke carefully, as if it wasn't easy to frame what she wanted to ask. "Fan—we are in some peril here. I need to know how far I can trust you."

Completely, I wanted to say, but it turned out I had a question too. "How far can I trust *you?*"

Her eyes widened. "What do you mean? Horses are to be used, you know that. They are *for* something—"

"As are young women?"

She flushed deeply. "I won't pretend not to understand you. Your marriage will be to our advantage—but mostly it will be to yours. If that were not so, *believe* me, I would not agree to it."

I did believe her. I'd known it already, and still, I was glad I had asked. "It's the same with me. If it was really *for* something, if a fast horse could truly make a difference, I would have let Cloud go. But it wouldn't! It will be days before Hancock gets to New York, on any horse. If it's six days and not five—so what? Whatever they do about this will take weeks to arrange . . . and for that, she's to be ridden to death?"

Mother's frown deepened. "Why should that happen?"

"You know the Wildairs. They're the gamest horses alive! They give until there's nothing left, and it's not worth it!"

"To you."

"Yes. To me."

There was more to say, but didn't it come down to this? I'd acted to save what was precious to me. Was it precious to her, because *I* was precious? Our country was on the brink of civil war. Were we? I would have said all that aloud, but I didn't dare, lest my voice quaver. I could only look her square in the face and read there the same reluctance to put power to the test.

A minute passed. Coals hissed and settled in the hearth. My heart beat strong and erratic in my chest.

A louder-than-usual shout from the street made Mother turn her head—or gave her the excuse to look away. "Now what?" She went to the front window.

Following, I saw that the crowd had swelled. We'd thought it was large yesterday afternoon. Now the men filled the entire space between cabins, Meeting-house and Court House, with more coming from both directions, jamming their way in. Almost twice as many, it seemed to me. I wasn't twice as frightened, though. There's only so much fear one can entertain, it seems, before additions become numbing.

I turned away, seeing the room, really seeing it, for the first time in days. Our portraits in their silken gowns looked down on a polished table lightly filmed with dust. The wine glasses were dusty too. That would never do for the judges, but the judges weren't coming. The cream of the county would likely never gather around this table again.

"What should we do?" I asked abruptly. "Shouldn't we be packing or something? If Ben Bellows takes us, we can carry more."

"I suppose that's true," Mother said. "Did you send Isaac away for the day, or will he be back soon? I want a small trunk from the attic, to pack your fa's papers in."

"I don't know when he'll be back. I sent him home to find out about his mother."

"The Lord protect her," Mother said simply, and stood quite still for a moment. Then she stirred. "We can get the papers ready, at least. I'll not waste another day staring out my windows at the mob. If they break in here, they'll find us going about our proper business."

Fa's study walls exuded the deep, settled cold of an unheated room in winter. Mother took the keys from where they hung at her waist and opened the locked drawers of his desk. Quickly she looked over each document and arranged them in piles.

"Tie these up, Fan. Nice tight bundles."

I went out to the kitchen for twine and scissors and set to work. Something hung in the chill air between us, unsettled. I wasn't sure exactly what it was, only that we were being careful with each other.

"We will be poor," Mother said, out of the blue. "Your fa's wealth is all speculative—land that must be sold or rented, and he will not be welcome here to do that."

"But—General Gage will send troops, won't he?"

"I don't think he can. Massachusetts and New Hampshire are in open rebellion, and this will only make it worse. Britain must send more troops—and that will also make it worse. It's only going in one direction now."

That sounded right. "But nobody knows the future, do they? We didn't know this was going to happen!"

"I've rarely gone wrong by being pessimistic! In the long run, who knows? But I see only upheaval in the immediate future." Mother pushed the drawers of the desk shut and handed me another pile. Slanting out of it partway down, I spotted familiar handwriting:

> *Intend Shortly visiting your Abode, Where we hope to Have the Honour of Presenting you with the beech seal . . .*

"Well, *that's* not going to happen!" I said aloud.

"What's not?"

"Ethan Allen presenting Fa with the beech seal. We worried about that, and it didn't happen."

That received only an ironic smile. I tied up the letter with the rest of Fa's papers. The bundles on his desk said it plain. We were leaving, and probably never coming back. The world had changed, and we'd been caught by it.

"Done!" Mother said at last. "Let's go make tea and sit by the fire. I'm cold."

I brought the tea canister from the pantry and took it back once Mother had gotten out what she needed. As I replaced it on its shelf, I spotted the round wooden box of cheese cakes. After a moment's hesitation, I carried it out to the table and opened it. That toasty aroma flowed out, the one that went with best clothes and Madeira and the starchy conversation of important men in the home of someone even more important than they were. I felt an unexpected twist of nostalgia for those dull evenings.

Mother looked in at the creamy cakes, crusted brown at the rims. Her mouth twisted in what was almost a smile. "Oh well, why not!" she said. "Who else is going to eat them? Bring two glasses in, Fan, and I'll get out the wine."

And so we sat there by the kitchen hearth, enjoying our cakes and wine. We drank to the King's health, and then we just drank, a little Madeira, a little tea, between nibbles of the savory cakes. There were periodic roars outside. We didn't bother going to look. We wouldn't know what was happening anyway. We talked little. "Be sure to pack your sketching materials," Mother said, after a long silence. "Spring is coming. You'll find plants to draw. Take your mandolin as well. We'll be civilized, no matter where we are."

That, too, skirted the important question we weren't opening. I was briefly tempted, possibly by the warmth of the madeira, to go into it, but before I could, I heard a horse outside.

I rushed out the back door. It was a gray, overcast afternoon, and she was like a beam of light slicing through the haze. Isaac sat on her back, gazing toward the Court House. I called his name, and when he turned toward me, I clapped my hands. "Oh, hurray! Your mother's all right!"

He grinned and nodded. He looked completely different now, face relaxed, eyes bright. Joy made him nearly handsome. I realized he'd been hiding anxiety, too. I'd lived with him for months, and never once known him.

"I'm glad! Very glad!" I held my hands out to Cloud, who blew her breath over them. Did she smell the cakes? I wondered if she'd like one. This close, I felt the strangeness of what I'd done: defied Mother, defeated her even, for the sake of an animal whom I knew less well even than I did Isaac. Her nature was not like mine, her beauty ungraspable. It pierced me every time I saw her, but I couldn't hold it, nor own it. Did I love her? Did she love me? It wasn't like that. I would never be able to describe the feeling.

I kissed her, right in front of him, and turned. "So, Isaac? A boy? A girl?"

"Girl," he said. "Anna."

"Every girl in New England is named Anna!"

"Not every girl. I know one named Fanna!" Now he was trying not to smile, which was rather adorable—and was he flirting with me? *Isaac?* I didn't know how to answer. I was aware all at once of hundreds of faces looking this way and stepped back, so I was sheltered behind Cloud. "Did I come back too soon?" Isaac asked.

"No, he's gone. He could never have ridden her anyway."

He shrugged. "Maybe not. I goosed her up before I brought her out—in case there was some kind of slip. I thought sure the old la—your mother would have figured it out."

"She did, but too late."

He slid down off Cloud and threw one arm over her sweaty back, looking down at me—yes, admiringly, but fleetingly, just one glance toward a might-have-been, and then off toward the Court House. "The Boys are here," he said. "Some of them."

"Ethan Allen?" Wild hope pierced my heart. He'd come after all! Something wholly unexpected might yet happen—

Isaac shook his head. "They say it's Robert Cochrane leading them."

So, no. No.

"Lots of men still want to burn the Court House down," Isaac went on. "That kind of talk. Won't happen. Bellows is there by the steps. He ain't going nowhere—so talk's easy. And they're digging French's grave, looks like."

I peeked under Cloud's neck. Over in the burial ground, just yards from the Court House, four men with shovels and mattocks attacked the frozen ground. Already there was a dark mound of soil beside them.

"I'd better get to my chores," Isaac said, and led Cloud toward the stable. I went back indoors and sat down.

"You smell like a horse, Fan!" Mother said.

"Mmmm." I sniffed my own hand. "Do the Buchanans have a large stable?"

She looked up, still and alert. After a moment: "I believe so." Her mouth wobbled. "Oh Fan. How can I be sure this is right? *I* married for love."

And look where it's gotten you, I wanted to say. I sat down and took another cake and ate it, the smell of horse mingling with the toasty smell of cheese. I felt light, as if all my burdens had dropped away. I didn't try to make sense of it, in case I scared myself again.

Isaac bustled around in a few minutes with wood and water. "Have a cake," I told him. "Did you use to snitch them ever?" He pressed his lips shut, but his eyebrows rose. "Get one now. Two! I doubt they'll ever be made in this house again."

He ate standing up, watching out the window. When he'd swallowed the last crumb he said thickly, "They're bringing him out."

Mother's eyes met mine. Without a word we went to stand on the kitchen steps, looking across to the graveyard. Militia men filled the space between it and the Court House. Many townspeople had gathered as well. Back against the Harlow's fence I saw Elizabeth's sky-blue homespun, motionless. At the head of the grave stood the Reverend Bullen, Bible in hand.

The street was quiet now. I heard the drone of his voice, but not the words. After a few minutes he stepped back, and a number of militiamen stepped forward. They stood in rank, loaded, aimed toward the western hills. Fired. The crowd grew silent. More men stepped forward as the first retired, and the guns thundered again. Once again, smoke drifted in the air above the dark, fresh-turned earth. For a moment time seemed to stand still, as if Westminster had been preserved under glass, a world in miniature.

And then the men with shovels moved forward, and Mother and I went back inside the house.

Late Spring 1783.
Westminster, county seat of Windham County, Vermont
and/or
shire town of Cumberland County, New York
to be determined

Part Three:

"A Mutable World"

Chapter 27

"She was stolen."

Hard words to say even now, but when the girl asked—a slender child in the early teens who ran across the yard of the Averill cabin to intercept me—I had to answer. Was glad to stop and talk, in truth. I'd dressed too warmly for the day, in my old green joseph. I remembered May being cooler here, and the joseph had felt just right as I'd set out from John Norton's tavern, determined to discover what changes eight years had brought to Westminster. But the sun had climbed the sky while I trudged up Court House Hill, and now I was in an unbecoming sweat.

Also: This girl running toward me shook me out of myself and back in time.

When she reached me, she looked as if she regretted it, but her tongue carried her along. "Aren't you Fanna . . . Mont-Montres—"

"Montusan. No. But I was."

She frowned, puzzled. "Where's your horse? That golden horse? I remember you riding up and down the street, in that very joseph."

Then I had to utter the words that still hurt. "She was stolen."

"Oh. I'm sorry." Such a frank face! I supposed I was like that at her age, when I rode a golden mare up and down the street. "So who are you now?" she asked.

"Fanny Buchanan. The widow Buchanan."

"Oh." She looked back at the cabin. Behind it a frame house was going up—slowly, by the look of it, the labor being squeezed in between farm work. "My father was widowed," she said. "Now I have a stepmother. She used to be Mrs. Peter Lovejoy."

176

"I know." That had been a painful part of our conversation yesterday, when Mother and I settled in for a reviving cup of tea with John and Anna after the tavern customers had gone home. "Who's died?" was the first question, and the list was long and wounding.

"I'm sorry too," I told the girl. "Your mother was kind to me, especially considering—you're Sperie, aren't you?"

"I'm called Experience," she said, becoming a bit more guarded.

"Do you remember that day? When I almost ran you down?"

Her eyes widened. "No. You did?"

"You darted under Cloud's nose and just kept running, off to meet your father. It was the Friday before the Massacre."

"I remember the Massacre. Who stole her?"

Back to Cloud. I opened my mouth and found that my voice was about to waver horribly. I took a deep breath and forced it steady, though I could only manage short bursts of words. "We don't—know. I saw her once—at the far end of a street. But then—she was gone from the city."

"You must miss riding," Sperie said. "*I* would." Her eyes kindled. She was off on a gallop in her mind, one probably inspired by Cloud. I changed the subject quickly.

"Your grandfather—we were sorry to hear about him."

She just nodded. Atherton Chaffee died seven years ago—half her life. I understood. My own losses dated from about that time, and I felt the pain only intermittently now. At twenty-three one expects to bear scars, one expects the heart to ache, and is beginning to be old enough to value distractions.

"Where is the printing press?" I asked. "John Norton told us Vermont is printing currency here."

"You mean, paper money?" She pointed across the street next to the blacksmith shop, where one of the old cabins had acquired an ell made of sawn timbers. There was no sign to mark the place out as a business, and no particular activity going on, but a new frame house was in progress next to it. "There's a newspaper too," Sperie said, "but I don't think—" Two barefoot boys came racing from behind the cabin, lugging a basket between them and prancing like a pair of ponies, perfectly in stride. "Crean!" Sperie called. "Come here."

The boys halted, tossing their heads and snorting, then minced up to us in a high-spirited way, champing invisible bits, while I tried to make sense of what I'd just heard. "Did you say *Crean?*"

"He's my uncle," Sperie said with a laugh, roughing up the little boy's hair. "Grampa Chaffee died before he was born, but he wanted the baby named Crean Brush if it was a boy."

"Crean Brush Chaffee," the boy said proudly, running it all together so the name sounded like Greenbrush.

"But—" I wrestled with the genealogy. Grampa Chaffee, Atherton Chaffee, had had a much younger second wife when we'd known him, and a large family of children. This boy must be Mary Averill's . . . half-brother, yes, so that did make him Sperie's uncle. The old man died in '76, after Bunker Hill and the Declaration of Independence. Fa was jailed in Boston at that time, his name the most hated in Cumberland County.

"*Why?*" I asked. "Crean Brush was my stepfather. Did you know that?"

Sperie shrugged. "I was little then. I don't remember."

"Well, I'm—" I pulled myself together. "It's very nice to meet you, Crean." He and the boy with him were complete Chaffees, with dark blonde hair like Sperie's and her mother's, and eyes that arched and narrowed when they smiled. Bewildering: time, wheeling around me like a gyre, had thrown out new children, new marriages, new houses, a new state, or whatever this *Vermont* was, a new country, in dazzling profusion. My life the past eight years seemed a simple straight line by comparison.

"I'm glad to see you again, Ex—no, you'll just have to let me call you Sperie. I knew you when you were a little girl. Only in private! In front of people, I'll say Experience."

That got a small, wary smile. Experience Averill, already a bit of a force.

I turned back up the street, feeling rattled and off-balance. I'd been eager to come up here, willingly trudged the steep slope of Court House Hill—*why?* To see what had changed, I'd told myself, but now I knew better. I had craved—I swallowed hard, pressing one hand to the base of my throat. I had hoped to find them here. Fa. Cloud. That young girl Fanny Montusan, or whatever her real name was. Find her as she was on that Friday afternoon before everything happened. But obviously I still carried her with me, still innocent, still tangled in illusion.

And now I had to walk back, past all the scenes of the old drama. The road west that I'd taken that night on Cloud. The Meeting-house, now surrounded with huge wooden rollers preparatory to being moved to the side of the King's Highway later this summer.

And our house. I hadn't looked at it on the way down the street; gazed east, told myself I wanted to take everything in its proper order, down one side of the street and up the other. Now here it was, giving its shoulder to the King's Highway in its old imperious way, tall and diamond-shaped and glittering with windows. We had lived in no better house in all these years. Simple though it was, the rooms had been large and spacious, and it kept itself apart from the cabins like a great lady who knew her own worth.

Now fire logs were piled on the place where my little botanical garden had been, and a vegetable patch fenced with upright sticks grew under Fa's study window. The stable door was open wide, and in my mind's eye I saw a scarlet cap, and a dancing blur of gold against the dark interior. But they weren't there. Of course they weren't.

Blinking away hot tears, I turned my head. *Fool!* That was now the home of Dr. Elkanah Day, a sheriff. *A* sheriff, not *the* sheriff. There were two of everything these days, according to John—a New York sheriff and a Vermont sheriff, New York judges and Vermont judges, a New York militia and a Vermont militia. It all sounded silly, but it was serious enough. Some thirty-six prominent citizens had been arrested over it a few years back and packed into the Court House cells so tightly they could only stand, suffering in the early summer heat. John had been among them—the one time his politics caught up with him! What it had been about I didn't know. Cows were involved somehow, and a clever young lawyer, new in town, had defended them—

But here I was already, nearing French's grave, now grassed over and marked with a slate headstone, the letters so crisply chiseled I could read them without leaving the road.

In Memory of WILLIAM FRENCH
Son to Mr. Nathaniel French. Who

Was Shot at Westminster March ye 13th,
1775, by the hands of the Cruel Minesterial tools

Of George ye 3d, in the Court House at a 11 a Clock

at Night in the 22^{d,} year of his Age.

I turned my head sharply, winking back more tears. Twenty-two. I was already a year older than he was, a year older than he ever got to be. I could see him in my mind's eye, striding up the hill with a stick of Azariah Wright's firewood in his hand—

HERE WILLIAM FRENCH his Body lies.

For Murder his Blood for Vengeance cries.

King Georg the third his Tory crew

tha with a Bawl his head Shot threw.

For Liberty and his Countrys Good

he Lost his Life his Dearest blood.

His dearest blood. In my mind's eye I saw that dark smudge on Isaac's handkerchief. The lump in my throat grew.

A rough fieldstone nearby marked where Daniel Houghton, the wounded man taken to the Harlow's cabin, had been buried. His blood had been dear to him, too, but he died anyway, days after the Massacre. He and French had lain in this quiet place the past eight years, mouldering into the earth, French remembered, Houghton forgotten except by his family.

Those years had passed me by as well. I'd spent them in other people's houses with revolution occurring just off-stage, turning me into a wife, widow, mother, and bereaved daughter. Then it dropped me and walked away, as a cat drops prey that is dead and no longer interesting—

"Miss Fanna?"

The voice came from the direction of the Harlow place. The old cabin was gone. In its place stood a large frame house, and rushing down the front path to intercept me came Elizabeth's aunt Rhoda, moving as quickly and lightly as Elizabeth herself. "Miss Fanna!" she said again, as I came near. "Or Mrs. Buchanan, I should say—"

"*Fanny*," I told her. How odd this was! In the old days Rhoda Harlow had little to say to me. I was a rich Tory girl, an outsider; she was a farm woman busy with her household and children. Now we were both women, equals.

"Come in and cool off before you go down the hill," she said.

Cool off. The very words to draw me in! And I was curious to see the house—which turned out to be unremarkable, but that was remarkable in itself. Westminster was slowly turning into the town Fa had foreseen. The sun streamed in through real glass windows. The little girls Elizabeth had cared for were teenaged and could be sent about their work in an actual kitchen, while Rhoda and I sat apart in another room with mugs of shrub.

To pay for the new prosperity and spaciousness Rhoda looked older up close—more lines, a tooth missing, a wide wing of gray hair. But she was hale and healthy, with a warmth in her eyes that I didn't remember. She asked about Mother. We were here together, yes? And she had remarried? Yes, she was Mrs. Wall now, Mrs. Patrick Wall. "Patrick is in Canada trying to get reparations for his war losses," I said. "He's a pleasant man. He makes us laugh."

A question rose to her mind. I could almost see it, and though she repressed it, I knew what it must be. Everyone wanted to know this. Did she really, did Margaret Brush *really* break her husband out of prison? Only to have him kill himself afterward, one cold morning in his lodgings?

What she asked was, "Do you hear from Elizabeth?"

"No. We moved about a great deal. Nobody would have known where to reach us with a letter."

"You may know that she left for her parents' farm the day we heard about Lexington and Concord. She married the next year. A widowed neighbor, a clockmaker."

"A clockmaker." Something about that sounded so . . . sober. *People should marry for love*, I remembered her saying. Well, I suppose one can love a clockmaker!

"We've had three letters over the years," Rhoda said. "She always asks for news of you. But it's a busy time in a woman's life, with the babies coming and everything to do. I wish I had a girl the right age to send to her, but I can't spare either of mine."

The talk of babies brought a crushed sensation to my throat. I changed the subject quickly. "They've grown so tall, your girls. Like Sperie Averill."

"I suppose they have," Rhoda said. "You don't notice the change so much when you see them every day. Will you and your mother settle in Canada?

Some Loyalists are going there, I've heard—or to other colonies, or even England."

I was surprised to meet such frank curiosity. People here used to wonder about us, watch us, but they didn't ask many questions. "No, Mother and I came here to recover our property. If we can get some land back, if we can put a roof over our heads, we'll stay."

Rhoda looked troubled. "I don't see how that's possible. The Loyalists who fled had their land confiscated, and it's all been sold. You may have to buy land."

"With what? All our wealth was in acreage! Since Fa—" My voice stopped. It was literally impossible to speak of Fa's death, even after all this time. I said after a moment, "Eight years ago we owned six thousand acres in Westminster. It must be possible to salvage something of that, even if it's only a house lot! Or do you mean we wouldn't be safe here, as Loyalists?"

"No. No, I'm not saying that at all. There aren't many Loyalists here, but we get along. Well, for instance—do you know who John's dearest friend is these days? *Ethan Allen!*"

Without my willing it, the mug paused halfway to my mouth. "Ethan Allen? Is *he* here?"

"Yes, quite often. He's the general of the county militia, and there's been trouble in Guilford and Halifax. And he comes to see his lawyer, Stephen Bradley. Bradley has the new farm opposite the tavern—and *he's* John's good friend too, though he fought with the Continental Army. So you see—"

I did see. Westminster was still Westminster, and John was John. "Well, we'll have one thing in common with General Allen," I said. "Stephen Bradley is our lawyer too!"

Chapter 28

I thanked Rhoda and promised to stop again and read Elizabeth's letters, then walked back down the hill, which afforded a fine view of the roofs of Stephen Bradley's farm—house, barns, outbuildings, all new and raw. He had built grandly, though according to John, he had no family here except his wife and one child. But he had made a big man of himself already.

When I entered the tavern, footsore and with a blister coming on, I heard Mother in the kitchen with Anna Norton imparting the cheese cake recipe. We could be traced as houseguests across Manhattan, Brooklyn, and Long Island by those savory little cakes. The recipe was always given early in our stay. Even when crowded households grew a little tired of us, they never tired of these.

I peeked into the taproom, hoping for a word with John, but he was nowhere in sight. Well, I could refresh my mind about one person in this drama, at least. I slipped quietly upstairs, shut our bedroom door, and dug the little book out of my trunk.

A Narrative of Colonel Ethan Allen's Captivity, Containing His Voyages and Travels . . . etcetera, etcetera, a paragraph-length title that crowded the front cover. This was what everyone was reading in '79—how, following his capture of Fort Ticonderoga and expedition into Canada, Allen himself was captured near Montreal and transported to England, escaped being hanged, and was shipped back to America, still a prisoner.

What had shocked us most was what he wrote about the condition of American prisoners. We'd all known the wounded among them were housed in New York churches; we hadn't known they were being literally starved to death. All part of a British plan, Allen claimed, to break the Americans' spirits. For this he hated Britain, but he hated Loyalists more. The book still fell open at the place that most grieved and shamed me.

> *. . . The hellish delight and triumph of the tories over them, as they were dying by hundreds: This was too much for me to bear as a spectator; for I saw the tories exulting over the dead bodies of their murdered countrymen......I have seen whole gangs of tories making derision, and exulting over the dead, saying there goes another load of damned rebels. I have observed the British soldiers to be full of their blackguard jokes, and vaunting on those occasions, but they appeared to me less malignant than tories.*

Our friends declared it couldn't be true. We represented *civilization!* We would never behave in such a vile way. I knew better. I could still hear the Cumberland County Tories mocking poor French's groans. Time and again we'd treated the rebels with the greatest cruelty, murdering prisoners with sword and pike, hanging them, or, as Allen showed us all, starving them in churches and sugar warehouses, leaving them to die in their own filth.

Yet peace reigned in Westminster, and the famous Whig Ethan Allen was a friend to Tory John. How was it possible?

Two small incidents in this book, two moments of grace, might explain it, and I flipped back hastily to find them. This was earlier in the tale, when Allen arrived in England starved, ill, covered in lice, and in imminent danger of being hanged. Despite his bravado and the several times he "came yankee" over his captors:

> *I could not but feel inwardly extreme anxious for my fate; this I however carefully concealed from the prisoners, as well as from the enemy, who were perpetually shaking the halter at me. I nevertheless treated them with scorn and contempt . . . and could conceive of nothing more in my power but to keep up my spirits and behave in a daring soldier-like manner, that I might exhibit a good example of American fortitude. Such a conduct I judged would have a more probable tendency to my preservation than concession and timidity. This, therefore, was my deportment, and I had lastly determined in*

my own mind, that if a cruel death must inevitably be my portion, I would face it undaunted . . .

For I reasoned thus, that nothing was more common than for men to die, with their friends around them, weeping and lamenting over them, but not able to help them, which was in reality not different in the consequence of it from such a death as I was apprehensive of; and as death was the natural consequence of animal life to which the laws of nature subject mankind, to be timorous and uneasy as to the event or manner of it, was inconsistent with the character of a philosopher or soldier.

I looked up from the page. One hand had pressed itself unconsciously to my heart. This stirred up all the pain of that time. Of our little family, only Mother had kept up a daring, soldier-like manner. I had drunk deep of despair over Cloud, and my marriage, and at my child's deathbed. Fa had found it impossible to keep up his spirits even after Mother rescued him, and by the time this book came out, he was dead. I'd known beyond doubt that it was possible to go under; it was the easiest thing in the world, and why not, when everything that was dearest had been ripped away? It took the words of Fa's enemy to stiffen my spine again and return me to a semblance of the girl I'd so recently been. Over and over, he played a role. *My extreme circumstances at certain times, rendered it political to act in some measure the madman . . .* With feigned lightheartedness, he tricked his enemies and laughed up his sleeve at them. *A conjurer*, he called himself, for *I had conjured them out of Ticonderoga.*

What he could do in the face of death, I could do to face down despair. I became known for a barbed tongue and highhanded manner which intimidated young officers hoping to get up a flirtation, and punctured several amorous senior officers who felt a young American widow was fair game. I laughed, I danced, I feigned gaiety, and gradually found how to lock my sorrows away, contained and at a little distance.

Now I would know the man who had taught me that. Though he lived on the other side of the mountains, his lawyer was our lawyer; his friend John was our friend John. We'd meet him—and he'd hate us on sight. Not once in his book did he say a good word about a Tory, and now he was a Vermont official, in a position to do us harm.

Mother was coming; I heard her speaking in the downstairs hall. Hastily, I flipped through the pages.

Here it was, the section that offered a crumb of hope. He'd gotten to know a British captain:

> *He was what we may call a genteel hearty fellow. I remember an expression of his over a bottle of wine, to this import: "That there is greatness of soul for personal friendship to subsist between you and me, as we are upon opposite sides, and may at another day be obliged to face each other in the field.*

Greatness of soul. I liked that, but it wasn't the line I was thinking of. Mother's foot was on the first stair as I turned back a few pages.

Here. The naval captain transporting Allen to New York had invited him to dine and gave orders that the ship's crew treat him with respect.

> *This was so unexpected and sudden a transition, that it drew tears from my eyes, (which all the ill usage I had before met with, was not able to produce) nor could I at first hardly speak, but soon recovered myself, and expressed my gratitude for so unexpected a favour, and let him know, that I felt anxiety of mind in reflecting that his situation and mine was such, that it was not probable that it would ever be in my power to return the favour. Capt. Smith replied, that he had no reward in view, but only treated me as a gentleman ought to be treated; he said this is a mutable world, and one gentleman never knows but that it may be in his power to help another.*

A mutable world. It was certainly that! And why should this passage give me hope? It did, though. The tears in his eyes—a man who would admit to them, in his tale of his own heroism, had a heart which could be touched.

But Mother was at the top of the stair. I stuffed the book under my pillow and bent over my open trunk, like a child caught in wrongdoing. She came in, the scent of cheese cakes lingering on her dress. "Can you find a *single* thing in your trunk?" I asked, looking up over my shoulder. "Even though we only packed them two weeks ago?"

She smiled faintly. "I can find everything in my trunk, with my eyes closed." Her eyes weren't closed now, though. I saw her notice the corner of the book sticking out from under the pillow. Naturally! I'd spent the last eight years in close quarters with this woman and rarely managed to deceive her. And why bother? I'd just been reminded *to keep up my spirits and behave in a daring soldier-like manner.* I pulled the book out and showed it to her.

She made a face. "Him again!"

I felt a pulse of irritation. Maybe I'd been a little too fascinated with Ethan Allen as a young girl, but we'd both better pay attention to him now. "He still visits John," I told her, "even though John's a Tory. And Stephen Bradley is his lawyer."

"I'm not surprised. They're both in the business of confiscating Loyalist property." She sat down on the edge of the bed and taking a lace-edged handkerchief out of her pocket, began blotting the dew of sweat off her flushed face.

"Should we use Bradley as our lawyer, then?" I asked.

"It takes a thief to catch a thief! John advised it—and as he knows them both and is our friend, I have to believe Bradley has no conflict of interest in taking on our case."

"You believe that," I said, slipping off my joseph. "I'll keep my eyes open!"

"That's the kind of belief I meant," Mother said dryly.

Of course. She was never one to be caught napping. I closed my trunk and draped the joseph over the top, so it wouldn't wrinkle. "Do you think they've gotten any of *our* property? Allen, I mean? Or Bradley?"

She shook her head. "I understand Bradley bought one or two of our lots, but Allen, no. John would have mentioned it."

"Well, here's something he *didn't* mention." I sat down on the bed beside her and took her hands. "Atherton Chaffee named his last son after Fa."

Mother's eyes widened and her face paled. "*Did* he?" she whispered.

"Yes. I met him. He's about seven years old and he looks like every Chaffee I ever saw! Crean Brush Chaffee. Old Atherton died before the boy was born, but that was what he wanted him named."

Mother sat shaking her head, gazing down into her lap and back in time. "Your fa wasn't easy to know, and most people didn't try. But he and Atherton Chaffee just *liked* each other, right from the beginning."

"But when he was born, Fa was the most hated man in Cumberland County! It would be like naming your son King George the Third Lucifer Satan!"

That startled a laugh from her. "Oh Fanny! *What* a rascal Chaffee was! I wish we'd known before your fa—I just wish we'd known. How he would have laughed! Well! This makes me feel we've done the right thing in coming back."

"Yes. Rhoda Harlow was very friendly to me just now. She never was before. I hope this Bradley is as clever as John says! If we can salvage a house-lot, and a few acres—"

"I intend to salvage much more than that," Mother said briskly. "We own six thousand acres in this town, and thousands more in other places. We got it lawfully, and if there's any justice in the world, we should be able to get it back."

Complicated emotions surged through me. I turned to look out the window at the tavern yard. A thin man with brown hair tied back was leading two horses to the trough. I watched them dip their muzzles into the water. The larger horse flattened its ears and bared its teeth. The smaller flinched back, and the big horse drank, ears flicking in time to each swallow. And drank. And drank some more, while the small one waited with a meeching expression. The thin man finally made the larger horse back up so the other could take its turn.

"I don't think there's such a thing as justice," I said. "Mercy, maybe. Not justice."

"Don't you?"

"Well—*whose* justice? Britain's? New York's? That was another world. This is Vermont now—"

"You're falling for their arguments, Fan, as you were always prone to do. This so-called *Vermont* is just a fancy, an invention, as airy as a meringue. It will not last."

I stifled a sigh. I'd listened to any number of her political predictions over the past eight years, and barely a quarter of them proved out. That was to be expected in a world so radically new as this, but it had eroded my confidence. And another thing: very few of those six thousand acres were hers. She'd forfeited the bulk of her inheritance when she married Patrick Wall. Under the terms of Fa's will, her former share went to me and Mrs. Norman, his daughter in Ireland.

Still, it was *our* land. We spoke of it as ours, and we'd traveled here to reclaim it as if it belonged equally to both of us. As a woman twenty-three years of age, a widow, a bereaved mother, I sometimes wondered how much the old loyalty still demanded of me. Might I not make my fortune elsewhere? Philadelphia, perhaps, or Boston? New York was loathsome to me, but for a young, attractive woman there was far more opportunity in a city. Yet here I was back in Westminster because I was the heiress, and my signature might be needed as we fought to reclaim *our* land. And for any number of other reasons.

"I'm going to see what help Anna needs," I said.

"She needs less help than we want her to," Mother answered, with a grim little smile. The problem of what to do with ourselves had presented itself over and over during the war years and rarely met with a satisfying answer.

"I'll go anyway."

She studied my face. "Come, Fan, we've done well, haven't we, cooped up together all these years? We're still fond of each other, aren't we?" As usual, she'd picked up something of my thoughts, and I understood, as I never used to, what she feared. Not having mothered me well enough. Not being loved enough.

"Much more than fond." I stooped to kiss her cheek.

But going down the stairs, I admitted to myself that despite my deep and abiding love for Mother, my solid sense of obligation—I was ready for a little elbow room.

Chapter 29

I sought out John, not Anna—John who knew everything about everyone in Westminster, and who certainly could have told us about Crean Brush Chaffee.

He was in the taproom changing out a cider barrel, and when he heard my question, he laughed. "Atherton loved his joke! And he always said the old devil—meaning your father—put this town on the map and ought to be thanked for it."

"But . . . but Vermont *exiled* Fa! After he was *dead!* They said they'd kill him again if he ever came back!"

"Oh, I'd never have advised *him* to come back here," John said. "But Westminster folks know a hawk from a handsaw, and a wife from her husband. Will you pass me that cloth there at the end of the bar, please?"

I got it for him; he mopped up his spill and then reached up for a couple of tankards. He drew a small amount of cider into them. "You'll sample this with me?"

I took a swallow of the tart yellow cider, prickling with tiny bubbles. "Better than champagne!"

His eyes narrowed in a smile. "Really?"

"I think so. I had champagne at my wedding—" and suddenly my throat was dry. I took another swallow.

"Not a happy memory?"

I set my jaw, looking into the tankard. "I wept the whole day long, John. But one good thing about marrying a soldier in time of war—he's not around very often!"

John was frowning deeply. "And—there was a child?"

I could speak lightly of John Buchanan. Not of my boy. A nod was the best I could manage.

"Now damn it, Miss Fanny—I mean, Mrs.—"

"Call me Miss, John, please. It was a *very* short marriage!"

"All right then, Miss Fanny, but—now I'm an admirer of your mother's. There's nobody like General Margaret. But what was she about, to allow that match?"

"*Allow* it? She *made* it, she and Fa. It was to keep me safe—*us* safe—with war coming on."

"Begging your pardon but you had an entire continent to escape into! You didn't need to be anywhere near the war."

"The Buchanans are wealthy. They have excellent connections. Mother and Fa thought—"

"They made use of you, Miss Fanny," John said. "They made use of you. You were too young to know what you were about. And yet, Margaret prizes you above anything. She always has. I don't understand it."

They made use of you. Well, I'd known that from the beginning. My marriage was to help us all. It had seemed perfectly natural; that was what arranged marriages were for. I'd *wanted* to be of use, and I took that brave leap—with my eyes open, as I'd thought. But I didn't know what I was doing, and they did, or should have.

"Never mind that for now, John." I pressed the tankard against the painful spot in the center of my chest. "Before she comes down, please tell me—is it true that Ethan Allen still visits you?"

His eyebrows popped up, and his eyes lit with curiosity. "Oh yes!"

"Even though—he's got some kind of position, doesn't he, dispossessing Tories? It seems to me I heard that."

"He's judge for the court of confiscations over in Bennington County—which courts he invented and pushed through the Assembly. Vermont's been financing itself by selling off the estates of Loyalists who fled. Ethan expanded that to take from the ones who stayed."

"But nobody's taken your estate!"

"Well, you see, Miss Fanny, I've always been open in my opinions, and people like me mostly got left alone. And besides—" He smiled, eyes merry, lips firmly closed. In a woman it might almost be called a simper, but in a broad-beamed, middle-aged tavern keeper, it seemed wise and above all, discreet. It would appear that Ethan Allen's friendship with John had been useful to both and could be useful to Mother and me.

"Does he call *you* a malignant Tory?" I asked.

"Oh, he calls me a lot of things, and then he calls for another bottle!"

"I've read his book! He hates Loyalists even more than he hates the British!"

"Oh now, *hate*?" John put his head on one side. "Ethan's no hater. Maybe when he first came back home, but . . . we've known each other a long while. He says a good deal more than he means sometimes. Why should you want to know, especially?"

I settled on a simple explanation. "He's been a threat to our family for years, ever since he wrote Fa that letter."

"What letter would that be?"

"Nobody ever told you?" I described the letter to the best of my recollection. Certain phrases remain burned into memory—land schemers, busy understrappers. The insolent postscript I could recall almost verbatim:

> *As a Testimony of Gratitude for the many unmerited Kindnesses and services you have Done us . . . we Intend Shortly visiting your Abode, Where we hope to Have the Honour of Presenting you with the beech seal . . . as a Mark of the high Esteem we have of your Person —We have the Honor*
>
> *Sir*
>
> *To be yours sincearly*
>
> *The Green Mountain Boys*

John laughed out loud. "That sounds like him! And it explains why your father took to wearing pistols. But he's gone now, and if Ethan does bear him a grudge, he won't take it out on you and Margaret. Someday no doubt you'll get to judge that for yourself. But his wife died in February, and one of the girls is dying now—consumption. So Ethan's sticking to home."

"I'm sorry," I said, rather mechanically. Ethan Allen a widower. The information had an impact on me, but I wasn't sure how or why, and there wasn't time to ask myself, with John still talking.

"Mary was a good wife to him. It'll be a sad household over there—two little girls with no mother, though I'm sure the older girls are taking hold. One's fifteen, I'm thinking, and the oldest would be about your age. Twenty-three? Twenty-four?"

I kept myself from saying anything, but I was daunted. The Robin Hood of the Green Mountains was literally old enough to be my father! Well, I'd always known that, too. "He has no sons?"

"Not any more. His boy died while Ethan was still a prisoner. Two of his brothers, too. A sad homecoming, to be sure."

His boy. I swallowed the aching lump in my throat. "When he does come, John, is he a danger to us? We're Loyalists, we're Yorkers; we have a large estate here if we can get our hands on it—aren't we just *meat* for a man of his views? Not to mention that we're the widow and stepdaughter of Crean Brush! Should we stay here? Or find someplace over in New Hampshire, so he can't get at us?"

John pursed his lips. "Well now, this is Windham County, if you go by the Vermont name, and Ethan only has jurisdiction in Bennington County, as far as confiscations go. That wouldn't stop him necessarily, if he really did have hostile intent. But he'd need to work all the angles, and you have the right lawyer to prevent that. Also—and this counts for something—you're friends of mine."

He twinkled at me, and I repressed a bitter smile. Once John Norton was happy to be *our* friend. We were the ones who conferred advantage. Now it was the tavern keeper who had the power to shelter and advise—a good man, a very good man, but I felt the difference. Truly the world had turned upside down.

Misinterpreting my silence for anxiety, John said, "Don't go too much by what Ethan might write in those books of his, Miss Fanny. Everything's simple in black and white—simple and clear. But in life, well now! It wasn't but four years ago I and a lot of others were on trial up there in the Court House, with my old friend Ethan raging against us and our artful young lawyer, Stephen Bradley. Oh, Ethan was on a grand tear that day! And now that same artful young lawyer is his own attorney, and here in my taproom with the cider flowing, there's no talk of Whigs and Tories among us three. That's all fading into the past, Miss Fanny, faster and faster. I wouldn't worry about Ethan Allen."

Chapter 30

We met with Bradley the following day, dressing in our best and walking across the dusty road from the tavern. The new house was large and rambling, set in a busy farmyard teeming with cattle, sheep, and oxen and smelling strongly of manure. It spoke of wealth without pretension, something of which Fa never approved. He believed in pretension. Wealth was for display, and display was for gaining power, and power was for gaining more wealth. Fa had been gone a long time now, but I felt him at my elbow this morning, could almost hear the dry little *tsk* of his tongue at all this rawness and lack of show.

Bradley opened his own door to us, a tall man of about thirty with strongly drawn black brows and a forceful nose and chin. Just the sort of man I could relish, except that he was married. His snapping dark eyes looked us up and down, and I felt that he saw both our air of fashion and all the little mends and darns which kept us that way.

"Mrs. Wall, Mrs. Buchanan. Come in. May I introduce—now where have they gone?"

At that moment a small child staggered into the room, only lightly supported by the leading strings that ran from the shoulders of his gown to the hands of the slender woman following him. She was laughing, pink-cheeked, but I felt instantly that she ought not to be quite so slender, and that it was the wrong color pink. Perhaps it came of knowing about the trouble in Ethan Allen's family, but I saw signs of consumption. Even so, it was easier for me to focus on her than on the child—a boy, I thought, judging by the high neck and buttons on the gown.

"My wife, Merab," Bradley said. "And my boy, William—"

"Blle!" the child warbled. My heart squeezed as I met his merry brown eyes. My boy was just that age . . .

"*What* did he say?" Mother asked.

"Mr. Bradley is enamored of Peter the Great," Merab explained, laughing. "I can't abide the name Peter, and so his father christened him William Czar."

"Bllzr!"

"Billa Czar," his father said, with a chuckle. "That's what he likes to be called."

I turned toward the window to hide my smile, avoiding Mother's eyes. How was *Peter* any worse than *Billa Czar*? And yet what a perfect name! Bouncy and cheerful, like the child himself. He was more dangerous to me than his father. I'd long made a point of not falling in love with married men, but this little boy was hard to resist. Also irresistible was the warmth between husband and wife, the atmosphere of fond, amused pride. This was what a proper marriage looked like!

Bradley ushered us into his office—a familiar-seeming room, lined with familiar books, the same books Fa had had. In fact, some of them might be those exact books. According to John, our former possessions were scattered in various houses around Westminster. Even the clock still chimed somewhere; he wouldn't tell me in whose home.

Once we were all seated, Bradley said nothing for a moment, looking speculatively at Mother. "Ma'am," he said abruptly. "I must ask. When you rescued Brush—your late husband, I should say—from prison, did you simply exchange clothing with him? Or did you wear another layer of dress over your own, or . . . what?"

Mother went still. The question verged on the improper, but she wouldn't care for that. It was the word *rescue*. She broke Fa out of jail in early 1777, remaining in his cell after a day-long visit while he walked out at dusk wearing her clothing and rode away on the horse she'd left. But in the end, she couldn't save his life. He killed himself in his chambers the following spring, with the very pistol Mother showed me the day before the Massacre, in despair over his property and the many insults he'd received. Years ago now, but it still scalded us both that her brave, reckless act had been in vain. "I really must decline to give you that detail, Mr. Bradley," she said.

He appeared to sense that he'd crossed the line. "My apologies, ma'am. I'm sure the memories are painful. But please know, your actions were much talked about here in Westminster, and . . . admired."

"Thank you, sir, but does that get us any nearer recovering our property?"

"It may help." He steepled his fingers and launched into an explanation of the difficulties. Fa's land had been confiscated in 1779 with the land of other Loyalists and was sold off to fund the new state. But by whom, and to whom, were difficult to discern. Leonard Spaulding had been in charge at one time—Mother sputtered indignantly at this—but was replaced by a new commissioner, Thomas Chandler Jr., son of the waffling old judge. After further irregularities, Nathaniel Robinson, the kindly Westminster revolutionary who'd owned the sawmill, was put in charge. Bradley himself had bought some of our land, he admitted, and facilitated the sale of other pieces. Buyers included William Willard and William Crook, and many of those parcels were already involved in lawsuits, with Bradley acting for one side or the other. Nonetheless, without exactly saying so, he made it clear that he considered the transactions final. The law was unambiguous. Inimical Tories who had left the state were subject to confiscation of property. We'd certainly left. We were almost certainly out of luck.

"However," he continued, "some plots were seized without going through the proper authorities. Spaulding, for one, is in possession some of your property in the north end of town that I believe he has no right to whatsoever."

I'd held my tongue as long as I was able. "No one has any right to it except us, under the terms of my stepfather's will!"

Bradley laughed. "Well, you see, Mrs. Buchanan, in a word—no. Fortunes of war. Your stepfather 'repaired to the enemy,' as it says in Vermont statute—"

"He stood by his king!"

"Who is and was the enemy of the United States of America. History moves, and with it moves property. But where there's a will, as I like to say—" he paused, waiting for a response, then gave a sharp-cornered smile. "Lawyer's joke. But stick with me, ma'ams. I don't despair of finding a *way*."

I smiled in spite of myself—more at his pleasure in the wordplay than at the joke itself, and he laughed, and the whole feeling in the room altered.

"This will take time, ladies," he said. "More time than any of us will like. I expect attitudes, and the law itself, to change with the ending of the war. Now it's in Vermont's interest to pull together and form a strong state, and so, while I make no promises, I by no means despair of being able to help you. Meanwhile, are you comfortably situated over at the tavern?"

"Oh yes," I told him. "John is an old friend."

"A friend to all he meets, the rascal. Very well, but if it doesn't suit you to live in a tavern, come over to me. I built this place big on purpose, and I rent rooms for not very much."

Mother said, "It would have to be not much at all for us to afford it at present."

"On account," he said, rather grandly. "We can settle all that later."

"Thank you," Mother said. "I can't slight John and Anna. We'll stay a few weeks with them, at the very least. But perhaps after that . . . I don't know when to expect my husband back from Canada, so it's hard to make a plan. He's gone to see if there's any chance of being recompensed by the government for the losses he's suffered."

"The government?" Bradley said. "Ah yes, the British government. Government is a noun that needs a modifier these days."

"What about Ethan Allen?" I hoped the question would surprise him, and it did, but I didn't learn anything by it. His face smoothed into blandness.

"What about him?"

"He's your client, too, I understand. He's in the business of confiscating the estates of Loyalists. You might recover our land only to turn it over to him."

Bradley flushed. I'd insulted him, which again, I'd partly intended. As well to find out early how he reacted. "If I recover any of your land, ma'am," he said, "it will be for yourselves alone. What happens afterward, what the court of confiscation may choose to do, we can't foresee, but I will be happy to act for you there as well. General Allen and I are friends, and I sometimes act for him, but I'm not bound to his interests in all matters and certainly would not be in this."

Honest anger and, I thought, an honest answer. "Thank you. Then I think we would like you to make inquiries."

There were papers to sign, and then Bradley ushered us out. The insult seemed forgotten, and he reverted to his slightly excessive courtesy. "I've heard many good things about Margaret Brush and Miss Fanny Montusan," he said, "and all are true of Mrs. Wall and Mrs. Buchanan. I look forward to meeting your third husband someday soon, ma'am."

As became women of mystery, Mother and I bowed our heads graciously, smiled with our lips pressed shut, and said not a word to each other until we were well out of earshot.

"Your *third* husband!" I said. "People still believe you were the widow Montusan once upon a time. What do you make of our new attorney?"

"He has a sharp mind, despite his social failings."

"He is a bit of a rough diamond, isn't he?"

"People said that of your fa," Mother remarked, the corners of her mouth turning down. I sighed without meaning to, glancing up at the Court House on the hill above us. What a comedown! Literally a comedown. Fa caused that Court House to be built and used it to rise to the top of county government. Now we were at the bottom of the hill, sponging on a friend. I couldn't wish Fa back in these circumstances. This is what he couldn't face, the loss of wealth and status. At least, I assumed this was what he feared. We couldn't know. He left no letter that day, only—

No. Don't think about what he left. His poor head, his brain that was so quick and subtle . . . Fa too lost his dearest blood, and we lost him.

Mother let out a sharp sigh. "And so, nothing is clear, even to Mr. Bradley. I foresee a long struggle."

With an effort, I brought my mind back to the property. "Is it worth it?"

"What else can we do? We at least have a chance here. Anywhere else we go, we'll have to begin again from nothing, and you may like the sound of that, but I'm a bit too old!"

Chapter 31

"What did you make of him, then?" John asked when we returned. I was surprised at the detail of Mother's response. She told him everything, including the way Fa's bequest was affected by her marriage to Patrick. She seemed to have decided to have no secrets from John, and I soon understood why. She wanted to consult Goldsbrow Banyar, Fa's old political patron, over in New York, and needed someone to go represent us. Bradley, with his ties to the Vermont government, might not be the best choice, if he'd even consent to do it. John was a businessman, a Loyalist, and a trusted friend, and agreed to make the trip after a bit of persuading, and the offer of payment, which he did not turn down.

He started a few days later. Speed was of the essence. Everything was in flux at the moment with the war so recently ended, and there might be opportunities that wouldn't come again. Mother and I helped Anna with the tavern work while John was away, and the thin man I'd seen in the stable yard took over the heaviest chores. He was Seth Arnold, a dour, silent Connecticut veteran who'd been a prisoner on one of the ships in New York Harbor during the war, the one that was burned during an escape attempt.

"Seth was badly hurt," Anna had told us, "and then he lost all his money, poor man, when the currency devalued. He was worth a thousand pounds before that, but he had only one pistareen in his pocket when he came to Westminster. He's working for John until he has the money scraped together to buy a farm."

For whatever reason, he had little to say to us, friendly or unfriendly, but it seemed odd to have him here, another yankee clustering around Tory John. Were people just tired of war, or was it something about Westminster? Many Whigs drank at the Tory Tavern now, including Stephen Bradley and Captain Wright, the latter much gaunter than I remembered him, with hollow eye sockets and a temper that flared easily. Anna was always nervous when he was in the taproom, pressing her lips together and glancing at us—wishing we hadn't appropriated her husband for our use, I'm sure, or afraid the captain might say something offensive. In fact he ignored us, as he had eight years ago when he bivouacked with his men at the end of our lane. From a man like that, it almost amounted to courtesy!

John was back quite quickly. It took him a little over a week to accomplish the journey and consult, and he brought no news worth having. Goldsbrow Banyar, who once had his fingers on the pulse of New York, was old, and bewildered by the new politics of the day. He had no suggestions as to recovering our property here in this new—or perhaps nonexistent—state or republic of Vermont—so declared here in Westminster in 1777.

"But the property farther west?" Mother asked. "Everyone agrees *that's* in New York!"

"He's not sanguine. New York confiscated Tory property too, and if it can be untangled at all, it won't be by the likes of Mr. Banyar. He's well past it."

"And if Vermont joins Canada? I've heard whispers about that, if Congress doesn't allow it to join with the other states."

"I don't know. No one knows. To all practical purposes, there's no government anymore south of Canada—thirteen different sets of laws and interests, fourteen if you count Vermont, and no higher power to appeal to. It's not the way I ever thought to live! As if someone had ripped the sky off. We'll all have to learn new ways, I guess, but I'm damned if I know which ones!"

"I put up overnight with Ethan Allen," he told us a few minutes later, having disposed of the business part of his news. His eyes flicked from Mother to me, checking for a reaction. "A sad household. His daughter is in a bad way, worse at the end of the week than she was at the beginning. Ethan doesn't often leave her side. It grieves him yet that he was absent when his son died."

Nothing was more common than for men to die, with their friends around them, weeping and lamenting over them, but not able to help them . . .

"It wouldn't have been any better if he was there," I said aloud. "When there's nothing you can do . . . my boy was so sturdy. I remarked on it every time I picked him up. But the disease made nothing of him, and he slipped away between one breath and the next." I was amazed to be able to say this, simply and clearly, without weeping. But it had been a long time now.

John looked down into his tankard, and I could almost see him choosing among his several thoughts. "You and Ethan will have something in common, when you finally meet," he said finally, "and I'm sorry for that."

"And when are we apt to meet Mr. Allen?" Mother asked.

"All in good time. The girl won't live much longer, in the nature of things, and then he'll want to stretch his wings. He never was one to bide at home over-long."

"Speaking of biding," Mother said, "we received an offer of hospitality from Stephen Bradley and I'm considering taking him up on it. If he can't recover our property, he can at least put us up for a time! But only if you and Anna won't feel slighted. We're occupying a room you could be paid for."

"I think it's a good idea," John said frankly. "You'll see a different set of people over there. Stephen's in with all the Vermont higher-ups, the judges and politicians. Well, he's a higher-up himself, and no doubt he'll be at the top of the dung heap before he's done. Barring the dung, it's more the level you ladies are used to. And he wants you. He's told me so himself."

"And you don't?" I asked, teasing.

John laughed. "I very much do, and if you don't come back and visit me at least once a day, Miss Fanny, I *will* feel slighted! But it pays to mix. You two living here along with me—that's a nest of Tories. Over there, you'll be showing the people who matter in this state, if state it is, that you are pleasant, intelligent women like their own wives and daughters, who'll make good neighbors once everything settles down."

"And you could use the room."

"I could use the room."

"Then we'll go," Mother said. "Do you want to be the one to inform him of his good fortune, or shall I?"

"Glad to do it," John said, and within a few days we changed abodes again. Bradly gave us two pleasant rooms just off the front entryway, the largest space we'd shared in many years. It amounted to an apartment, where we were finally able to unpack our trunks, the few things we'd saved from the house here and the even fewer we'd accumulated since. There was a cupboard for china and glass, and against Mother's wishes, I put our few mismatched bits on display. "What's the sense of having them if we can't see them?"

"They'll need dusting."

"Then we'll have something to do at least once a week!" We had our old trouble again—too much idleness. Merab had plenty of household help and was mostly absorbed with Billa Czar. He liked me and often tried to get me to play. Too painful. Also, I felt strongly that the child should spend all the time he could with his mother. If I was right that Merab wasn't long for this world, it was important for Billa to have strong memories of her.

We attended Meeting for the first time the following Sunday. Before that, we'd used fatigue from our travels as an excuse, and with John gone, not even Anna had made the trip. Now we found ourselves following Stephen, Merab, and Billa Czar into the building, out of summer warmth and bright sun into shadow, floating dust motes, the rustle of garments, and a very subdued murmur of conversation. I found my heart beating hard. I hadn't been in this building since the day before the Massacre, since which I had developed a strong aversion to church buildings. Our own church in New York had been converted to a prison; I hadn't seen it with my own eyes, but I had vividly through Ethan Allen's. I found I was breathing through my mouth to avoid an expected stench.

The Bradley pew was the large one up front that once belonged to Bildad Andros, who no longer lived in Westminster. John Norton's was next to it—Tory Tavern owner and Revolutionary soldier side by side before the whole town. Turning as I arranged my skirts, I saw that all eyes were on us. Some seemed wary or hostile, which I could understand. Everyone knew why we were here, and many in this building held some of the property we hope to recover. But some people seemed truly glad to see us. There were smiles, little nods. Sperie Averill poked her stepmother and pointed, and the new Mrs. Averill bowed her head to me.

I let myself breath through my nose. Of course there was no smell other than the fennel seeds some were already chewing. The room was pleasantly airy with its open windows. Discreetly, I pointed out Crean Brush Chaffee to Mother. She studied him keenly, but there was no difference between him and any other Chaffee.

Through the service, whenever we stood to sing or sat back down again, I took the opportunity to glance back at the room. So many more children! And old people too, though they, I gradually realized, were the middle-aged people I'd known eight years ago. There were several strangers—single men, once a rarity in this frontier town. Wars always cut people loose from their homes; many former soldiers had come north after serving in the army or navy.

High in the balcony, I finally spotted Isaac's family. I recognized his mother first, short, round, red-faced, carrying yet another baby in her arms. Her girls were all around her, and her husband behind, grayer and more stooped. But where was Isaac? I didn't see him. There was a little family beside theirs, a tall, broad-shouldered young man holding a baby, and a heavily pregnant girl at his side. He looked a bit like Isaac—

No. That *was* Isaac.

He was taller than he used to be, fresh-faced, heavy-chinned, with something of that bovine look that I used to mistake for stupidity. And married—unless that was one of his sisters?

No, it obviously wasn't. I could tell by the way he turned and handed her the baby, adjusted her shawl, stooped to say a word in her ear. There was a tender connection between them, as sweet as the one between Stephen and Merab.

He turned back toward the pulpit and suddenly met my eyes. Color came up in his cheeks. He nodded briefly and bent his head to look down at the baby again.

I didn't hear the rest of the sermon. I rose and sat when Mother and the Bradleys did, and at one point, noticed that I was singing along with a hymn, but all the while I was thinking: *He has his baby. I lost mine.* That wasn't the only source of the pain I felt, but it was the biggest.

After the service, as we stood at the fringe of the people around Stephen Bradley, saying hello to former neighbors we hadn't seen in eight years and being introduced to newcomers, Isaac came up to us with the baby in his arms again, and the young woman at his side. "Hello," he said—not to me, to Mother.

"Oh, it's you, Isaac," she said in surprise, and to her he introduced "my wife, Anna." He didn't say my name to her, and I saw no sign that he remembered our last conversation, when I'd said that every girl in North America must be named Anna, and he'd professed a fondness for the name Fanna. But something about the way he didn't meet my eyes reminded me that we were never very good at detecting Isaac's thoughts and feelings. He didn't choose me to know them now, and I didn't. But I might have been distracted by the child's head snuggled against his shoulder, showing just one pink, downy cheek. About a year old—the age when I began to know that I loved my boy. *Don't look*, I told myself. It was a mutable world, and children, young children, were among the most mutable and vulnerable creatures in it.

Resolutely I turned my gaze away, and discovered Isaac's wife looked at me with round, opaque gray eyes. I didn't have the least idea what she was thinking, even when she glanced at the details of my gown. Did she see the style, or the mends? Or both? Her own gown had no style whatsoever, though all its mends were neat enough to be nearly invisible. I could see the wear on her lacing, showing how slim she must be when not with child. In her tired eyes and rough, reddened hands, I read a life I most certainly would not want.

Oh well, I didn't want my own life either in its present state, and I was starting to feel a familiar irritation with her husband, who had yet to say a single word to me. "What's the child's name, Isaac?" I asked, pitching my voice a bit louder than normal so everyone around us could hear.

He flushed, meeting my eyes with a look not exactly amused, not quite angry. But his wife was the one who answered, in a clear, calm voice. "Frances," she said. "But we call her Fanna. Because Anna is quite a common name, my husband tells me."

"*Does* he?" That almost startled a laugh from me, but that would never do, outside the Meeting-house on a Sunday. "That's not very kind! Oh well, your two names rhyme. Isaac can write poetry to you."

A mischievous smile crossed her face. "He does have a little verse he likes to say—"

"You must be tired," Isaac said, taking her arm. He swept her off toward the horse blocks, giving me a boding frown over his shoulder. But I could see that he had to prim his mouth up to keep from grinning. *Oh Isaac, you may have chosen very well!* In my heart I released him. That last conversation we had, eight years ago, could have served as the beginning of something if I had stayed. I didn't, and now that was another world, and we were different people. But he remembered. I hoped his Anna wouldn't come down too hard on him.

Now his father joined us, bent with years of work, like an axe handle polished and hardened by use. "Good afternoon, ma'am," he said, addressing Mother. "Is it true what they're saying, that you've come to recover your husband's lands?"

"Yes," Mother said, "though in some cases we would be happy to sell people the property—"

"I bought my property three times over," he interrupted. "I had a grant from New Hampshire, I paid your husband quit-rent, and then I bought the place again at vendue."

Mother said cordially, "The vendue auctions weren't all as regular as they should be—but time will tell. Meantime, tell me about your family. Some of your girls I haven't met before. And is Isaac still on the farm?"

"Isaac has his own farm, out in the western part of town. One of your husband's plots. Bought it the same day I did mine. Nathaniel Robinson ran the auction, and if you think there was anything irregular about it, you can take that up with him. I'm sorry if that leaves you a pauper, ma'am, but there's nothing to be done about it."

His wife stepped into the conversation. "And no need to be unpleasant about it, either. Mrs. Buchanan, this is *my* Anna, the girl I birthed right after the Massacre. Raised on tales about you, night-riding the countryside on that mare you used to have. Anna, this is Miss Fanna that Isaac told you all about."

Night-riding. I glanced toward Mother. Even now I didn't want her finding out about that ride. But she wasn't paying attention. "Anna," I said, somewhat at random. "That's a fine name. The old plain names are the best, I think. Anna, and John." The little girl sank her chin into her chest, looking up at me with wide solemn eyes. What had Isaac told her about me? With Mother standing so near, I wasn't going to probe. "Someday we'll talk," I told the girl. "Isaac doesn't know *all* the stories." She didn't respond except by pressing back against her mother, and I turned away so as not to overpower her.

So I did have a hold on Isaac's imagination! One wanders this mutable world never guessing if one makes an impact, but it appeared I had.

Chapter 32

My legend lived not in Isaac's family alone. Sperie Averill found one pretended errand after another to bring her to the Bradley farm over the next several weeks. At first I assumed she was interested in one of the farm workers, but she gave no sign of having a preference. The person she always maneuvered to see was me. She keenly observed what I was wearing, offered to help when I was mending my garments, scrutinized the construction closely. Soon I observed a change in her appearance, new touches and tucks that brought her closer to New York fashion as exemplified by one impoverished young woman who must make over her old clothing instead of buying new—but for all that, a noticeable improvement.

Having furbished up her gowns, Sperie was perfectly willing to plump down on her knees in them and help me garden. Merab had happily given over her herbs and flowers to spend her time with Billa Czar. But there's only so much that needs doing in a small garden, so after transplanting the rosemary into its summer bed, I offered Sperie one of my sketch pads. She covered the pages with brown thumbprints and rough, angular sketches, while I tried to guide her observations. "Look carefully at how the leaf joins the stem. Can you get that exact shape? It's the details like that which distinguish one species from another."

That wasn't what she was here to observe. She wanted to know about me, about us, about New York during the war, culminating in this question as we rested in the shade, sketching on an August afternoon. "Did you feel safe in New York after the British came? Because you were Tories?"

Were Tories? I wondered why she put that in the past tense, but let it stand. "No. We weren't safe. There were battles. The city burned. The churches were turned into charnel houses, and . . . I had a baby."

"You did?" she asked, eyes huge and round. "Nobody here knows that!"

Then John hadn't told anyone. A true friend. "Let's keep it that way. It's something I'd rather not talk about."

She nodded, looking sober. "It's terrible when babies die. But you're a widow, so . . . after your mourning was over, did you go to balls? With British officers? What were they like?"

What a useful reminder! One's sorrows matter mostly to oneself! "British officers? Let me tell you, Sperie, nothing is more disillusioning than continual close contact with an army. One gets a front row seat to cruelty, boredom, and incompetence. Even the young officers one likes, the good, intelligent ones, are terrified to go against the will of their commanders. They'll tell one—oh, how they love to tell one—how everything can be done more efficiently or humanely, but by the time they rise to higher rank and are in a position to implement their reforms, they've learnt to be just like the people they replaced!"

"But were they handsome?"

I had to laugh. "Do you know, they aren't anywhere near as good-looking close-up as they are at a distance. It's chiefly the uniform, I find. Anyway, it doesn't matter. The way things have turned out, I doubt you'll ever in your life encounter a British officer."

She looked mysterious. "You'd be surprised!"

"They're leaving! They'll all take ship by the end of summer, and there will only be Americans left."

"Maybe I've met one already!"

"Well, if you do meet one, again—and I don't see how it's going to happen—remember that they're a long way from their homes and families, and the people whose good opinion they care for. They're apt to make promises to young women that they've no intention of keeping!"

"Oh well, the one I saw was quite old, and he was—but I'm not supposed to say." And to her credit, I couldn't get another word out of her.

Amazingly, there turned out to be some truth to her story. I visited Rhoda Harlow to find out how to direct a letter to Elizabeth, and we ended up sitting together gossiping as we shelled beans. When our talk turned to the British departure, Rhoda said, "I wonder what happened to our soldier."

"Your soldier? The one you nursed after the Massacre? He died, didn't he?"

"Daniel Houghton. Yes, but he wasn't a soldier. Just a farmer, just a man who expected Britain to treat us like citizens."

She was trying to turn my attention. "Then what soldier?" I asked, pressing the way Sperie would.

She hesitated. "Not many know about it and . . . I'd just as lief they didn't for a while yet. But you won't tell."

The story was an improbable one. Two weeks after the battle at Bennington, where General Baum was defeated by the Americans, Rhoda went out to pick some green corn for supper and found a wounded redcoat hiding in her field. He was a prisoner being marched somewhere who had escaped and was trying to make his way to Canada. The Harlows hid him in their barn and tended his wounds—this at a time when nearly thirty Westminster men were away fighting Burgoyne's army.

"Why did you do it?" I asked. "Why didn't you give him up?"

She sighed. "I don't know. He was hurt and I helped him, and—he was a decent man. We liked him."

"And you healed him?"

"Yes. When he was well enough, we sent him on his way."

"Would Sperie Averill have seen him?"

Rhoda frowned. "If she did, I never knew it, but she and my girls are of an age. I can picture them taking her to have a peek at him. What did she tell you?"

"Just that she'd seen a British officer once. And he was old."

Rhoda laughed, and sighed. "I suppose it doesn't matter anymore. It's all sliding into the past already. It makes you think, doesn't it?

Chapter 33

Isaac missed Meeting two weeks in a row in August. His mother told us that his Anna was delivered of a boy, and both were doing well. The third week Isaac came in without her and, after Meeting, happily received congratulations. He was indeed to be congratulated. His life was well-begun. A wife, a farm, a growing family—what more could a person want?

I congratulated him among the rest, expecting that to be the end of it. But when I started to walk back along the street—I made it a habit to walk home from Meeting, for exercise and solitude—suddenly he was there beside me. He strode along well-separated from me, hands at his sides twitching slightly, as if he wanted to be doing something. He never did care for the enforced idleness of a Sunday.

"So—Cloud," he said abruptly. "And Joost too—you don't have them anymore?"

"Mother sold Joost in New York. Cloud . . . was stolen."

"No!" He stopped in his tracks and turned toward me, face flushed and grieved. "*Really?* Damn! I never figured I'd see her again, but when I saw you in that coat I thought, 'Maybe I'm wrong. Maybe they do still have her.'"

"Only the joseph. It's better for riding than walking, but—" I didn't finish the thought. Beggars can't be choosers, true enough, but they needn't angle for sympathy.

"What do you think happened to her? Was she taken into one of the armies?"

"No," I said firmly. I saw my child die before my eyes. I knew what irrevocable loss of hope was. There was hope for Cloud, and it wasn't at all unreasonable. "If she were with the British Army, I would have heard. I believe she's in Connecticut, or the Bay. Several good horses were stolen in

New York and brought to New England for breeding, and Wildair stock is coveted."

He nodded. "Makes sense. I always thought a cross between her and Joost would make about the perfect horse. Still—" His shoulders rose and fell on a big sigh.

"We'd have had to sell her soon anyway. After my husband and boy died—" I paused and took a deep breath, hoping it would steady my voice. "And Fa—"

He slanted a glance at me, looking troubled. For once I could read him clearly. He wanted to ask about my marriage; he'd known the circumstances eight years ago and disapproved. But in the end, he spoke of Cloud. "I bet you're right. I never saw the man who could ride her at a militia muster, let alone a battle—not even me! If she went into either army she came right out again. But anybody with eyes in his head would want a foal out of her."

"Mmm." I bit my lips to drive back the tears. Time for a change of subject. "So—tell me about your farm."

"Why?" He looked at me directly. "You want it back?"

There he was! The Isaac I knew, the Isaac I never knew, hard as granite and not even a little bit mine. He loved Cloud. He came to like me and perhaps I was his friend, but like a man friend, the kind he wouldn't hesitate to fight.

All right. I'd rather have that than pointless sentimentality. "I don't even know which lot it's on, Isaac. We had so many! And if that sounds like bragging, I don't care. Fa did service to New York. He earned his reward. But I have no interest in a hill farm."

"Not good enough for you?" He put quite a top-spin on the question. I'd angered him.

"It's not the life I'm suited to. Mother may try to get it back. Or she may not, I don't know. She was fond of you in her way, and now you have children. Bring them to Meeting as often as you can. Let them win her heart!"

The corner of his mouth quirked; suddenly he was fighting back a smile. "She's got a heart?"

"Ha!" But it was the Sabbath. I probably shouldn't laugh out loud. "I wouldn't worry, Isaac. This thing is an impenetrable tangle, as far as I can tell. Stephen Bradley has hopes for certain parcels, but he hasn't mentioned yours."

"I ain't worried," he said, raising his eyebrows at me. Cocky and belligerent, just like always, only now I didn't have the authority to quash him. How strong he looked! Like a young ox. The privations of war did nothing to stunt his growth.

"Did you fight?" I asked, marveling in a back corner of my mind, at how free I seemed to be with my questions. I just didn't care. If I offended him—well, he was offended. He'd get over it.

"Nope. Nope, I didn't fight."

"Why not? You were furious after the Massacre. I imagined you at Bunker Hill, at the very least."

"No, I didn't go. A bunch of men from the west part of town went, and Billy Crook. He was fifteen, like me, and they sent him back home before the battle. Don't know why they even let him march, but they sure didn't let him fight. And in '77, his *dad* went to fight Burgoyne, and he's old! But somebody had to stay to run the farm and mill, and that was Billy."

So neither of those boys took a man's role that summer of '75, when we were all fifteen. Only I took the role I was supposedly born for.

But those were thoughts to avoid. I challenged him. "So you didn't go to Saratoga either?" Oh, I *was* like Sperie! I knew just how Isaac felt—crowded!

He looked away, considering an answer. "Dad wasn't feeling too well that summer. He hurt his back, and we had an ungodly amount of hay to put up."

"Oh. I see."

"No, you don't!" he said abruptly. "I don't know about you, but I have nights even now when I sit straight up, thinking I hear French. I hate Britain like poison, but I ain't going to march off to shoot some soldier in the face! If they come here, all right. That's different. Anyway, that's how I felt in seventy-seven, and how I feel yet."

Now he'd surprised me. Why? Because he was male, did I think he was made of different stuff than I? We walked quietly together for several paces.

"Does it strike you, Isaac," I asked, "that we live in a mutable world?"

He rolled the word around in his mouth. "Mutable. Mutable."

"Changeable. Fickle."

"Oh, hell yes! Oops—it's Sunday. Yes."

We'd reached the graveyard. I turned to look back along the street, broad and peaceful. Hard to remember it packed full of angry men with guns. That was the beginning of something, the moment when people here understood that they'd have to fight if they really wanted their liberty. They didn't fight, that day. They prevailed by peaceful means. But that was the day we all knew it.

"Was it worth it?" I asked. "All the deaths . . ."

He sighed and started to answer, and sighed again. "I guess so. It's over now, anyway. My boy and girl won't know war. We've taught Britain to leave us the hell alone."

"Oh, don't underestimate what it takes to teach the English something!"

"Well, I don't know. It's better to be free, I guess. Now we have to make something of it. Anyway, I got to get back. Anna's got her sister with her, but they like a man to boss around."

"We all do, Isaac!"

"Then I hope you get one," he said, with a little half-bow, and strode off down the street.

Chapter 34

S perie still haunted me, though I was sure her stepmother had plenty of work for her at home. It was exhausting being someone's heroine. I took to leaving the house early in the morning and going down by the river to sketch and write to Elizabeth. Curled up under a big willow, writing with my drawing pencils so I didn't have to manage ink and quill pens, I brought her to mind—the friend to whom I could open my heart. Letters weren't the same; it was too easy not to say certain things.

Said:

My belief in the superiority of the British did not survive intimate acquaintance with them. There was something hideous to me about the parties and balls, officers dancing and flirting while in churches all over Manhattan they were starving American prisoners. New York burned, it festered, it decayed, and still it danced. I no longer cared for dancing—but the tone of my mind was not gay at that time . . .

Not said:

The tone of my mind was *gray* at that time, mud-colored, like one of those November days—no, weeks—we got here in Westminster. After Fa died, and the child, I didn't see color, any color, for at least a year. And I lived in a town full of redcoats!

I did say this:

I found solace in gardens—those of friends, or at houses where we took refuge. Cultivating plants, drawing them, some watercolor

painting. If ever I see you again, I will give you my little painting of
a flax flower. It's just a scrap of a thing, but I've kept it through every
move, because it reminded me of you in that blue homespun you used
to wear.

Eventually I did force myself to write the hardest truth:

Helping Anna Norton with her little one, and Merab Bradley with
hers, is almost too much for me. Both are the age my boy was when
some contagion out of the camps swept him away from me. I never
wanted him, Elizabeth. He was as unwelcome to me as his father.
But when I was over the shock of his birth, I began to say I was fond of
him; and when he was gone, I knew how much more than fond I was.
People ask, or politely don't ask, but delicately attempt to discover,
what I did these last eight years. Honestly, I don't remember much. I
broke, and put myself back together, with Mother's help, and here in
the clear air of Westminster, I feel finally reborn.

I sent the letter, and she wrote back—a short note, obviously penned in
haste, and also joy.

Pay me a visit, Fanna, a <u>long</u> visit. That's selfish of me. I've so much
work with all the children, and I'll put much of it off on you if you
come, but my husband is a serious man and I long to laugh. It sounds
to me, if I read aright, that you're in sore need of a laugh as well. Do
come if you can, if being around children won't wound you. I want
to tell you everything, but there's so much, too much to write. I didn't
marry for love either—at least, it wasn't first love, and I didn't think
it was best love, but I love him now, so after all, your mother was
right. But didn't it work that way for you?"

That last line was crossed out, so unlike neat, skillful Elizabeth. I
imagined her life behind a clockmaker's shop with—how many children?
I couldn't quite tell. She named four as well as "the babe," but was he (or
she) one of the four, or number five? And the clockmaker wasn't her first

love? Who was? French, probably. I'd always suspected she hadn't told me the whole truth about him.

I wrote in answer but felt reluctant to ask Stephen Bradley to frank another letter for me. We were under increasing obligation to him as the summer stretched on. So I let the pages pile up.

Some day, Elizabeth, I will visit, but I don't know when. For the moment we are fixed here in Westminster, waiting for Patrick to return, for Stephen Bradley to perform some legal miracle, for the day to come when we are finally settled in a house again, instead of being perpetual guests. Life is slow. I had not remembered Westminster as being so large, so flat, so dull. Yes, I waxed eloquent about the clear air in an earlier letter, and it is clear, but is that enough? After a month or so, one wants more.

Not having a horse changes everything. To exercise or socialize, we must walk. When the days are hot it's impossible to get up into the cool hills, except by special arrangement to hire a cart, or borrow one, and we don't like to beg too many favors, so we sit and fan ourselves, and are dull.

I want an adventure, Elizabeth! I'm 23. Other women have husbands, households, children, but I don't see a husband here for me. I'm not suited to scraping a farm out of the wilderness. I need a different sort of man, someone like Fa who will take me to the center of things or bend the world around himself so that <u>he's</u> the center. Women can't be in the Assembly, or even vote, but Mother exercised some power even so. If <u>I</u> were queen of the circle around an important man, I'd find a way to raise the level of discourse, broaden their viewpoints, sooth their tempers with music, green plants, good wine and cheese cakes . . .

And I know you'll point this out, so I'll beat you to it: This mythical man would also broaden <u>my</u> viewpoint, bring books and ideas, and dare to quarrel with me, because he'd take my opinions seriously.

Fa did that when I was a girl. John does it now, but in a tavern keeper's way. He's wise—but I want <u>dash</u>, Elizabeth, I want <u>flare</u>, and tenderness too, I think. What I experienced with John Buchanan was called that, but it wasn't. Tenderness, and children, lots of children, so that I'm too busy even to come see you until we are old ladies with scarcely a tooth in our heads. Then we'll gather to cackle and tell our tales, and I'll be Mrs. . . . . I don't know. I have no real candidates. There's only Lot Hall—the right age, an attorney. Already something in Vermont government.

But he's too much the lawyer, always at daggers drawn with Stephen over someone's cow or right of way, and he talks like a Cape Cod sailor. Not exactly to my taste. And there's this, Elizabeth, another insurmountable obstacle: Apparently, I'm not to his taste either!

"There's always Billy Willard!" I hear you say it, so I'll save you the trouble. He is one of creatures in this mutable world who is <u>not</u> mutable. The same cocksure braggart, still under his father's thumb. And even he isn't interested in anything more than a flirtation. That tells me more about the lay of the land than all Stephen Bradley's law-talk. Billy doesn't think we'll get the property back—or more probably, his father doesn't.

And so . . . and sew, and sow. We wait for Patrick. I know Mother has decided to settle here. Patrick will get a trifle in recompense from the government, enough to buy a house lot, or if Mother can swing it, maybe to buy our own house back. But am I, the witty and attractive Widow Buchanan, to go into that house and close the door, and abide with Mother forever? As long as I live, I'll owe her for my every breath—but I've already lived with her forever.

I want something to <u>happen</u>, Elizabeth! I want to <u>do</u> something, before I burst. I want to pick a fight with someone—isn't that awful? But it's all I can do not to make really cutting remarks to Mother, so an actual enemy would be a great relief.

Maybe Ethan Allen will visit.

And literally as I wrote that, down by the river, Ethan Allen did visit, and I missed him.

Mother caught a glimpse, but she wouldn't say much. "Thin," she answered, when I asked how he looked. "Bald."

"*Bald?*"

"Well, bald*ing*. And loud, though Stephen held his own, I must say. Of course I didn't listen, so I've no idea what they discussed. And then he went over to see John—or John's rum!—and then back off over the mountains, not twenty minutes ago. It was entirely uneventful, Fan. You didn't miss a thing."

Just then I heard Billa Czar's stumbling feet, and the next moment in came—

"What? Who is this?" The boy was a British officer in miniature, in breeches and a scarlet coat—and a scarlet face too, glowing with pride. His mother followed, with a laugh that turned into a cough.

"Look what General Allen gave Billa! His first suit of boys' clothes."

"But—a *British officer's uniform?*"

"Well, the war is over, he said, and these things don't matter as much as they once did. I don't know where he came by the suit, but doesn't Billa look splendid?"

"Splendid indeed! And walking by himself!"

"Yes, I haven't had time to sew on the leading strings. Maybe I won't need to."

"Maybe he should have been out of them already," Mother commented, aside. In her view Merab was a bit too doting.

Later in our rooms, she said, "It does make me wonder, Fanny, if there's truth to the rumor that Allen is secretly trying to return Vermont to Britain."

"He would never do that," I said, as authoritatively as if I really did know the man. "If there are secret talks, I'm sure he's just planning to 'come yankee' over them again. But it might explain where Billa's suit came from!"

Chapter 35

A nd more time passed. This was a busy house. Stephen was the Vermont attorney general, or had been last year and would run again next; I was never certain, because he held so many posts in succession or all at the same time. He was a judge, a general of the Vermont militia, a Westminster selectman, and part of the continual negotiations to get Vermont officially out of New York and admitted as an American state. A good percentage of his business was conducted here at the dinner table or over at John's tavern, in private discussions among gentleman where the rum and cider flowed and floated the intellect.

It took some time for me to understand why all this made my heart ache—and then one morning, I woke up knowing and had no idea why I hadn't seen it before. It should have been Fa at the center of all this. This was his kind of world, the one he'd raised me in. Now in it as members of Stephen's household, but not of it, Mother and I were irrelevant. Nobody bothered to despise us or suspect of anything. We were simply of no consequence. The knowledge bit deep and added to my growing restlessness.

On a cold day in October, when the maples blazed red and orange, and the migrating pigeons cast long flowing shadows over the fields, I put on my joseph and walked across the road to visit John. Or to help Anna. Or just, to be honest, to get away from Mother. She was in an impatient mood, too, these days, but with winter coming and Patrick so long delayed in Canada, it was impossible to buy or build a house. Stymied, she said things she regretted later, and I responded in kind, or took another long walk, or went again to see John, who appreciated my wit.

Coming into the yard, I saw Seth Arnold watering a horse, a fine stout chestnut of Joost's stamp. We didn't see Dutch horses east of the mountains very often. They were more common in the Hudson Valley, and around Bennington.

"This boy's come a long way," I commented to Seth.

He turned his eyes toward me and thought before he spoke, as always. "Aye. From Arlington."

Arlington. "Is it . . . General Allen?"

Seth nodded. My heart did a small somersault. Now I knew how all the rich abbots felt when they heard the name Robin Hood.

But we weren't rich, not now. We had nothing; therefore, he could take nothing from us—and anyway, I'd like to see him try! The mood Mother was in, General Allen might finally meet his match. I took a moment to steel myself, to remember my rights and loyalties. Then I walked steadily toward the side door, and let myself in.

A tall man in a hemlock-green uniform coat stood at the bar talking, while John drew him a noggin of something. From the doorway I assessed him.

Balding? Ridiculous! He had a high forehead, that was all. He was thin, with a strong line drawn down alongside his mouth. That was from imprisonment, and suffering. A jutting nose, a firm chin, broad shoulders—

"Any of those little cakes, John?" he asked. The voice was slow, deep and vibrant. His eyes lit up when the plate of cheese cakes arrived; his fingers trembled slightly as he picked one up. He'd written in his book of being "in great measure" restored to health, but I could see there were empty places in him that he had yet to fill.

John turned to reach for something behind him and noticed me in the doorway. His eyebrows rose, asking a question. I nodded, and only then did he speak. "Oh hello, Fanny! Let me introduce you to General Allen. I believe you've heard his name once or twice! Ethan, this fair young lass is the widow Buchanan, Fanny Buchanan—and you've heard a bit about her, no doubt."

Allen turned a trifle stiffly as I advanced into the room. His face was deeply tanned. His brown eyes were alight with the fire of sociability, but they slowly darkened as he contemplated me. "Are you the daughter of that Tory miscreant Crean Brush?"

I made a point of pausing before I answered. "Mr. Brush was my stepfather."

"Of all the landjobbing Yorker blackguards that ever contaminated this green earth!" he said. And there was more, much more. Uninterruptible; I didn't even try. I would have liked to say: *My stepfather came here from Ireland. He was in service to the King there; why should he not be a king's man here? He didn't owe America his loyalty.* But there wasn't the slightest chink in which to insert a word. It all felt well-worn, phrases the man had repeated many a time, and yet I could tell that he was intoxicated with them, carried away by his own flow.

How disappointing! I'd wanted him to be a fine talker, to live up to his book and the anecdotes about him, not to rave away about things that were now many years in the past. Was there any way to stop this, and actually gain his attention? Or at least give him a retaliatory tweak?

Yes, of course there was! Did I study his book for nothing? I waited, preserving a smooth-faced equanimity, until his throat got dry, and he buried his nose in his tankard. Then I said, "Ah well, this is a mutable world, is it not?"

His eyes widened. He swallowed audibly, his Adam's apple bobbing, and turned his face toward mine.

"'There is a greatness of soul for friendship to subsist here,'" I continued, "'as we are upon opposite sides—'"

The hard brown face relaxed into a smile that deepened the creases beside his mouth and exposed a chipped front tooth. "You're quoting my own book at me, young woman!"

I smiled politely. "I know it well, sir, and therefore, I already know what you think of Loyalists."

"Not every Loyalist," he said, with a laughing glance at John.

"John is always an exception. But you believe it's a game of hazard between Whigs and Tories—that we would have taken your property had we won, and that therefore, you Whigs have a perfect right to ours."

"I do believe that," he said. "I heard Tories often enough, totting up the rewards they'd reap when Britain won the war, and the Whigs' estates were confiscated. But you didn't win, and it's no more than right that you should pay the penalty you intended for us."

"It's a game for you," I said, "who are—what's the term? *Land-jockeys?*" His head jerked back. He appeared affronted. "It's what you called my stepfather once, in a very polite letter that you wrote to him. But aren't you yourself a land-jockey? Who owns more acres here in Vermont? But you have a roof over your head, and if you lose it, can repair to any of your thousands of acres and put up a cabin with your own hands. My mother and I have no roof, and no skill at all with axes—"

"Your tongue's sharp enough, by God!" he said, no longer smiling. "Yours is a pitiful plight indeed, ma'am, but had you seen how your people reduced the young men of this country to skeletons, had you heard the mockery as their bodies were carried out for burial, had you endured the sufferings—"

"But I have heard the dying mocked, sir! I heard William French in his death agonies, and I heard them laugh at him. It was an injustice, a—" my voice caught, which I did not intend. "A *profound* injustice. But my mother and I had no part in it, nor did my late stepfather, who also suffered in prison."

"Not as our prisoners suffered! Not as I suffered! I never heard that *he* was starved—"

"He was kept in close confinement for many months, deprived of light and writing implements. He . . ." I paused, swallowed, collected myself. "Robbing my mother and me of a place to lay our heads will do nothing to mend any of it!"

That brought back a wry warmth to his eyes. "Too true, too true. The past is done, and nothing can alter it, and as a matter of fact, the focus of my *land-jobbing* is elsewhere at the moment. Come, join us, won't you? And have one of these excellent little cakes."

"They're good, aren't they?" I lifted my eyes to meet John's. "A specialty of the house, I understand."

"A recent specialty! I never had them until a few weeks ago. You've been holding out on me, John!"

"New times bring new ways." John drew me my customary half-noggin of cider and slid it over. Allen lifted his tankard to me in salute and drank deeply.

"You're here to recover your stepfather's land," he remarked. "You won't do it."

"Stephen Bradley has hopes—"

"Stephen Bradley is an artful lawyer. I hope he hasn't sunk his hooks into you too deeply."

"There's nothing to hook, sir. We are objects of charity. Pretty good for people who once had title to 6,000 acres in this town."

"As much as that?" He looked interested. "I'd forgotten how well Brush did out of old New York."

"Well—that proved mutable too, didn't it?"

He looked at me more deeply, as if trying to see past my face, my exterior, into my heart and mind. "The word strikes you, doesn't it? It did me. I've always remembered him saying that. 'This is a mutable world, and one gentleman never knows but that it may be in his power to help another.' It brought tears to my eyes—"

"I know."

He did love to repeat his stories! But how mutable both our worlds had proved. Fa, John, and Johnny gone: Allen's son, his wife, his daughter. And yet he seemed lighthearted. How was that done? And why did I feel so shockingly at ease with this man?

I pushed that question aside. The moment demanded my full attention, because his mind, when distracted from his rants and tirades, was flexible and swift, doubling back on itself. "Most of Brush's land must be occupied," he said, returning to the earlier topic.

"Not so. Mother has a list. Some is, but much is in the hands of speculators." *Like yourself.* Would I say that? Deliberately provoke him? "Like yourself."

He smiled, and didn't answer directly. "Something might be done. Speculators are always moved by money."

"Which we lack. If the people who occupy our land could be brought to pay—but they've already paid once, and there's no one to make them do it again."

"And it wouldn't be right. Well, it's a problem, and I don't see what Stephen plans to do about it, but he may find a way to come yankee over somebody. He's a sharp one!"

"That's why I advised going to him," John said. "More cider, Miss Fanny?"

"No, I should be getting back." Why did I say that? There was no real reason. Mother had no need of me and wouldn't be at all concerned at my absence. But I was too comfortable with this man, and more cider would only loosen my tongue—and I felt that the scene should end now, before new topics could be opened.

Allen drained his tankard. "I'll walk over with you. I've business to discuss with Stephen."

So the scene was not ending—and he knew where I lived. Avoiding John's eyes, I stepped outside. After the darkness of the taproom, the brilliant red of autumn maples and fresh leafy scent on the crisp air struck me with sudden delight. I drew a deep breath, tipping my head back to watch the big Vs of geese drift down toward the river.

Allen had lingered inside for a last word with John. Now he joined me, not offering his arm, but walking close enough that I could take it if I chose. "'Miss Fanna,' he said, but I was sure John introduced you as Mrs. Buchanan."

"I was married. Briefly."

"Ah." He looked off at the surrounding fields and trees. I expected him to say more, but he simply paced along beside me, admiring the day.

When we entered the house, Mother was coming from the kitchen. "Mother, this gentleman is General Ethan Allen. Sir, let me introduce my mother, Mrs. Patrick Wall."

"Mrs. Wall," he repeated. He knew the name. Stephen or John would have told him.

"General." Mother nodded graciously, not betraying the slightest surprise.

"I understand we share a lawyer," Allen said. "And a common interest in Tory property!"

Her eyes narrowed to gleaming slits. She studied his face and permitted herself a slight smile. "I suppose we do, sir,"

"Damned right we do! Well, to the victor goes the spoils. I'm sure your former husband would have happily beggared me! But I hope Stephen earns his fee for you. He usually does! Good-day, ma'ams." He sketched a bow and walked into Stephen's office. Mother closed her lips firmly, thinking her own thoughts—and keeping them to herself.

Chapter 36

He was back in two weeks. Did I see that horse go by, and follow him to the tavern? Or did I come upon him accidentally? Good questions. Excellent questions. Did he ask them? He looked up when I came in, and I thought he seemed pleased, but almost at once he launched into a rant.

Unappealing, at first, but after a few minutes I ignored the words and centered my attention on his eyes and the blood flaming his cheeks. He had looked wooden when I'd first walked in, travel-worn. Now he came alive. This was how he stoked himself. *There!* Now he was burning bright, now he'd brought his spirit to the pitch where he felt most himself and was capable of greatness. It was that way with Fa. His own eloquence was a fuel to him.

And now he was talking *about* Fa—I didn't know how why; I hadn't been following. "Your father—the late dishonorable Crean Brush!—had the typical British inability to distinguish between *meum* and *tuum*. He showed his true colors by his crimes in Boston—"

Putting aside for the moment the slight pleasure of having Fa's enemy insult him in Latin, I thrust myself, not without a certain flutter of pulse, into the turbulent stream of talk. "Crimes? My stepfather was ordered by General Gage to sequester Whig property so it couldn't be used by the enemy. He was doing his duty."

I'd crossed his line of talk and actually stopped him, or else he'd made himself thirsty. He took a long pull at his tankard of cider, and I pursued my advantage, substituting boldness for conviction; Fa's actions in occupied Boston were certainly open to interpretation, and it was a topic I preferred to avoid. "When the British left Boston, that property went with them. Of course it did. It would have been used against us—"

"People's *china teapots?*"

"I don't know what was put on board that ship! I don't think Fa did. He worked without sleeping for the three days before they set sail—"

"*Thieved* without sleeping!"

"—and he wasn't entirely in charge—"

"He was utterly and completely a rogue!"

I had not often been bellowed at. Those who had done me harm did so quietly. To my surprise, I wasn't intimidated. On the contrary, I found General Allen's noise wonderfully stiffening to the spine. Pitching my voice clear and piercing, I said, "He was a loyal servant to his king, sir, acting under orders in a time of war. You may quarrel with that king and those orders, but you may not impugn his character to me."

"Oh, I may not?"

"No, sir. A gentleman does not traduce the name of a dead man, not to the people who loved him."

He looked at me under frowning brows. He cared to be thought a gentleman and treated as such; I remembered that from his book. He meditated a response, started to say something, stopped himself. I met his eyes with as much seeming calm as I could muster. Off to the side I sensed John standing quite still, possibly holding his breath. This might be an epoch-marking event. Could I be the first person to ever stop Ethan Allen in full flow?

"No," he said eventually. "A gentleman does not. I apologize."

I nodded, gracious. The hollows of my elbows felt hollower; my knees quivered. I didn't think I was afraid—I *wasn't* afraid. But this was an event, certainly!

Having him off-balance, I supposed I ought to keep him there. And possibly a little off-balance myself, I revealed something I rarely disclosed to anyone. "My father did harm you, actually—my *real* father. Captain John Montresor, the Royal Engineer. It was his map of Canada that led General Arnold astray, so that he missed rescuing you. Without that map you might never have been sent to England—"

"Your real father? I knew your mother was a widow when she married Brush—"

"You never met my mother. She was led astray by Captain Montresor as a girl of fifteen, and abandoned by him, and she died."

Anger was back in his face. "I wasn't the best husband to Mary. Often absent—*always*, she'd say—and by my own choosing. But I always left her provided for. Any man who treats a woman otherwise is a hound!"

"There we agree, sir. Though my poor mother wasn't John Montresor's wife, she was deserving of his protection. Mother—Mrs. Wall—is her older sister. She raised me as her own—as did Fa, fully. They are my parents, not by blood, but by deeds."

He nodded. "I see. I stand corrected, and that's not something I submit to often, ma'am. I will have to consider that your stepfather's faults resided solely in the areas of politics and property."

"Consider what you wish, as long as you take care not to mention your opinions of him to me."

He took a long draft from his tankard, looking at me over the rim. Gradually his eyes warmed and began to twinkle. Emptying the tankard, he set it down with a bang. "Well, I've got to go across the road and see my lawyer. Are you coming?"

This took too much for granted. I shook my head. "I came over to—" do something for John, I would have said, but General Allen turned abruptly and stalked out the door.

I took up the cloth and began mopping the bar, as had become my self-appointed task. Did I make a mistake there? I'd thought to manage him, turn him aside and stop him from presuming too much—not to make him leave. I began searching my mind for an excuse to go after him.

But no. No. There was a balance of power to consider.

The man drinking at the back table drained his own tankard and went out. John took the bar rag from my hand. "You're going the right way about this," he commented. "Ethan doesn't mind a sharp tongue on a woman, if she's got a sharp mind to go with it."

"I didn't need you to tell me that, John. And I'm not *going about* anything!"

He smiled, shaking his head. "So you say. Well, Fanny, if you marry Ethan Allen, you'll be queen of a new state."

"And if I marry the devil, I'll be the Queen of Hell!"

He let out a big crack of laughter. "Oh, that's good! The Queen of Hell. That's very good."

Chapter 37

Too good not to share, apparently. "The Queen of *Hell?*" Stephen whispered, as he handed me a cup of coffee the next morning. Sperie repeated it later in the day, as we sat stuffing herbs into pillows to keep out the moths.

"Those aren't words your father would want to hear from you," I said.

"Oh, he doesn't care. Are you going to marry Ethan Allen?"

"I've met him *twice*, Sperie! Both times we quarreled. Why should anyone think that means we're going to marry?"

"Because you're—" Sperie paused, shook her head, trying to come up with words. "Because you're *you*. And he's him. Who else would he marry?"

"He's old enough to be my father! Literally—he has a daughter my age."

"Oh, people marry older men all the time," she said, impatiently.

"And then they write songs about it. 'Maids when you're young, never wed an old man.'"

"Ethan Allen is not an *old man*!"

"Certainly not. But Sperie, if I marry him or if I don't, he'll always be twenty years older than me. When I'm forty, he'll be sixty—"

"And he'll still be Ethan Allen!" she said, eyes sparkling.

"This is absurd. There's no possibility—"

"If he asks you, will you say yes?"

I looked at her helplessly—this girl, the age I was when I recklessly agreed to wed John Buchanan. Someone should have told me not to. What should I tell Sperie now? Whatever I did—supposing Allen had any sort of intentions towards me, or I toward him—she'd be watching. She'd take it to heart. If he did ask—and why should anyone think he would? We had literally met twice! But if he did, what would I want her to see me do? I'd never council someone her age to marry a man of his years. But I wasn't her age, I was *my* age, and no one had asked me, but if he did—he wouldn't, but if he did—

"You haven't said anything for five whole minutes!" Sperie crowed. "You're just sitting there, looking at your hands and blushing."

My fingers were twined into each other. I unknotted them and looked her full in the face. I knew I was blushing, but I didn't try to hide that. "Sperie, it's wrong to encourage a woman—any woman—to imagine a romance that might not exist. It can raise unwarranted hopes and cause damage, if the man has no intentions toward her. Do you understand? You're making too much of a joke between myself and John Norton, and if you keep doing that, I won't admit you to these rooms again. Do you understand?"

She smiled mischievously. "I understand."

"No, you don't, my girl. And you're thinking far too much of this. You're only fifteen—"

"*You* were married at fifteen!"

I knew it! She was fascinated by me, in part because she was now the age I had been when I was married. Nobody would let her do as I had done—at least, I didn't think so—but I must do my part to make sure.

"That was the worst mistake of my life, Sperie. Whigs like your father used to speak of how the British wanted to turn Americans into slaves. If paying a tax on tea is slavery, then what is it to be given away to a man you don't know? He will assume all rights over you, *all* rights. Your very mouth is his if he wants to kiss it, and your everything else."

She jutted her jaw to one side, looking down. She *was* thinking about that, and it was exciting to her. So I drove the point home, mixing lies with truth and sacrificing John Buchanan's reputation willy-nilly. Why not? I owed him nothing. "Suppose he *smells*, Sperie? Suppose he's very stupid? Suppose he beats you with his fists?"

"Some husbands do. Captain Wright did—"

"And his wife filed suit. The point is—marriage is unequal. You want to be strong going into it. You want to learn everything you can—how to hold your own, how to stand on the rights you do have, how to make yourself respected. And then choose wisely, of course. Marriage should be for love."

She was sitting bolt-upright, hands stilled in the big bowl of fragrant herbs—eyes wide but not looking at me. She was seeing the story of my marriage—mostly wrong, but not far wrong. I never did get the chance to become accustomed to John's pomade, and he was only a little dull, not imbecilic . . . but for the rest, I'd rather not remember. Marriage should be for love.

"At fifteen you don't know enough. When I was your age, I knew a great deal more than you do—and it wasn't enough. Tell me that you understand that, girl!"

"How can I understand it? I don't know enough!" Under the saucy tone, though, I sensed that I had finally gotten through and at least given her something to think about. So good, I'd done my duty. Now I could think about my own prospects.

No, not prospects. It was absurd to think that. We were strangers to each other—though I was more a stranger to him than he was to me. I had studied him for years, and our two short encounters proved to me that I did, in some degree, know him. That must be the source of the unusual comfort I felt in his presence, even when we were sparring.

Unfortunately, my words to John had created an atmosphere around our acquaintance. At Meeting the following Sunday, I caught many more people than usual looking at me—some disapproving, others laughing, maybe even a little admiring—but all thinking about the possibility that Ethan Allen might be interested in, might *marry*, Fanny Buchanan. It was unfortunate, it was mortifying, it was tantalizing—and it was much too late to do anything about it.

Meanwhile Mother kept her own counsel, and kept it, and kept it, until I finally confronted her one morning as we sat mending a tablecloth for Merab. "You don't say anything about General Allen. Why?"

She smiled slightly. "Am I making you nervous?"

"Yes!"

She sobered. "I don't want to influence you, Fan. I did so once, and you suffered for it."

"Influence? That was *influence*?"

"What you don't understand, Fanny, is that I was blind with terror that whole time just before the war. I wanted to stop it all from happening. If I could only get the sheriff to act, to throw out the protesters . . . Failing that, I could marry you off and keep you safe. You were *fifteen*, Fan! Fifteen. The age your mother was, the most perilous age for a girl, and men know it, the wrong kind of men. Ready for love and completely ignorant about the ways of the world—exactly the sort of lass to become a soldier's sweetheart, and I could see that the world was soon going to be full of soldiers. I wanted to shelter you with someone steady, and John had that reputation."

"Oh, he was *steady!*"

"Yes. I know. But I didn't then, and I wanted desperately to prevent what happened to your mother from happening to you."

"So something else did!"

She made a rueful face, conceding the point. "At least you were protected. That was all I could see at the time. The Buchanans gave you a home. Your child was also theirs and they did all they could—"

"Which was nothing!" But that was unfair. Children of all degrees were lost in that epidemic. Wealth and care could do nothing for them. Without Mother's pressure, I would not have had a child to lose. That's what she cost me, and what she gave me.

She said, "I saw how unhappy you were. I took a vow when Buchanan died that next time, I would give you your head."

I felt myself bristle. "You don't *have* my head. I'm not a horse, and you don't have a bridle on me. I'm an adult woman, free to do as I choose."

"I know that. I'll be frank, Fan. I understand that opposition from me could push you straight into Allen's arms. But that's not why I haven't said anything. I simply don't know what's best." She was frowning intently at the tablecloth as she said this. "I've read his book. After his most recent visit, I borrowed it. You didn't know that, did you? I do see the appeal. There's a mind there, and a heart. Another rough diamond, like your fa. But the age difference, Fanny! He has a young spirit, or at least a brash one, but—still, you know your business best."

Just what I'd been about to say, but she got there first, leaving me deflated. "I don't know. He might be flirting. He might have no intentions toward me at all."

"That's not what John thinks."

They'd been talking about me. Everyone in Westminster had been talking about me. Let them! That had been true my whole life. "You really don't have an opinion?"

"Of course I have an opinion. It varies day to day, sometimes hour to hour. I'd like best to have you live near me, which would mean marrying someone from Westminster—"

"*Ouch!*" I'd run the needle into my finger. I stuck it in my mouth and sucked it to take away the sting and avoid spotting Merab's cloth. I mumbled around it. "You don't want me to live *with* you?"

"No."

No? I'd always known, to my bones and to the marrow of my bones, that I was Mother's dearest treasure. But now, shockingly, she said, "We've lived under the same roof the best part of twenty-three years. I've a fancy for a trifle more elbow room."

I couldn't hold back a crow of laughter. "I've been thinking that *exact* thing! I want more elbow room!"

We met each other's eyes across the table. Mother's narrowed warmly. I felt myself smiling. We each understood what the other was saying, and what she was not saying.

But she went on. "Lot Hall, now. You might make something of him. Or—Merab's brother will be coming to visit. Not a Westminster man, but he'd be strongly connected to the town."

"Lot Hall! Reuben Atwater! Just because they're lawyers? Is that the governing principle behind your choices?"

"*Your* choice, Fanny. But an older man can be domineering. That wouldn't suit you."

"Ethan Allen?" I teased. "*Domineering?*"

She smiled briefly, but she wasn't finished. "These May-December alliances are rarely happy, at least for the woman."

"I have lived twenty-three years with someone old enough to be my parent!"

"And is it a parent you want?"

It wasn't; not at all, but I couldn't answer. I suddenly saw what she was doing: seeming to give me my head, but all the while pointing out every drawback Ethan Allen possessed. We didn't want the same thing, even if we used the same words—and she was still very powerful. Still my mother.

I looked down. The needle trembled slightly in my hand.

"I've said too much," she said. "I knew I would. You make your own choice—and if that's General Allen, well, I have faith that you'll hold your own. John says you have a way with him."

I set a careful stitch in the tablecloth. "He's not a horse either, Mother, not a creature to control. He's a person."

"As long as he sees *you* as a person."

"Of course he does. I *am* one."

But did he? I didn't really know how he saw me. I'd only met him twice. Mother I'd lived with almost every day of my life, and she continually surprised me.

Marriage should be for love. Those words spoken by Elizabeth so long ago, had faded to a soft hue, like weathered homespun, but they held up. The real question—was this love, or anything like it?

You don't even know if he's inclined toward you, I scolded myself.

But I did know. He was.

What he meant to do about it? That was another matter.

Whatever he meant, he seemed in no hurry. A monotonous winter set in. Poor traveling conditions and a cold kept Sperie home. It snowed, and thawed, and froze, eventually creating road surfaces perfect for sleds and sleighs. We rode, creaking up the hill to Meeting with the snow flying back in our faces. Sleighing parties formed on the frozen river. The men went ice-fishing and hauled in next winter's firewood. Mountains of logs grew in Stephen's yard; a young farmhand was injured scrambling about on them, and Stephen warned everyone to keep a sharp eye on Billa Czar, lest he emulate the feat.

"He certainly doesn't seem to be in a hurry!" Mother burst out one evening as we sat over our needlework. Neither of us had said a word in possibly half an hour.

"I know! He does mean to come back, doesn't he?"

Mother stared. "Of course he does! I'm impatient, that's all. I suppose the weather in Canada is much worse than here."

Canada. She was talking about Patrick. She must know I was talking of someone else.

He didn't visit for weeks. Christmas passed, and part of January. Mother got a letter from Patrick, who had finally received his reparations and would be joining us in Westminster as soon as he was able. He was eager to buy a lot and start planning a house. Mother's plans differed from his, and she talked them over with me as if it would it be my home too. It wouldn't.

I was determined about that, no matter if I never saw Ethan Allen again. If I had to throw myself at Lot Hall, or even Billy Willard, I would be my own mistress, run my own household, rear my own children—but I waited, not throwing myself at anyone, while the long days passed without a visitor, until one afternoon when I was mending a stocking in the clear light coming in the front window, and a fine chestnut horse flashed past.

I couldn't follow him to the tavern, not a third time. I'd raised enough speculation about myself. Besides, I needed to know what his inclinations were, unaided by any lures from me. Marriage should be for love. If he loved, he would pursue. I took up my needle, with fingers that seemed a trifle shaky, and resumed darning. Mother sat frowning over her house plan. She didn't seem to have noticed anything.

Would he ask John about me?

Why should he?

Would I ask John about *him*, once he was gone again? Better not. Too much had been said already, and if there was anything to tell, John would—

"Tea, Fan?" Mother asked. "I'm thinking of making a pot."

"Yes, please. Tea would be . . ."

Footsteps crunched on the snow outside. I didn't let myself glance at the window.

Footsteps in the front hall. I heard his voice, and then a knock on our apartment door. Mother went to open it.

He filled the doorway, tall and broad-shouldered in that green uniform coat. "Good day, Mrs. Wall, is Fanna at home?"

"Yes," she said, and I looked up from my work, as if just noticing that he was there. He was all brown with outdoor living and bright with cold, more alive than anyone else I knew. The age difference? I snapped my fingers at it.

"John says the cold is keeping you home these days," he said. "But the sun is out now, and the wind's died. Will you walk with me? And perhaps take a hot toddy afterward?"

"But the walking is dreadful!" Mother said. "All snow and ruts—"

"Well, perhaps it will be a short walk, and a long drink."

I stood up and took down my joseph from its peg. "I'd be happy to walk, at least as far as the tavern, and perhaps farther."

"I found it easy enough," he said. "Just pick a sled track and follow it."

As we stepped out the door, the wind came belting unobstructed across the Flats, swirling my petticoats and making him grab for his hat. "*Died down?*"

He laughed. "I lied!" We walked together. He was on my windward side, but not being a broad man, he didn't offer much shelter. "So," he said after a moment. When he didn't go on, I looked up. He was half-smiling but looking hesitant—a new side of Ethan Allen.

"Yes?"

"The *Queen* of *Hell?*"

John had been very busy spreading this story. My face heated, but I tipped my chin up. "Anyone who married the devil would be, would she not?"

"She would, she would." He didn't seem to know what to say next. Nor did I, so I gestured at the new farm we were passing. "That's one of Fa's lots—fully occupied, as you can see. Stephen says we're unlikely to get it back. What do you think?"

He shrugged. "Even if you do, it won't do you any good. I own thousands of acres, but I can't realize a profit on them. No one can afford to buy. Still, anything might be possible, if you know what wires to pull. And I might. I'm a useful friend for a Loyalist to have, you know."

"You? You're *skinning* Loyalists! You'd leave us without a rag to our backs or a shilling to scratch with!"

The slight vulgarity made him laugh. "You at least have few rags left, ma'am." He flicked the sleeve of my joseph with one finger. It was the first time he'd touched me. My next part in the conversation should have been some tart, witty remark, but my tongue suddenly refused to move. I had nothing to say.

"We all gambled," he said, apparently at random. "Had the war gone differently, you and John might be skinning me, with Stephen acting for both sides. The lawyers always profit, no matter who else loses."

This way of looking at it—amused, not at all bitter—felt refreshingly philosophical, and accorded with my own thinking. "All life is a gamble," I said. "We place a bet and toss the dice and live by the result."

"Do you think so?" We'd reached the tavern gate. Sled tracks, crossing and recrossing each other, caused me to stumble. He offered his arm, and I took it, leaf-green sleeve winding through hemlock-green. "The walking isn't very good, is it? And your nose is red." Evidently he was looking at me. I didn't look up; couldn't. "I like it," he said. "But come inside and have a hot drink."

I walked into the taproom, feeling the warm air on my face. I couldn't afford to look at John just then. I sat down with General Allen and waited for hot mulled cider to be brought to us, and cheese cakes, and we talked.

About our children, about our spouses. John Buchanan, drowned crossing a river. Mary Brownson, dead of consumption. "I didn't think she *could* die," he said. "She was strong—almost till the end. We didn't live in each other's pockets. Mary always said she was glad to see the back of me after a few days. But . . . I can't speak of her. No doubt it's the same with your husband."

"Not if you loved Mary," I said, bold and clear, startling him. "I married to oblige Mother and Fa. It was a mistake."

"Was it?" He looked a little blank.

"Marriage should be for love," I told him.

"I agree. I do agree." He looked at me searchingly. His eyes were bright and soft. I met his gaze, and held it, and it was he who looked away first.

"Now I have two little girls at home," he said, "and two older girls, and a cousin living with me, and sometimes one of Mary's family. It's a busy house, and small. Nothing like Stephen's place. That's why I like to get away. I might go north, up by Champlain. I've got land there, and . . . I could start again. Live more quietly, more at home."

"With all your girls? You can't demand that your older daughters postpone starting their own families."

"No, I can't. I can't do that. They have their plans, and . . . the great difficulty is to do right by all of them, the little ones and the older ones, when their needs are so different."

We sat looking into our tankards, and then, at the same time, sneaked a look at one another, and hastily looked down again. *There is one obvious solution. You need a wife.* I was bold enough to frame this in my mind, but not to utter it. He sat gazing into the depths of his cider, and I didn't know at all what he was thinking. He was not too old for me. That was decided when he walked in the door over at Stephen's. But perhaps I was too young for him?

And what else? What was Mother's caution?

Oh. *Domineering.* I stole a look at him, and what I saw was a man afraid, a man unwilling to cast the dice. Uncertain how I might respond? If I knew that, I'd find a way to encourage him. But would that be right? If he was afraid of making a mistake he couldn't go back from, then how could I attempt to influence him? It might very well *be* a mistake. About that, I knew no more than he did.

When our drinks were finished, he didn't order more, as I had expected. Instead he walked me home, saying little. I sensed that he was thinking, hesitating: not giving me his arm again, and I chose to like that, because I had to like something on this bleak, unsettling afternoon. He wasn't casual, not a flirt. Indeed, none of the stories I'd ever heard about him involved anything improper with a woman.

He said goodbye at the door, shaking my hand, looking hard at me, then walking quickly back toward the tavern.

"Did you get chilled?" Mother asked, when I stepped into our apartments.

"It's very windy out." I went to the fire and stretched out my hands to it. That was the hand he shook, and that was the hand that rested on his arm as we walked, and both were trembling, though not with cold.

Chapter 37

And now what? A week crawled by. I avoided the tavern, and John was too busy to come over; winter was traveling season. But I saw him at Meeting, and everyone in Westminster saw me, sitting up front in Stephen Bradley's pew. I could feel their thoughts, pelting my back like hailstones.

The Queen of Hell . . .
out walking with him
She's a proud one. Very sure of herself!
Maybe she'll have a fall.

Maybe she would. Maybe she had. After Meeting, Isaac was my refuge. Living out of town, he arrived too late to hear the gossip. He greeted me as he always did, as I imagined a brother might, a brother with whom one has a friendly but rather distant relationship.

His wife's cloak was disarranged; I looked a question at her and held my arms out for the baby. Without hesitation she handed him over, a warm, comforting little bundle. I bowed my head over him to hide unexpected tears, and he stared me in the face with his dark, opaque baby eyes. Who would he be? What force of personality incubated within these wrappings? When she had her cloak in order, I was glad to hand him back to his mother, and sorry too, an aching mix of feelings that had me watching the road as we drove home, for a horse and rider.

It was Sunday; no one traveled on the Sabbath. But he was not religious, famously so. Might he . . .

But he didn't travel, at least not to Westminster. Not Monday either, nor Tuesday. Wednesday Mother and I made cheese cakes for the Vermont judges who would arrive in a few days for the superior court session. I'd been making cakes for the judiciary half my life.

239

Then somehow it was Saturday: another whole week, and he hadn't come. Mother asked no questions. I found that more painful than if she had. At Meeting the next day, people were discernibly less interested in me. My drama had already peaked; they expect nothing further. The great interest was politics. The towns of Guilford and Brattleboro talked of seceding from Vermont, to rejoin New York or somehow exist independently. Some of the men were angry about that—the women too, but with a difference. Rhoda Harlow said it best: "I'm tired of all this dividing everything smaller and smaller, and fighting for every scrap of liberty. Let's settle down and *live!*"

Other women gave downright nods. "Yes, we've had enough division," the new Mrs. Averill said, by her look drawing Mother and I into the group. "Let the women settle it!"

I saw Mother's cheeks flush, and her words, hurled at Paterson and the others, came back to me down the years. *If you weren't women in men's clothing . . . you have only to contend with traitors who'll run at the sound of their own voices . . .* Women make mistakes too, I thought, and probably some women in Guilford were giving speeches very similar to Mother's, to their lagging menfolk. But it felt good to be included, and neither of us brought up the past.

Sperie caught up with me as we were leaving. I braced myself for questions, but she didn't ask any, which was much, much worse. She gave me a look of such compassion that I was ready to sink into the earth and followed that with an encouraging smile. *Oh Lord, protect us from our friends!*

That afternoon I pulled out the long letter to Elizabeth, which had been mouldering in my trunk for weeks. I'd told her nothing about Ethan Allen; I stopped adding to the letter at the time of his first visit. I took up my pencil to write:

> *It's intolerable to live in a place where there are only one or two eligible men. One cannot avoid occasioning gossip if one even speaks to them. Everyone speculates, when it probably means nothing. I'm beginning to seek ways and means of going to Philadelphia in the spring, where the population of eligibles is—*

No, I wasn't. I was waiting, right here. I folded the letter and tucked it away deep in the trunk.

Monday morning the justices began to arrive, making the house loud with their laughter and self-confidence. We kept to our rooms so they could get through their business—though they didn't sound very businesslike! They were much occupied in playing with Billa Czar and seizing every excuse to shout out his improbable nickname, while he showed off in his little uniform. They were all Ethan Allen's friends, especially the chief justice, Moses Robinson, and I hated hiding from them, hated knowing that I was hiding, hated them knowing it, as they probably did. I would have taken refuge at John's, but the tavern was full, too, and I didn't like the way John smiled at me these days, as if he was happy for me. I was fairly sure by this time that there was nothing to be happy about.

I lay awake that night in the bed beside Mother, still as a stone so as not to wake her, as I'd done so often. As I did the night poor French was killed. Everything brought that time back—the cakes, the judges, the cold and snow, my own unhappiness, searing along my breastbone with a pain that couldn't be swallowed.

Of course my hurt was nothing, compared with what happened to French. How beautiful he'd looked, that young farmer, marching up the hill with all the rest. From the moment the posse arrived with the guns Chandler had promised they would not have, everyone's lives were set on a new course. We didn't know the full meaning of it yet. Perhaps we never would.

Did Elizabeth grieve French long, I wondered? Or did that preference extinguish itself in caring for Daniel Houghton, and in the war, and in the clockmaker? How long did it take for a preference to extinguish? Or was that even possible?

I stifled a sigh. Mother turned over in her sleep and put her arm around me. I listened to her breathing until my mind finally loosened and I fell asleep, to dream of nothing in particular.

The first morning of the session dawned bright and cold. We breakfasted early, before the justices were down, and retreated to our apartment. Mother pointed out that the glassware needed dusting, as she'd predicted when I put it out. It was something to do; we dusted it.

I was standing on a chair, taking pieces from Mother and arranging them on the top shelf of the cabinet, when sleigh runners squealed across the snow and stopped outside. Boots squeaked up the walk, thumped on the hallway floor, and Bradley shouted from the dining room, "Ethan! Join us for breakfast!"

Ethan.

My chair wobbled. He'd go on through. He was here to see his friends—

"I breakfasted over at John's," he said. "I'll step into Mrs. Wall's apartments and visit the ladies."

There was his knock, and Mother let him in, dressed for travel in his hemlock-green military coat. He brought with him fresh air and the scent of coffee—handsome and bright-looking, but his mouth was tense. I hastened to lighten his mood.

"See this?" I held up our cracked decanter. "A man would have to pour quickly, or his drink would run away from him across the table!"

He laughed. "Yes. Well. Fast is best, sometimes." He glanced out the window. I saw two black horses hitched to a sleigh. One pawed and tossed its head; the other stood with ears flattened, disapproving. Fine creatures—not Cloud's equal, but unless I missed my guess, there was a touch of Wildair blood—

"If we're going to be married," he said.

Time stopped. I re-heard, as if whispered from a distance. *If we're going to be married . . .*

". . . now is the time, for I am on my way to Arlington."

Now is the time.

If we're going to be married, now is the time, for I am on my way to Arlington.

I met his eyes. They sparkled, but I could see he wasn't sure of himself. This was bravado. I knew this man. . . . *my extreme circumstances at certain times, rendered it political to act in some measure the madman . . .*

Extreme circumstances.

He was afraid.

My heart swelled with an almost painful tenderness. From my height on the chair, I was aware of Mother over near the door—a small figure in the background, a gown, a pale face. My eyes wanted to sharpen on her, check her reaction—

But no. This, at long last, was a decision to be taken without reference to Mother. Taken now. Taken swiftly.

I stretched out one hand and laid it in his palm, looking down into his eyes. Suddenly his were bright with tears, and I felt my own tears start.

"Very well—"

My voice wobbled. I closed my eyes and swallowed hard. When I opened them, his face was transformed. I'd never seen anyone smile like this, with such strong, spontaneous joy. The blood pounding in my ears, I gave him my other hand and stepped down off the chair. Breathing in the cold air and woodsmoke from his coat, so near my face, I said,

"But give me time to put on my joseph."

Epilogue

Fanny and Ethan walked into the next room and asked Chief Justice Moses Robinson to marry them. Once wed, they packed her trunk and mandolin into the sleigh and drove over the mountains to start a new life. Soon the couple moved to a cabin in Burlington overlooking Lake Champlain, with Ethan's children and other relatives and employees. In November 1784, Fanny gave birth to a daughter, Frances Margaret (Fanny) Allen. A son, Hannibal Montresor Allen, was born in 1786. The couple's marriage was reportedly happy. Ethan did far less traveling and politicking and focused much more on his farm.

In early winter of 1789, while sledding hay across the lake, Ethan Allen suffered what was probably a stroke. He died several hours later, leaving Fanny pregnant and widowed at age twenty-nine. Ethan Alphonso Allen was born that October. Fanny and the children came to Westminster to live with her mother. In 1793, at age thirty-three, she married Dr. Jabez Penniman. They moved to the Allen farm for a few years, but debts forced them to give it up. They returned to Westminster, until Stephen R. Bradley, then a U.S Senator, used his influence to gain Dr. Penniman the lucrative post of Vermont Customs Collector. The couple moved back to Burlington in 1806.

Fanny had four more children with Jabez. With one of her daughters, Adelia, she established an herbarium and studied botany; she was one of the first woman botanists in America. Another daughter, Frances, became a Catholic nun; Vermont's Fanny Allen Hospital was named for her.

Fanny died in 1834 at age seventy-four, and is buried in Elmwood Cemetery in Burlington, Vermont, under a horizontal gravestone which gives her maiden name as "Montezuma," a woman of mystery to the last.

Historical Notes

The Westminster Massacre was well-documented at the time it took place, but some details remain unclear. Was the Connecticut River frozen over? Accounts differ. I chose to have it frozen in this novel, as was normal for March, but there's some evidence that it was a warm, dry winter and spring, so there may have been open water and no snow on the ground.

Was the protest primarily against British tyranny, or the New York courts? All contemporaneous accounts say the former, and I've gone with the opinion of the participants.

Were the Whigs armed on March 13? They said they were not, and that seems most plausible. They were following the example of the Massachusetts Farmers Rebellion protests, which were intentionally nonviolent. Protest was illegal. Armed protest was punishable by death. No arms were reported confiscated when the posse retook the Court House. The Tory participants who claimed the Whigs were armed had a strong interest in doing so; they did not want to be charged with murder. The Whigs and their descendants always stated in the strongest terms that they had no guns; indeed, one man who wanted to bring a sword to the protest was forced by his companions to leave it home. Once the posse had fired on them, though, the Whigs went home and got their guns.

Following the Massacre, some of the imprisoned officials were released. Others, including **William Willard**, **Sam Gale**, and **Sheriff Paterson**, were transported to New York for trial following the outbreak of war the cases fell by the wayside. Many of the prisoners submitted bills to New York government for their expenses during the Massacre period. Most notable is Paterson's large bill for the liquor consumed at the Tory Tavern. Willard returned to Westminster with a new coat, said to be his reward for killing French. He lived a long life, but died insane, which many felt to be poetic justice. Gale moved to Canada, as did his father-in-law, **Judge Wells**, and many of their family. Paterson's movements after the Massacre are unknown.

Three couriers including **Joseph Hancock** rode to New York City. They told their story to Crean Brush and Samuel Wells, who crafted some of the details ahead of the couriers' depositions before New York judge, Horsmanden. The initial volley that went high was transformed into humane "warning shots." Great emphasis was placed on the violent language of the crowd, and no emphasis on the fact that all the bloodshed was inflicted by the posse. The Assembly voted one thousand pounds to put down the rebellion, and General Gage, according to one account, had placed arms on a ship, *The King's Fisher,* bound for New York in preparation for an expedition to Westminster. Before that could happen, the battles of Lexington and Concord plunged America into war. New York immediately sided with the colonies, without giving up its struggles to regain the land in what soon became Vermont.

Though it has often been conflated with the struggle between New York and New Hampshire over what would become Vermont, both sides made clear at the time that the protesters were motivated by the struggle against Great Britain. As **acting governor Cadwallader Colden** wrote to Lord Dartmouth on April 5:

> *A number of People in Cumberland, worked up by the example and Influence of Massachusetts Bay, embraced the dangerous resolution of shutting up the Courts of Justice. . . . It is proper your Lordship should be informed, that the inhabitants of Cumberland County have not been made uneasy by any dispute about the Title of their Lands; those who have not obtained Grants under this Goverm(t) live in quiet possession under the Grants formerly made by New Hampshire. The Rioters have not pretended any such pretext for their conduct. The example of Massachusetts Bay is the only reason they assigned.*

After the Massacre **Fanny** and **Margaret** made their way to New York, where Fanny was married to **Captain John Buchanan**; by her own account she wept the whole day of her wedding and soon fell pregnant. Buchanan died during the war, perhaps by drowning; accounts vary and are not to be relied on. Their son, **John**, died very young.

By autumn of 1775 **Crean Brush** was in occupied Boston, commissioned to receive and protect the personal property of Bostonians in whose houses the British army were quartered. His own property was marooned in hostile Westminster. He hatched a scheme to raise a body of men and occupy posts on the Connecticut River, which came to nothing. When the British evacuated Boston in 1776, Brush received permission to seize more personal property and had it all stowed on the brigantine *Elizabeth*. Sailing north to Halifax, the heavily laden ship fell behind the convoy and was captured.

Brush was placed in solitary confinement in Massachusetts, denied pen, ink, paper, or candles, and forbidden to speak to anyone but his jailers. He spent a year and a half in prison, apparently often under the influence of strong drink. Margaret began to visit him in early 1777, and in November of that year broke him out of prison by allowing him to walk out at dusk wearing her gown. He escaped to New York and died there in early 1778, apparently by suicide, though accounts differ as to the method. Despite recent speculation that Ethan Allen may have murdered Crean Brush, no credible evidence supports this theory.

News of the April 19, 1775, battles of Lexington and Concord reached Westminster the following day. Nine members of Azariah Wright's militia, all from the western part of town, joined Putney minutemen in a rapid march to Cambridge, where most of them joined the Continental Army and fought in the Battle of Bunker Hill on June 17.

Captain Azariah Wright, with a couple of other Westminster men, marched to Canada with an expedition in 1775—a disastrous, ill-planned attack that resulted in many deaths from cold and hunger. The men were forced to eat their own leather pouches and cartridge boxes. Wright never fully recovered from his privations and became even more eccentric and dangerous. Nonetheless he lived many more years and died in 1811 while milking a cow.

Fanny's biological father, **Captain John Montresor**, returned to England with his family in 1778 and retired from the army. Irregularities in his army accounts led to an embezzlement charge, and the government confiscated his estates. He died in 1799 in Maidstone Prison, imprisoned for debt. The portrait of his wife, **Frances**, is often misidentified online as being his daughter Fanny. There is no portrait of Fanny as a mature woman, only the one painted when she was twelve; with the portrait of Margaret and one of **Jabez Penniman**, it forms part of the Fort Ticonderoga Museum collection.

Judge Thomas Chandler became a firm supporter of the American cause after the Westminster Massacre but faced opprobrium for his role in the latter. He became impoverished late in life, was imprisoned for debt in Westminster Court House, and died there a pauper in 1785. A legal superstition of that time was that by touching the body of a debtor you could inherit his debts, and that by carrying a body past the bounds of the jail yard, you would be regarded as conniving at an escape. Chandler's body rotted in the June heat until the jailer, measuring the bounds of the jail exercise yard, stretched the surveying chain enough to make the jail yard overlap the cemetery grounds. A grave was dug slantwise across the boundaries, and at midnight, a few hardy souls put Chandler's remains into a rough box and slid it to its final resting place. The grave was never marked, and its whereabouts are unknown.

Stephen Rowe Bradley became one of the most important Vermont politicians of his day. He helped guide Vermont to statehood and was one of its first U.S. Senators, serving one four-year and two six-year terms. He was twice Senate president pro tem and drafted the Twelfth Amendment to the Constitution, which established the system of vice presidential and presidential candidates running on a single ticket. Bradley's first wife, **Merab**, died young. He then married Gratia Taylor, more commonly known as Thankful, who also died of consumption; Stephen's third wife was Melinda Willard, daughter of **Billy Willard**. She was thirty-one years his junior, and two years younger than his eldest son.

William Czar Bradley (Billa Czar) became a prominent Vermont lawyer, served in Congress, and was charged with surveying the Maine section of the U.S./Canadian border following the War of 1812.

Margaret and **Patrick Wall** lived the rest of their lives in Westminster, in the crooked house once owned by Crean Brush. Margaret died in 1805, Patrick in 1815; they are buried next to each other under a pair of horizontal gravestones.

Experience Averill (Sperie) married Abraham Nutting of Westminster. Her great-grandson was the lumber magnate and philanthropist George Dascomb, whose charitable foundation supports many organizations in Westminster, including the Historical Society. Their descendants still live in Westminster.

John Norton lived a long life in Westminster, a pillar of the community, and is buried in the Old Cemetery alongside many veterans of the American Revolution who took the other side in that conflict.

Vermont declared its independence from New York at the **Westminster Court House** in January of 1777, naming the new entity "New Connecticut." There was already a New Connecticut, and the name Vermont was chosen when the declaration was ratified that July in Windsor. Westminster remained an important town in Vermont for many years, hosting the legislature in 1789 and 1803. However, the county seat was moved to Newfane in 1787, and the Court House, no longer useful, was dismantled in 1806; timbers and doors from it are built into many local houses, but the old front door and lintel, with the hole made by a musket ball on the night of the Massacre, were preserved, and are on display in the Westminster Historical Society museum.

For more, go to www.westminstervthistory.org[1].

---

1.   http://www.westminstervthistory.org/

Author's Note

The chance discovery that Fanny Montresor, future wife of Ethan Allen, witnessed the Westminster Massacre at the age of fifteen was the impetus for this novel. Fanny told the story to the *Vermont Phoenix,* a Brattleboro newspaper, in 1805. Fanny and her stepmother provide the only female voices ever associated with this lethal pre-Revolutionary conflict, which resulted in the immediate overthrow of New York and British government in what is now eastern Vermont.

At first I discounted the story. Why wouldn't Fanny and Margaret be in New York with Crean Brush? But I came to understand that men attending court or the legislature stayed in lodgings, and their families stayed home. Also, it's likely Fanny and Margaret would not have been welcome in New York high society. They were an embarrassing reminder of John Montresor's sexual indiscretions, which was why the family moved to Westminster in the first place. Further, John Hancock, one of the couriers who took word to New York after the Massacre, mentioned in his deposition being in the Brush home on March 14. It seemed unlikely he would have been there in the absence of the family.

What was the Massacre like for two women living so near the courthouse? Why would Margaret have incited the sheriff to violence, while Fanny tried to hold him back? How did this village full of young families—the wives, sisters, and children, and neighbors of the combatants—experience the protest and the aftermath? These kinds of question guided my writing and deepened my understanding of the Massacre.

Fanny and Ethan's courtship was described to historian Benjamin Hall in the 1850s by William Czar Bradley; the account is worth reading for its glimpse into Allen's religious philosophy. Recent historians have poured scorn on the story, as Billa Czar was only two years old at the time of the wedding. However, in his adult life Bradley was a friend, neighbor, and attorney to Fanny and Margaret. He would have heard the story retold by them and by witnesses like his father and the lawyers and justices who became his colleagues. Details may have become polished with retelling, but there is no reason to discount the essential truth of this oral history.

Only three lines, spoken or written, are attributable to the historical Fanny—her own account of what she said to Sheriff Paterson, her "Queen of Hell" remark, and her answer to Ethan Allen's proposal. All were spoken in Westminster, and those three lines dictated the shape of the novel.

Did Fanny have a horse? We don't know. The famous joseph is a possible clue; a joseph was a fashionable riding habit in England and colonial America, and we know she had one in 1784. Her New York background would have acquainted her with the fine horses being bred there. Cloud's fictional breeding is based on the race horses raised by James DeLancey in the Bowery. One of DeLancey's stallions, True Briton, was stolen in 1780 and brought to New England, where he sired Figure (later named the Justin Morgan horse, after his owner), progenitor of Vermont's famous Morgan horse breed. The Dutch Haartdraaver breed, exemplified here by the fictional horse Joost, was also part of the mix that created the Morgan horse.

Finally, the cheese cakes.

What we would call *cookies*, colonial Americans called *cakes*. I developed these savory cheese morsels from a recipe in *The King Arthur Flour 200th Anniversary Cookbook*. They would have been well within the scope of a colonial housewife's baking using a brick oven. They should be regarded as fictional and enjoyed with a glass of wine or cider.

Cheese Cakes

1 C flour—fluff it up, spoon it into the cup measure and level with a knife. If you like, remove a tablespoon or two and replace with whole wheat flour

8 T butter, well-softened

2 C grated cheddar cheese

¼ t dry mustard powder

a few grains cayenne

½ t Worcestershire sauce

2 t caraway seeds

Mix all ingredients together until well combined and easy to handle.

Form into small balls, about a half-tablespoon's amount of dough.

Flatten slightly between your palms.

Place on an ungreased baking sheet and flatten with your thumb, as for thumbprint cookies. Bake at 375ºF for 12 minutes, and cool on a piece of absorbent paper.

Acknowledgments

My late father, Robert Haas, first got me interested in the history of Westminster. He had a passion for the American Revolution and the Westminster Massacre, and a vast collection of books, photocopies, and handwritten notes. Whatever I needed to know was usually in one of Dad's folders. I'm sorry he never got to read this book, and happy to remember talking about it with him just days before his death. My mother, Patricia Haas, shared Dad's interest in history and is still a trustee of the Westminster Historical Society. Many thanks to both of them.

Among the books and papers in Dad's collection were the following: Ethan Allen's *A Narrative of Colonel Ethan Allen's Captivity*; the depositions of Oliver Church, John Griffin, and Joseph Hancock sworn before Judge Horsmanden on March 22, 1775; Benjamin Hall's *History of Eastern Vermont*; Reverend E.J. Fairbanks's *The Double History of Westminster, Vermont: The History of the East Parish*; *Vermont Historical Gazetteer*; and R.S. Safford's "Remarks on Vermont's Centennial Celebration." The Westminster Historical Society provided access to David Bryan's unpublished manuscript, "Mother and Daughter: The Lives of Fanny Montresor and Fanny Allen." Reuben Jones's *A Relation of the Proceedings of the People of the County of Cumberland and Province of New York,* written on March 23, 1775, was published in Slade's *Vt. State Papers,* American Archives, Fourth Series, 1775, Journals of the General Assembly of the Province of New York, and was available through the Brooks Memorial Library in Brattleboro, Vermont.

The Westminster Historical Society gave me the opportunity of studying and writing about my town through a generous grant from the Dascomb Trust. In the archives, the unpublished manuscript "Mother and Daughter: The Lives of Fanny Montresor and Fanny Allen" was very helpful, as was the book *Crean Brush, Loyalist, and His Descendants,* by Jane Norman Smith. Special thanks go to Alice Caggiano, who provided several folders full of information, along with encouragement. Racheal and Sonia Scott were very illuminating about the clothing a young woman wore in 1775. I'm grateful to the Society for its support over the years, and for the indispensable work it does preserving Westminster history.

I would also like to thank Heather Taylor, editor at Blue Heron Images and Words; James F. Brisson Book Design and Production; Alan Berolzheimer, managing editor at the Vermont Historical Society; Glen Fay and Angie Grove of the Ethan Allen Homestead Museum; and Tabitha Hubbard and Miranda Peters of the Fort Ticonderoga Museum.

Through the long process of finding the way to tell Fanny's story, my writing group has been crucial. Their questions, suggestions, and interest kept me going and gave me faith that I'd find the way through to a last line that was always pre-ordained. Pam Becker, Nancy Detra, John Gurney, Andra Horton, the late Sara L. Miller, Kim Peavey, Jeanne Walsh—we've been through some hard things in the last few years. I'm so glad we were able to keep meeting throughout, and am eternally grateful for your insight, suggestions, and support.

Michael J. Daley. What can I say? You are my true love.

About the Author

Jessie Haas grew up in Westminster, Vermont, on a farm once owned by a member of Azariah Wright's militia, in a farmhouse built by a great-uncle of Benjamin Hall, the eastern Vermont historian. A graduate of Wellesley, she is the award-winning author of forty-two books for children and adults including *Revolutionary Westminster* and *Westminster, Vermont, 1738–2000: Township Number One.* She is current president of the Westminster Historical Society, lectures frequently about the Massacre, and was interviewed extensively for the Ethan Allen Homestead's film biography *Frontier & Flowers: The Story of Frances Montresor Brush Buchanan Allen Penniman.* Haas and husband Michael J. Daley have lived in a 450-square-foot, off-grid cabin next to the family farm for over forty years. She is an equestrian, cook, knitter, environmental journalist, and political activist.

Read more at https://jessiehaas.com.

www.ingramcontent.com/pod-product-compliance
Lightning Source LLC
Chambersburg PA
CBHW070511030726
47503CB00004B/1239